Pavitra in Paris

Dear Shushma ji,

It is my great pleasure to send you my collection of short stories that were inspired and written in your breathtakingly beautiful province of British Columbia. I'm sure you'll enjoy my stories that are gaining acclaim from politicians, media, authors and readers alike.

Happy Reading!

Warmest regards to you & your family,

Vinita Kinra

www. VINITAKINRA.COM
email: KINRAVINI@GMAIL.COM
Tel: 1-647-712-0149

Pavitra in Paris

stories for life

. . . .

Vinita Kinra

www.vinitakinra.com

Greengardens Media
Toronto, Canada

For my husband
Pankaj and our daughter Veda

Acknowledgements

Pavitra in Paris has been an incredibly memorable journey for me. After God, I would like to thank my husband Pankaj Kumar—my friend, my mentor, my inspiration and my toughest critic—for his tireless support in helping this book emerge from my dark drawers after 5 long years, and breathe in the light of the day. It is his baby as much as it's mine, and together we have brainstormed for its name, awed over its beauty, cried in its myriad emotions and helped it patiently through its countless teething troubles. We have seen it grow, page by page, under our loving care and supervision. Slowly, our baby found its extended family in Mr. Ramtirth Prasad Singh, my father-in-law and an avid reader, who has unflinching faith in my writing abilities, and my mother-in-law Mrs. Indu Devi who kept a keen eye on its progress.

I would also like to thank Sunil Mantri, our friend, who compared Pavitra in Paris to Buddha's enlightenment, and saw the need for the wisdom contained in this book to be disseminated across the globe. With this aim, he suggested valuable technical and marketing strategies.

Finally, Dr. Nancy Mitenko (gynaecologist at St. Paul's Hospital, Vancouver) and her team gave me a second life in the summer of 2008, when I was rushed into an emergency surgery after suffering internal hemorrhage during my first pregnancy. She not only helped me heal physically, but also provided moral support by reassuring me that soon a healthy baby would play in my arms. Accordingly, she delivered my daughter Veda in the winter of 2010. Thank you, doctor! I'm indebted to you for two lives.

Contents

The Curse of a Nightingale

"**I** was as beautiful as my name, *Nargis*: a poet's daffodil. My complexion rich and creamy like its blushing petals; my almond-shaped sapphire eyes fanned by copious lashes subtly curved like its tender filaments; my innocent youth blossoming like its lingering fragrance. Until everything changed. Not gradually, like God wills beauty to wither with the creases and wrinkles of old age, or the twinkle of the eye to fade by a vision of the fleeting world, or the curtain of coal black hair to be stripped white by the stresses and grief attendant on human life. But by a sudden brutal incident which was uncannily frequent in my hometown of Bamiyan in Afghanistan.

"School had just got over, and my sister Laila and I were exiting the ramshackle white building where two dozen girls learnt to read the Qur'an and write Afghan alphabets on a bullet-pocked blackboard surrounded by windows of shattered glass—grim reminders of Taliban attacks to prevent girls from getting an education. We spilled out on the dusty, rutted street like a black tent in the middle of a desert, our teen bodies cloaked under life-size burqas, fearful eyes forever vigilant behind its transparent grey eyepatch.

"We scurried like rats on a sinking ship when we noticed the pickup truck rumble towards the school, black beards flying on white robes amid a haze of dust cloud. Our black tent was pulled in different directions, as if by a powerful dust storm; muffled screams rent the air like the desperate grinding and scratching of rats running for dry ground, water lapping dangerously all around them.

"Then, the unthinkable. Scenarios that had unfolded countless times in our minds, of ruthless reprisals for defying the *Taliban Law* of attempting an education. Reprisals of falling dead to *Taliban bullets*, if you got lucky; but if death passed you by—missing you narrowly—you would be bound to the back of a pickup truck with a coarse rope handcuff and dragged across the rough terrain until blood oozed from your viscera like water and stained the sand black; or you would slowly bleed to death, standing in a neck-deep trench, with only your masked head exposed for better impact to heavy pelting rocks.

"But in all scenarios, I had imagined myself dead. Never alive to nurse or live with wounds, gashes or scars. Just soaring up to heaven in the same pristine body God had endowed on me at birth. However, even the most meticulously conceived scenarios change—subtly but surely—just like among the billions of humans on earth, no two are *exactly* alike.

"So, my preconceived scenarios betrayed me. It was my sister Laila who was immediately liberated. Falling to the ground after random bullets sprayed by the Taliban struck her chest and abdomen. Distraught, I slumped to the ground beside her, pressing her quivering hands to double the force over gaping holes of her body that oozed blood with the same ferocity that a nozzle oozes water when the faucet is separated from its head. I had lifted our veils, and noticed the light fade from her hazel eyes in sync with her fading screams of agony. Her hands lost their grip around her wounds and hit the sand, blood-soaked. I looked around—traumatized—yelling for help. Laila's faucet had cured itself to a trickle around coagulated lumps of red blood cells. But mine had just been let loose. Saline water ran steadily through my sapphire eyes that saw several Lailas sprawled on the sand, whining and cringing. I wondered why *I* had been spared by Allah.

Why *me?*

Then, I got the answer.

"The same pickup truck roared furiously towards the school a second time. Black riffle muzzles penetrated the smog of dust suspended in the air as the truck veered and reversed, its tyres screeching and brakes wailing. Gut wrenching screams tore through the oppressive hot air, as survivors, thus far tending to the injured, used the bullet-riddled bodies of their loved ones as shields to protect themselves.

"Surprisingly, not a single shot was fired this time. Much to my chagrin. I was the lone survivor who dared to stand amid horribly twitching bleeding bodies, my veil upturned and my chest thirsty to be pierced by the deadly rain of forceful metal heads, so that I could join Laila—wherever she had headed—and make sand castles with her.

"But that was not to be. Outraged by my audacity, the truck rolled impatiently towards me, squealing the brakes to a halt just an inch before its heavy tyres could run over my slippered feet, full of red sores in the blistering heat. Then, my eyes locked the spiteful intent gaze of a gaunt turbaned man in his twenties, his pointy bird-like features adding to the disdain in his sharp eagle eyes, as he screwed up his clawed nose like looking at me had somehow made him unchaste.

"I continued staring at him defiantly, temporarily deaf to the incredulous chanting of *Stone the Slut!* by his fellow comrades of the beard patrol team. 'This shameless slut should be stoned to death!' came the unanimous sentence to my effrontery.

"Death? I smiled in gratitude. They snickered, scouring the landscape for solid pointy rocks. Just then, the bird-faced Taliban waved his hand authoritatively. He stretched the same hand. The long, white sleeve fluttering in the air, along with thin wisps of curly mud-brown hair swaying under his turban gave him the appearance of a cult leader. A small glass bottle with a viscous, dark brown liquid was handed over to him subserviently.

"I wanted to scream the loudest scream my throat had ever known. But I couldn't. I felt my temples pulsating violently; massive waves of hot blood were rushing to my head and making it throb with a dull crushing pain as if a concrete boulder had landed on all its nerve cells, squishing them to pulp like defenceless earthworms under a speeding car.

"I wanted to cover my face with my hands and roll over in the sand. But I didn't.

My hands felt numb.

Immovable.

Frozen.

Despite my body's refusal to gear up its defences, my eyes held on.

Unwavering.

Unblinking.

To watch the ghastly spectacle of my daffodil face wilt and peel. Not gradually, like God wills flowers to wither and droop under the vagaries of nature: petals to fade under the scorching sun, or stems to hunch under the weight of snow, or leaves to succumb to a thunderous rainstorm.

"My cheeks melted instantaneously under the impact of the scorching, viscous, dark brown acid thrown at it. My body wobbled

and hunched under the weight of wildly stinging burns eroding my garden of youth.
I succumbed to the shock of the attack and excruciating pain.
I passed out on the burning bed of hot sand.

"I came to—after what felt like an eternity of hallucinations of floating on dark, icy waters—with the shrill bleeping of an ECG machine, whose sharp green waves across a black screen were only faintly visible to me. Suddenly, the hallucination broke when the icy water feeling of the translucent gel on my face and neck gave way to relentless searing penetrating my bones and jaw. I screamed out loud, forcing my eyes to open beyond the slit view through the left one. A familiar hand pressed the exposed fingers of my bandaged arm which had pulled the tube connecting it to the IV. I reached my free hand laboriously over my right eye. It was pasted shut; its skin smoothed out and ironed over by the semi-solid cold gel. I pressed hard to feel the protrusion of the eyelid, but couldn't. Reassured by the touch of at least some scant, coarse bristles of eyelashes, I sank back into my delusion—falling flat on my back to the icy depths of the dark ocean.

"When the blissful sleep induced by morphine wore off, my mortal body rose effortlessly above the dazzling shapes and colours of starfishes and corals and octopuses. It left behind the enchanting phosphorescence of what is mistakenly perceived as obscure underwater life, to enter the deceptive realm of flashy colours on earth, which—in reality—is all black.
At least for me.
"I wished earnestly I could camouflage myself as a cuttlefish and become a rock, or wrap my arms around algae and blend into my surroundings like an octopus. For, I didn't know how I looked. Like a half-eyed monster, maybe. Then, the same familiar touch pressed

my hand. My mind drifted instantly to a loss far greater than my external beauty. Laila, I whispered. No sound emerged from my mouth: only the tip of my tongue touched the roof of my mouth, twice. My mother understood my question. Cloaked in a sky-blue chador, her shrivelled body had further emaciated as she clutched the metal frame of my bed with her gnarled hand to keep her frail body from swaying. From the slit of my left eye, I saw her skeletal hand wipe her drooping, wrinkled eyes that had been elongated vertically after her skin sagged and merged her cheek bones with her toothless jaw. This time, *I* pressed her hand, albeit more forcefully than I had expected. She turned her face and lowered her head. I pressed her hand until I feared her dry bones might crack and snap. She turned around and shook her lowered head.

"'*Over; it's all over,*' she waived her fleshless hand dismissively, and narrated amid loud sniffles how the Taliban had dumped the dead bodies of the school attack at an undisclosed location for vultures and wild dogs to feast on, instead of letting the family members provide them a decent burial.

"*Allah!* I muttered, and longed to take refuge once more in the cold, wet embrace of the underwater world, but the sweltering, arid reality of Afghanistan clawed me back to my piteous existence. Vivid memories of *that* haunting night came flashing to my mind as soon as I closed my left slit eye. In two split seconds, I had retraced two long years. I was 14 then. Laila was only 10. We were making sand castles outside our modest mud hovel that evening when the motorcycle almost rammed into our hut. Laila started crying when the intruders stepped on her castle, flattening the royal abode of her dreams under brutal footsteps. I remember hushing her by plastering my dirt-coated hand over her cavernous mouth. Together, we peeked through the little window of our hut. Mother—shaking with fear yet brave in demeanour—continued stirring the big brass casserole containing our repetitive dinner of watered-down lentil *shorba* from the night before.

"'Nargis!' barked the bird-faced Taliban pointing to the door. Horrified, I pulled Laila forcefully below the window, and huddling together in fear, we hid at the back of our hut which stretched out to a vast dump yard that we scavenged everyday for survival. We slid back into the hut—panic stricken—after ten minutes when we heard the *phutt phutt* of the motorcycle fade away. Mother was wiping the tears that glowed like transparent beads on her hollowed cheeks in the orange light of the clay stove. When I insisted, she hugged us both in one tight maternal embrace, her warm tears streaming down our necks and rolling off our chilly spines.

"'No more attending that charity school.' Her hoarse voice resounded a paradox of resolve and resignation. 'We Hazaras are born to starve and die like dogs.' She tightened her embrace and growled like a protective lioness. 'I will not let them have you after they widowed me.'

"But *they had had me now*—albeit partially—and reduced Laila to cold meet for scavengers. I cursed and swore at myself for fighting my mother's decision back then to stop us from attending school. I had won. But did I, *really*?

"Discharged from hospital in a few days to make room for the perennial wave of critically burnt women—most of whom had tried self-immolation to escape domestic violence and abuse—I returned to our hut with my mother. The stones that had served as chimneys and doorways in Laila's sand castles were still strewn about haphazardly outside our hovel.

"My external wounds healed gradually, leaving my face looking like a blind, scaly fish with ochre-yellow scabs pocking it like mould on rotting food. My eyebrows were gone—burnt to their roots—so that the right side of my face was one continuous scaly patch, as if the eye had never existed. I couldn't smile, either. Not that I had anything left in life to smile about, anyway. A loose flap of skin hung over my lips, left to its fate by doctors who were too ill-equipped for plastic surgery.

"So, the only time I smiled—through a twinkle in my left slit sapphire eye—was a full year later, when I stumbled upon an old, abandoned harmonium, discarded by roaming gypsies in the dump yard behind our hut. I slaved at its keyboard night and day until the pads of my fingertips felt sore. My mother remarked that I made strange gestures with my hands in the air even when I slept. After two years of my insane obsession with synchronising the notes of the keys and the wind in the bellows of the harmonium to my own vocal chords, I took to the streets of Bamiyan to sing religious songs as a panacea against our impoverishment.

"Initially, I attracted more disdainful attention than charity, but gradually Afghani coins jingled in my ragged chador, and I afforded my mother the rare luxury of kebab and naan once a month. From the netted window of my black cloak, I saw that my surroundings had become a veritable sanctuary for the homeless and destitute: limbless men, widowed women with starving infants, and shrivelled bodies debilitated by old age, hunger and disease. Their sorrows seemed to be uplifted like the comforting lyrics of my songs riding on the melodious drone of the harmonium. I sometimes donated a few coins to these luckless patrons who marvelled at my fate once the songs ended and their trance broke. Even though the Taliban regime had been ousted from power, I remained on my guard for random patrols of agents of the moral police of Propagation of Virtue and Prohibition of Vice. I didn't fear death, but found myself less forthcoming now to join Laila in the dead world, for it meant leaving behind my old and ailing mother to suffer alone in the living world.

The Curse of a Nightingale

"So, on the fortuitous day, when my repertoire of:
Allah created me for a reason,
He made me poor for a reason,
He masked my face for a reason,
He gave me this voice for a reason,
He makes me beg for a reason,
He makes you give for a reason;
Please give whatever you can—
For, He wants me to live for a reason
was abruptly broken by two non-Muslim looking men, I almost fell into the ditch that was my stage, cushioned with the bridge of a long, flat slab of stone.

"'Don't be scared, sister,' said the older of the two, evidently embarrassed at catching me off guard. They both wore white uniforms with an emblem embroidered in orange, white and green on their right chest pocket, which—I learnt later—was to represent India.

"'We are part of the reconstruction team commissioned by the Indian government to restore the legendary beauty of the Buddha statues demolished so brutally by the Taliban.' My pace slackened, as some words addressed to me reverberated in my ears until a cold sweat broke on my non-existent brow, despite the sultry pre-dusk humidity that hung low over the narrow streets of the crowded bazaar we were crossing.

Restore the legendary beauty demolished so brutally by the Taliban.

"If only the demolished beauty of living humans could be restored as flawlessly and painlessly as those of stone statues, I mused ruefully, passing my fingers over the jagged outlines of the flap of skin covering my lips.

"The two men threw occasional cursory glances behind to ensure I was following them, as they didn't want to lose me among numerous other black burqa-clad women. Why or where they were taking me, I hadn't a clue; however, I did start regretting the fact that I had left my harmonium unattended, succumbing to the authority projected by these two uniformed men I was now following.

"Maybe I was going to be thrown into a dark, dank prison where my voice would be stifled until it could no longer break into a song. But, I discovered the contrary upon reaching the official headquarters of the restoration team—a heavily guarded stark white two-storey building—a short car ride through the outskirts of the city.

"At first, I was rather intimidated by the presence of only men— lots of them—wearing different uniforms and pacing around the neat offices with an impending sense of fear and foreboding. Only a few days back, a car laden with explosives had detonated not far from this office complex. The white-skinned men with short cropped hair I recognised as Americans, who occasionally patrolled the bazaar streets, and threw a coin or two into the outstretched hands of the desperate beggars. The Indian men finally introduced me to two women and three other men. I must admit that seeing the women infused in me a sense of instant relief, even though they spoke fluently and supported no head covering.

"'We are making a documentary on Afghan women,' explained a charming, sultry woman with arched eyebrows over curious, jet-black eyes. The men in the crew just nodded respectfully in consent, pointing to their cameras, life-size mirrors and flashlights.

"'You can take your burqa off,' suggested the other woman amiably. She was middle-aged and dignified, with pepper-and-salt hair pulled back on either side of her middle parting. I didn't realize how violently I shook my head at that suggestion.

The Curse of a Nightingale

"'As you wish,' they spoke together, apologetic expressions sweeping their calm visages. Hence started my bizarre tryst with destiny that saw me sing song after song in the comfortable confines of that white building, even as my mother languished in the hovel after I forbade camera crews from filming her for reasons of security.

"After two weeks of glaring spotlight, time came for me to return back to my life: a life that was unchanged in every aspect, except that I had some disposable cash now. I learnt that the documentary was entitled, *Nargis—the masked nightingale.* I smiled through my slit eye from behind my burqa on contemplating the title. *Masked.* This word kept swirling in my head until I felt dizzy. I remembered how disenchanted I had been when mother first imposed the burqa on me. I despised the merciless cloak that caged my blooming beauty in its shapeless prison. My sapphire eyes felt barred behind its netted window. My vision of the world was suddenly reduced to a small square—suffocated and forever fearful.

"Yet now, the same prison was my refuge. Nobody could guess the horrifying face this shapeless cloak concealed. Nobody could see the browless slit eye behind its netted window. The blotches and scaly scabs were smooth and seamless under its uniform yarn; the loose flap of dappled skin, even and shiny like its fabric. It was indisputably my *best friend* now. It prevented people from pointing me out from far, just like a good chum shields you from bullies. It deflected startled gazes of pity and terror by reining in my monster face. At least until my final day of departure from the white building, when I myself let go of its equitable embrace for the lust of stealing a clear and comprehensive glance at my dehumanised face in the life-size mirror of the camera crew.

"It so happened that everybody had gathered in the dark room on the other side of the building to view the rushes of the documentary. I never used to participate in those viewings, loathing the idea of *looking at my masked face from behind my masked face*. So, when I was alone in the room with the life-size mirror, I crumbled—cracking like a nest egg that releases its fledgling, knowing full well how fragile it is to confront the harsh realities of the world. Yet, I peeled away the burqa clinging to my body and let it fall in a heap at my feet. Stepping on it, I pressed down my blistered heels spitefully, for, even though it had guarded me from scornful eyes, it had also prevented awestruck gazes when I was a blooming daffodil. So much so, I was its slave without ever realising it—depending upon its ghostly sweep for my very own identity. It didn't let me be the pretty girl I was, and wasn't allowing me to assume my present monstrous identity. I didn't want to limp across the world with this crutch, I resolved to myself, as I inched towards the mirror, putting every iota of courage I possessed to open my slit eye. I was going to be reintroduced to myself, after the disbelieving and reluctant reflection I had seen—years back—like a patchwork of browless eyes, jaw and neck from the broken palm-sized hand mirror of the hospital. I would not run away from myself anymore, I reassured myself, as I opened my slit eye gradually.
Silence.
Complete silence ensued.
My heart stopped beating.
My pulse stopped throbbing.
Just one furtive glimpse at my own reflection battered my resolve, shattering it to infinite pieces I could never gather in a single lifetime. Releasing my feet, I tiptoed over the burqa respectfully, and hunching down, wore it with my back towards the mirror.

Never, since, have I looked at my reflection again. Never, since, have I despised the burqa again.

"That moment onwards, my focus shifted from *masked* to *nightingale*. A tiny, black, insignificant bird that would have flown across the face of the earth without making a single head turn, had it not been for its melodious voice. That's who I wanted to be now—insignificant and all black in my burqa, yet making an indelible impression with my voice. Maybe even winning a Grammy award for a self-composed song, as the documentary crew had encouraged me to do.

"I was walking quietly through the maze of sparkling tiled hallways, so wrapped up in alluring fantasies of the new harmonium gifted to me by the documentary team, that I failed to perceive the hastening footsteps behind me. They finally caught up with me at the reception, where I halted momentarily to hand back my security pass to the uniformed guard.

"'Ma'am,' he gasped for air as he hastily drew out a small card from his breast pocket. From my netted window, I observed a white bald man in his fifties, with a posture so erect and a physique so stout that would put many a young men to shame. I raised the card to my netted window and noticed a few English alphabets with dots in between, followed by a few numbers, neatly spaced after a long name scrawled beautifully in cursive gold print. '*Jonathan Lonsdale, M.D., M.S., Plastic surgery*,' he reiterated, hands clasped behind his back and eyes lowered respectfully. 'Call that number whenever you need me,' he whispered. 'Most procedures are almost painless and flawless, and we can even work on the missing eye.'

"I dashed out of the building—bursting through the heavy front gate—and ran as if my life was in danger. The realization of what that fleeting, moss-green reflection in the life-size mirror had been, lifted me over the scorching, unpaved street almost weightlessly. I clutched the front of my burqa so the gushing hot wind wouldn't blow it off my face. The man in the moss-green uniform was an army doctor, afterall! Could he really gather the wilted dry petals, broken stem and withered leaves to sew them back into the blooming daffodil my face, neck and eyes had once been? Could I really woo the world with my stunning voice and captivating beauty all at once?

"That night, I dreamed the song that brought me today in your midst for this grand gala of the Grammy Awards night. I thank you all from the bottom of my heart for your dedicated attention and interest in my extraordinarily long gratitude speech. As promised, I conclude my speech with the same song you all honoured as *the best song of the year*. And yes, after the song, I will discard my veil *forever* and let the world embrace my beauty, just as dew drops embrace that of a daffodil.

Am I dreaming or awake?
I see Afghan women rising to take—
Charge of re-writing their fate;
To make our nation proud and great.

I'm still a blooming daffodil,
Abbu's not persecuted against his will;
Laila's busy making sand castles,
Ammi has conquered poverty and its battles.

Girls go to school at dawn,
Without fear of acid, gun or stone . . .
Corroding their beauty, stealing their life;
They are human again: a daughter, sister and wife.

The Curse of a Nightingale

Allah and Buddha embrace in Bamiyan,
There's no place for fear of Taliban;
Sunnis and Shias, Pashtuns and Hazaras,
Pray in the same mosques and offer Namaaz.

When the wind blows from craggy brown mountains,
It smells of pure desert sand, not missiles or machine guns;
When it wafts through the crowded bazaars,
It tickles the taste buds with the scent of kebabs.

No rockets, no car bombs rob life or limbs,
No widows, no orphans beg for alms;
No, I'm not dreaming—I have both sapphire eyes and not a scar,
For, Afghanistan is peaceful and not at war."

Thunderous applause resounds in the glittering auditorium as Dr. Jonathan Lonsdale rushes up the plush red carpeted stairs of the Grammy Awards' podium, a yellow spotlight suffusing his stout body and moving in pace with his elegant stride.

He reaches for the black veil concealing the genius of his craft that has transformed a crushed daffodil into a blossoming one.

"Are you ready?" he asks the public that's applauding uproariously in standing ovation.

"Are *you* ready?" he whispers to Nargis and pulls off her veil like a gallant soldier draws his infallible sword from the scabbard.

There's a loud knocking on the door and Nargis turns her side, smiling, considering it to be an extension of the uproarious applause at the world's premier awards night function honouring her golden voice and gusto.

But the knocking continues, and finally, she's jarred awake by gunshots followed by screams that chill the blood under her skin. She is completely disoriented. Not sure if she was dreaming about the awards night, or hallucinating about the massacre outside her school that snatched Laila from her life.

Running her shaking cold fingers across her face puts things back into perspective immediately. The skin feels bumpy, one eye is still missing, and the loose flap over her lips, intact.

Paralysed by fear, she gropes her way in the dark, when her feet suddenly freeze by a warm liquid gushing with the same ferocity that a nozzle oozes water when the faucet is separated from its head. Splashing through blood, she stumbles upon her mother's dead body, prostrate towards the west, as if she were offering *Namaaz* in Red Sea. She inches lifelessly towards the broken wooden door and steps out into the silence of the night. Her slit eye traces the shattered pieces of her harmonium in the pale moonlight, until the haze of a gigantic dust cloud blurs everything except the dispersed headlights of a pickup truck roaring alongside the ancient caves of the disfigured Buddha statues.

"Allah! Why did you spare me again?" she screams out loud, falling to her knees and challenging the sombre sky.

"Why *me*?"

This time, she gets no answer.

Kamini

Kamini smiled wistfully as she pulled the divine smelling kebabs off the skewers and arranged them mechanically on the silver aluminium foil laid on the sunmica kitchen table.

Mani, her husband of seven years, was preparing to leave for Darjeeling on a routine supervision of his sprawling tea estate nestled in the enchantingly pristine foothills of the Himalayas. She knotted her straight black hair into a bun, to no avail, as it uncoiled moments later to hang obstinately over her damp white bathrobe.

She bent furtively to glance at her reflection in the hazy stainless steel of the grill, still steamy from the kebabs. What she saw made her simper: she looked way younger for her thirty-eight years, her fish eyes alluring enough to arouse the carnal instinct of the most staid of people; her sun-kissed dusky complexion was at once provoking and mysterious, and her rod straight hair that fell over her streamlined body resembled that of a mermaid's, beguiling unsuspecting sailors.

She chastised herself by looking away from her image and slumped into a leather chair of tan colour and utmost comfort. She wouldn't go to the club today, she decided. Dreary talk of jewellery and fine linen choked her. She surprised herself by this sudden change of heart. Until two weeks ago, she longed to go there—her only source of entertainment in the otherwise monotonous routine of being an opulent new mother. When her two-year-old son Ankur slept through the mercilessly long afternoons, she escaped to the club to play cards, or swim, or languidly watch silver-haired men bending over golf clubs for eternity, before striking the ball with a meticulously measured upward swing of the arms. For two weeks, she had concocted every excuse she could conjure, to avoid just one round of bridge or a brief game of bingo with the women in her kitty.

Mrs. Sinha had cajoled her puckishly the other day by repeating incessantly, "Top date, number 38," after noticing the number on her unhidden bingo ticket. As Kamini stared at her ticket without scratching out the number with her pencil stub, Mrs. Sinha had called, guffawing, "You're late, number 38!" When none of these efforts yielded the desired result, Mrs. Sinha waved her hand right in front of Kamini's diaphanous eyes, breaking her reverie and making her blink repeatedly. All other women had burst into a paroxysm of laughter when Mrs. Sinha tapped on Kamini's ticket while doubling up with laughter on asking, "Do you have a date, number 38?"

Kamini had immediately become grave. She had excused herself on pretext of a throbbing head and walked straight to the spa. She had to press her fists to her temples to obstruct wayward thoughts from invading her mind. What she found most irksome was the brazenness with which Mrs. Sinha had repeated *thirty-eight*.

"Was she taunting at my age?" she had questioned herself rather nettled. She pictured Mrs. Sinha's playful eyes sparkling over chubby dimpled cheeks. She dispelled her doubts by remembering instances of her charity, when Mala (who refused to be called *Mrs.*

so and so to maintain her own identity), was advocating *the proper age to have kids*. As the debate veered to Kamini, who had recently given birth to her first child at age thirty-six, Mala was inexorable. "I am thirty," she had proclaimed proudly, knowing full well that most other women in the group were on the wrong side of forty. "My daughter is ten." Mrs. Sinha had dived in to rescue Kamini from her assailant in her trademark hilarity by quipping, "Your identity, then, is by your *daughter*, not your *husband!*" While this light-hearted twist to the rankling discussion left everybody smiling, Mala had sprinted off like a stag.

Kamini let out a sigh as she subconsciously pressed the kebabs before bunching the foil around them, and tying an elastic band on the neck. "How, then, had Mrs. Sinha conjectured that she might have a date?"

"Memsahib, *rava dosa* is ready," Rampyari said tediously, placing the semolina crepe carefully on the glass top of an elegantly carved birchwood dining table. She stood there, untucking the pleats of her synthetic sari and covered her shins.

"Go call sahib for breakfast." Kamini's tone was gripe at the intruder who had interrupted her soliloquies.

"Stop; I'll call him myself," she rambled, her mind swirling round and round in eddies. "You can go and wake Ankur, and give him milk."

Rampyari scratched the wart on her chin whose long hair tickled her blotched neck. She paused, her thick brows knitted in an effort to remember the most recent instructions. She then disappeared as abruptly as an airplane goes off the radar of the monitoring crew.

Mani was poring over the pages of a gilt-edged diary in the light of an incandescent lamp on the table in their bedroom. He looked typically South Indian: his forehead was smeared with sandalwood paste after his morning prayers, and he wore an off-white *lungi* with a black floral silk border. Silver rimmed spectacles sat askew on his nose as he smiled ingratiatingly at the contents of his book.

Kamini knew this ecstatic expression all too well. Mani was passionate about tea. "It's much more than a mere drink," he would say with conviction. "'It's a solace, a mystique, an art, a way of life, almost a religion.'"

Kamini had thought his list of superlatives describing the beverage was exhaustive, for Mani would close his eyes as if in spiritual contemplation, and at every adjective, mentally savour the infusion in its different incarnations. When he was not at his tea estate in Darjeeling, he would sit for hours at the same desk, under the light of the same lamp, wearing the same smile, as he filled pages upon pages of his gilt-edged diary with punctilious details about planting, picking, harvesting and processing the aromatic leaves. The lure of the leaf was as intoxicating for him as the grape is to a wine connoisseur.

Kamini had vivid memories of her wedding night, when she sat, stooped under the weight of her cranberry red bridal sari bedecked with semi-precious stones and sequins, on a rose coloured chenille bedspread patterned with dreamy lilacs.

The snug ambience of the room was mysteriously aphrodisiac, with mauve curtains of lustrous satin flowing smoothly over sliding windows, all the way down to the traditional Persian carpet woven in intricate geometric motifs. On one side of the bed, on the mushroom-shaped lacquered table, lay a big, stainless steel glass full of whole milk, prepared with generous quantities of crushed almonds, cashew nuts and condiments, traditionally believed to invigorate the groom to consummate the nuptials. Finally, her languorous eyes had fallen on the table, which now she had come to despise, but back then it had intrigued, even charmed her. She wondered what lay hidden in the thick volumes of hardbound books stacked one on top of the other, almost touching the stenciled flowers beneath the ceiling. The soft glow of the lamp that now made her glower, had then enchanted her, casting dancing shadows through the sliver in the curtains as the tall peepul trees swayed in the backyard, doped by the warm spring air. She couldn't remember how the tea conversation began, to never end, but to dominate all aspects of their intimacy. So much so, she was convinced that Mani was lost in the aroma of green oceans of tea gardens, even when he delicately inhaled the fragrant jasmine flowers braided in her hair.

Before the night ended, she knew all about the fine green and white teas of China, the crisp blacks of Sri Lanka and the sophisticated greens of Japan, instead of knowing her life partner.

At dawn, when he entered her splayed legs silently, she moaned, not out of pleasure but out of anguish, at succumbing to parental pressure to enter matrimony with an alliance of their choice.

Her parents had been unequivocal about the reasons influencing their choice: the boy (although Mani was forty-one then, but since he was unmarried, he was still referred to as a *boy*) was well settled, with immense ancestral property to feed their generations to come; he lived independently in his luxurious bungalow in New Delhi, so Kamini would be the sole mistress of the house, visiting her in-laws in Kerala only occasionally. Moreover, she could visit her parents anytime she pleased, as they lived in the adjoining city of Faridabad. What they didn't articulate explicitly, but what Kamini knew was the real reason for her sacrifice, she thought, was the fact that she had crossed marriageable age eons ago (she was thirty-one at the time of her marriage) and not only was she faced with a lifetime of spinsterhood, they were doomed to die without cradling a grandchild.

She parried nagging thoughts that her parents' sole consideration was their exoneration from dowry. She had often overheard snatches of conversation between her parents, when her mother averred, "What can we give them? They have many times what we have, and more." To this, her father had concurred, "They are decent people and only want a bride in three pieces of sari."

As Mani dipped the crunchy pieces of *dosa* in thick coconut chutney—licking his fingers after each bite—Kamini observed him with forced interest. In a few minutes, he would place a neatly folded shawl on his left shoulder and pinch the baby's cheeks before routinely examining his briefcase. She could bet on all her valuables that his parting exchange would be one of the following: "You should've come too; fresh mountain air is rejuvenating," or "You must go to the club; it'll change your thoughts," or "I'll call upon reaching."

She was outflanked and too stumped to answer when Mani asked, "Why don't you go watch a film?" gently stroking her arm swathed in the towelled bathrobe. Making a gargantuan effort, she mumbled inaudibly, "I don't know who to go with—"

At this, she expected more persuasion from his part, but he boomed, "Alright then," and jabbed Ankur in his tummy, making him gurgle and dribble.

She waved long after the flashy Mercedes had driven out of view, reduced to the size of a toy car in the densely crowded streets of the capital. As she handed Ankur back to the maid, holding him by his fluffy arms, he kicked his cottony legs about, wanting to stay out longer. She took him back and sat him on her lap as she slouched in the hammock hanging in the garden.

Kamini

At first Kamini was uncertain whether the soft sprinkle of water on her face was drizzle from the sky, or if the draught of wind had forced the fountain to spit on her, while bathing a nubile marble statue of Venus, flanked by cockle-shells; the erotic goddess of love was covering her taut breasts partially with one hand, while her gingery brown hair twirled around her supple waist, veiling her pubis.

The rocking of the hammock had lulled Ankur to sleep, as she dawdled, immersed in fleeting thoughts.

She wondered if she would be a heretic to go to the movies with Nikhil, her neighbour's eighteen-year-old son.

"Was she in denial?" she asked herself rather sternly. "If not, then why everyday, for the last two weeks, did she yearn to go to the spa instead of meeting her friends at the club?" When the aesthetician had painted her face with soothing emerald-green cucumber mask and placed circular wedges of citrus orange on her eyes, she had visualised the evening with Nikhil when he came to watch the cricket test series between India and Pakistan. She had felt like a school girl herself: skin soft and radiating after multiple exfoliations at the spa, and every muscle of her body relaxed and pliable after being massaged with essential oils soaked in rose petals and herbs.

She repudiated the maelstrom raging in her mind by pressing Ankur to her bosom, and rained kisses on his cheeks until her nostrils were filled with the overbearing smell of curdled milk. Pleasant thoughts of Nikhil were beginning to ebb from her system, only to surge back with increased velocity and drench her completely. From across the parapet wall shrouded in purple bougainvillea—climbing the roof and spilling over adjoining trees— Kamini saw Nikhil's back, resembling a camel's hump with the school bag secured over his shoulders. He wore spotless white school uniform contrasted by a black leather belt buckled at his waist.

As the rain started beating down her head, she realized why Nikhil had dashed off so quickly. She covered Ankur with both her arms and was about to enter her roofed verandah when Mrs. Menon, Nikhil's mother, stopped her.

"Kamini *ji*, so good to see you," she said sycophantically, smiling broadly at her affluent neighbour.

Kamini tried to look nonchalant, wiping her wet face with the sleeve of her bathrobe. As she debated on the best topic to initiate a conversation, Mrs. Menon obliged. "I saw Mr. Subramanyam leave in the morning," she said amicably, arranging the damp clothes she had piled from the clothesline on her left arm that she now held as if in a sling.

"Yes, Mani left for six weeks," came the prosaic reply.

"I wanted to ask you about Nikhil—" Mrs. Menon paused, blushing slightly, that made Kamini's heart gallop like a racehorse. She caressed Ankur quiveringly to evade eye contact with her neighbour. She thought it implausible that Nikhil would confide to his mother that while the two of them watched cricket, seated side by side on the warm red velvet sofa, there seemed to be nobody else in the house. Didn't she always make sure that Rampyari was sent out for long errands with more money than she needed, Ankur tucked in bed with dimmed lights and the phones put on *silent* mode? The seconds that separated Mrs. Menon's explanation only amplified the doubts that assailed Kamini. Yet, she resolved to wait for an explanation rather than offer one herself. Mrs. Menon bore a humble look on her face as she spoke, "I mean, I hope he doesn't disturb you with his cricket mania." She shook her head helplessly and added, "He's a bright kid and does well at school; however, I want him to excel—this year being his board exams."

Kamini

Kamini was familiar with the vicissitudes that had blemished Mrs. Menon's once carefree life. After her husband's accidental demise nearly ten years ago, she had steadfastly undertaken the herculean challenge of fending for her only son, Nikhil. Not being educated, she roamed houses resiliently, offering her services and collecting orders as a seamstress. Late at night when Kamini ambled in her balcony, unable to sleep alone, she could hear the monotonous drill of a foot treadle sewing machine.

Kamini was faced by a strange quagmire: should she inform Mrs. Menon that the match this evening had been indefinitely postponed due to the rains? She vetoed this thought that menaced the only palliative to her vacuity. She hoped Nikhil would not get wind of it in school. She visualized him, his spotless uniform sullied by unexpected splashes of rain, and dull yellow half moons under his armpits from dried sweat.

She smothered a smile on remembering how he jumped lightly on the couch, fists clenched, rhapsodizing with the commentator when the Indian batsman hit a sixer, or when the Indian bowler routed out a Pakistani contender. She was secretly impressed by his profane yet imperious voice, when the Muslims in the colony would rent the air with deafening firecrackers upon Pakistan's victory in the match. "They should live in *Pakistan*," he would decree peremptorily, with an air of masculinity that stimulated her, and she longed to be protected by him.

"No, she wasn't trying to decoy him," she affirmed silently, salving her conscience of any culpability. She decided to switch on the television when he would come, and wait with the same ardour for a game she barely understood or cared about. She would propose they go to *Dilli Haat* to compensate for the inopportune turn of events.

At five-thirty that evening, as the two waited impatiently for the cricketers to appear, adjusting their accoutrements and occasionally dropping on the field for some impromptu push-ups, Kamini disappeared into the kitchen and returned with a plate full of the morning kebabs and coconut chutney.

Nikhil was flinching, his brow puckered. There had been an announcement that the match would resume tomorrow, weather permitting. Kamini was elated at how the appetizing odour of the kebabs whittled his disappointment and cheered his waning spirits.

"Mummy says South Indians can't eat meat," he remarked astringently, popping a third kebab into his mouth.

"South Indians have an age-old predilection for coffee, yet your uncle Mani touches no beverage other than tea." Kamini's tone had an unwavering aplomb that advocated gratification of the senses without constraint.

"I'm going to *Dilli Haat*," she mentioned rather casually to Nikhil when he had finished the last kebab in the plate. "Do you want to go, too?"

Not getting a chance to sit in a car very often, except when his rich friends offered him a ride back home from a birthday party or a get-together late in the night, Nikhil accepted the proposal by rushing towards the garage without waiting to check if Kamini was following.

They bent under several thatched cottages and kiosks, mostly marvelling at, but periodically purchasing ethnic mementos and handicrafts from the zealous craftsmen of *Dilli Haat*.

Unable to resist the rhythm, they began to dance by stamping their feet at first, as a huge crowd circled a young girl wearing a long black skirt embroidered with silver ribbons. She was spinning sinuously to the high-pitched notes of the snake charmer's *been*. As the dance caught momentum, the dancer reeled in circles, her elastic body bearing semblance to a slithery snake.

Kamini did not realize when she and Nikhil held hands, to lose themselves in the frolicsome ambience. When everybody had dispersed, they were still swaying—hand in hand—floating in clouds of dust.

As they headed to the food stalls, coughing from the dust and laughter, Kamini was suddenly consumed by the urge to skulk into oblivion.

"Who do I see here? How are you Kamini?"

Kamini craved to annihilate all vestiges of her existence as she stood facing Mala and her petite ten-year-old daughter.

Taking no notice of Nikhil, who got magnetically attracted to a stall displaying hand-spun caps with cricket symbols like the bat, ball and wickets embroidered colourfully on their visors, Mala continued her interrogation.

"I say, you haven't been coming to the club of late; is all well at home?"

At this point, Nikhil turned around and joined them, sporting a white cap embroidered with the lettering *India* in deep saffron, under which the icons of a slanting bat and a flying ball shone in grass green, thus weaving together the near-obsession of the nation symbolised by the tricolour, with the game that sometimes transcended sporting spirit to assume communal colours.

Mala looked around momentarily to ascertain who the boy belonged to, but asked finally, "So you have relatives visiting you?"

Kamini's sodden countenance betrayed no expression as she replied in a rasping whisper, "Nikhil is my neighbour. His mother is purchasing some handicrafts from a nearby stall and we are going to eat together." She had no antidote should Mala want to join them for some snacks at the food court, but the exaggerated confidence in Kamini's tone left no room for suspicion.

"Okay, then," Mala sighed, wrapping her arms around the puny figure of her daughter. "Maybe I'll see you in the club sometime." Kamini did not stay to respond to this comely parting phrase, but strode along, wiping the beads of sweat on her thinly arched eyebrows with the edge of her georgette sari.

She collapsed like an empty bag on a wooden bench facing billowing steam emanating from large flat woks of a Chinese food kitchen. She experienced deep turmoil as she looked at Nikhil sauntering in nearby stalls.

Math was not her forte, but numbers drifted through the currents in her mind, lucidly. If she would have given birth at Mala's age, her child would be exactly Nikhil's age today.

She banished these incriminating thoughts from her mind as Nikhil came and occupied a seat opposite her.

"You have to promise me, aunty," he said in earnest, his dark features blending with the indigo sky beyond.

The salutation that would have otherwise gashed her soul and inflamed its turbulence, evoked no impact on Kamini. He was right to address her as his aunt. He was right to seek a promise from her to never engage in insidious flirtations with him. He was also right to want to confess their frivolous encounters to his mother. She dared to look into his eyes—innocent as they were—in the cover of darkness.

"Please don't tell mummy that I ate meat."

She stared long at his pearly-white teeth bordered by fine sprays of adolescent moustache. As they laughed and chatted over a hearty Chinese meal of piping hot spring rolls, garlic chicken chop suey, and golden sizzling noodles, Kamini threw reconnoitring glances around her, every now and then. They abandoned their chopsticks and voted for forks instead, coiling their noodles on the fork in a competition to finish first.

The red light flashing on her phone indicated that there was a voicemail when Kamini returned home after nine in the evening. Ankur resembled a sleeping cherub ensconced in the folds of a seashell, with wide-laced pillows flanking the side of his bed unprotected by the wall. Kamini opened the fridge brimming with glass casseroles that preserved dinner prepared by Rampyari. She tentatively lifted the lid from one, and bent forward to sniff the delectable odour of fried lentils cooked in coconut milk. Replacing the lid with a distracted clang, she returned to her bedroom.

Mani's voice seared with fervour as he spoke to Kamini in monologue through the perforations in the phone.

"I reached the land of thunderbolts around seven in the evening amid pouring rain. We head out tomorrow to sample over 500 different varieties of tea. I can scarcely wait to distinguish the bold from the bright, the cloudy from the coloury, the flowery from the fusty, the wild from the—"

There was a pause.

"Am I boring you?"

Kamini started in alarm and looked around to ensure it was the speaker of her phone and not Mani in person who was talking to her. She had subconsciously been pressing her wrist at the spot where Nikhil had held it in the dance.

Mani's habitual roaring laughter struck Kamini as grotesquely sneering and she freed her wrist from her clenched hand.

"Okay, I won't bore you anymore, and will probably call in a day or two."

The long bleep indicating the termination of the message did not pierce Kamini's abstracted musings that now wandered to her blissful college years.

She was extremely popular among friends—especially males—owing to her seductive charm and extrovert ways. She wondered what had become of Rishi, a friend she was particularly close to, and even contemplated marrying at one point. Memories pounded her mind in much the same way the rain was beating against the windows in conjunction with the howling winds outside.

The storm raging within her assumed monstrous proportions as she lay tossing and turning on her velvet smooth bed. Flashes from her buoyant past came back to torment her, leaving her limp and emotionless.

She remembered how she had clasped Rishi's hand and pressed it apprehensively when Tom Hanks, in the dramatic role of Chuck in *Cast Away*, had set afloat on an amateur raft in the mighty ocean after four years of being marooned on an isolated island. She reminisced with bittersweet joy the day they had exited the movie theatre, unable to speak, totally mesmerized by the benign alien of *E.T. The Extra-Terrestrial*. Besides Hollywood, they also shared a passion for multicultural cuisine. They relished equally Japanese sushi, as they did Italian pasta or a non fussy McDonald's burger with fries.

Although she had once been fond of the exotic South Indian food, seeing Mani eat it ritualistically thrice a day, snuffed the longing out of her.

She throttled her surging desire to stroll on the balcony for fear of hearing the drill of Mrs. Menon's sewing machine.

Kamini

Kamini didn't realise how fast the week passed, as if in the twinkling of an eye. Rampyari had perceived a discernible change in her mistress' temperament, who now smiled and joked, though she couldn't comprehend her newfound love for kebabs. So, she made a fresh batch of Shish kebabs everyday that Kamini and Nikhil savoured while watching the spirited game of cricket.

A few weeks into the odyssey, Kamini was plagued by a crippling fear. Nikhil's interest seemed to be ascending its summit, as India and Pakistan were to play their final match the following day. Her heart scalded at the thought that the innocent world she had wrought to evade her solitude, would soon be reduced to naught.

The next evening, Kamini's heart was a kaleidoscope of emotions as she sat lackadaisically, staring blankly at the television like a mute marble statue in a pure white chiffon sari.

She feigned interest by smiling feebly when Nikhil cheered the Indian team ecstatically after they won the toss. She couldn't vouch that his love of kebabs would be a potent vector in continuing their innocuous rendezvous, as Nikhil was too preoccupied to be swayed by the tantalizing odour of the snack, sitting on the edge of the couch, his bated breath broken only by intermittent applause.

With her modest knowledge of the game, she could sense that stakes were high for both sides in this fiercely contested match. Nikhil buried his face in his lap—covering it with both hands—as a shrill whistle from the referee rose over the din of discordant exchanges from players, resulting in the expulsion of a stellar batsman from the Indian team. Though he had racked up an impressive tally of runs, his exit cast a gloom over the likes of Nikhil, nationwide. In less than half an hour, another formidable batsman got bowled out at a furiously hurtling ball by the Pakistani team. As the vanquished Indian batsman stooped to pick up his paraphernalia scattered close to the stands, Nikhil fell back on the couch and bent his head. The pace and intensity with which the game was being played gnawed at Kamini's optimism—shredding it to microscopic bits—as the possibility of a draw seemed remote. She understood enough to know that a draw would mean playing more to determine a winner, thus opening the floodgates for more cricket the following day.

Adrenalin came rushing back to Nikhil in overdoses as the Pakistani captain, who had flung every ball to sixers and boundaries like an automaton, collapsed finally to an impressive ball by the Indian side. With less than an hour to close, the competition was now neck-and-neck. Nikhil slid back excitedly to the periphery of the couch, and Kamini noticed a soft pulsate through his cheek that comes from clenching of one's jaw.

Frenzied yelling from the crowd, coupled with the zealous voice of the commentator heralded the ousting of the second last Pakistani batsman. Though Nikhil's face was inscrutable and the scores painting the screen didn't mean much to her, Kamini could foretell, in her own layman way, that all was not lost for the Indian team. The rivals had to make only ten more runs, but they had no other batsman than the one on the field, in their arsenal. She had heard of seasoned batsmen making centuries before getting ejected from play, but some even succumbed in their first innings to a steadfast bowler. In the final moments of the match, Nikhil closed his eyes frequently in prayer for a miracle to wallop the last impediment standing between victory and his motherland.

The Indian bowler had an unyielding look on his rugged face as he sprinted, stopped, rotated his arm and propelled the ball with a velocity that sent the wicket flying, amid roaring cheers and seismic firecrackers. Nikhil sprung up from the couch, jumped euphorically, and embraced Kamini in a tight hug as the players lifted the star bowler and bathed him with champagne.

Kamini's smouldering primal instinct surfaced as the touch of their bodies warmed her viscera. She felt his breath on her nape as her buxom chest flattened against his. A medley of feelings floated across her mind like potpourri in a glass, as she fought back concupiscence for Platonic love.

A juggernaut of libido pulverized her half-hearted attempts at staying demure to stave off the wanton overture. Initially diffident, Nikhil reciprocated by unhooking the panels of her blouse when she touched his groin. As they wedged into the couch, Kamini could tell it was his first time, by the way he insinuated into her before giving her the bounty of his ultimate passion. She lay in the same position—long after he was gone—moist from the climax, yet unsure of the denouement of this liaison.

Kamini seemed to have found the elixir of life in her frequent coitus with Nikhil, who treated it like manna to explore his newfound sexuality. She saw a stark analogy between her and the legendary Cleopatra, although she found no likeness between Mani and Julius Caesar, or Nikhil and Mark Antony. She subconsciously obliterated the gruesome end of the Egyptian queen and her lover from her psyche, replacing it with gratifying thoughts of her harmony and unison with Nikhil.

Days rolled into weeks, and Kamini condoned her impulse for jouissance in its myriad avatars with Nikhil, in the confines of her bedroom. One evening, as she approached the lamp to turn it off, in the backdrop of the rumpled bed after Nikhil's departure, she stood transfixed, reading the diary where it lay open, pressed down by a steel pen next to the cylindrical spiral of wire. She clutched the chair close to the table to stay steady, as what she read made her head vertiginous.

"You twisted my tongue and burnt my mouth with your scorching touch—you full-bodied siren! When you're dry, you're soft, delicate and mellow; but when I drench you in water, you take me on with the power and grace of Artemis! You become strong, dark and seductive."

Kamini sank in the chair heavily, staring at the stenciled flowers that seemed to smile at her predicament. She turned her vacant gaze to the ceiling. Suddenly, she started leafing violently through the pages of the diary. The same excerpt stared at her tenaciously. She took the pen, and holding it like a knife, slashed the text again and again, until she reached a line in fine print, close to the end of the page that read, "To you I raise a toast my Darjeeling, you are truly the champagne of all teas!" That night was a twilight zone for Kamini, between marked apathy and excessive concern over her future.

She went about her life perfunctorily, casting forlorn looks at the clothesline on the other side of the parapet wall several times a day, through gaps between the curtain of riotous bougainvillea that separated her house from her neighbours'. Nikhil's white trousers swayed in the brisk autumn wind, serving as a grim reminder of their temporary severance, owing to his board exams. She darted back into the house on hearing the phone ring.

"Kamini speaking." Her voice resounded a strange alibi for an unknown accusation.

"Kamini, Mani here." His voice echoed inexplicable exaltation.

"I can visualize my long nurtured dream coming to fruition."

Kamini grimaced as she struggled to decipher the intent of her husband's speech.

Kamini

"Over the course of intensive executive meetings, I have thrashed out a plan to move permanently to Darjeeling."

Kamini's head swam in a welter of emotions as she grasped the enormity of the situation.

"We will live—you, I and Ankur—in the shadow of the snow-carved *Kanchenjunga*, on the roof of the world! Never again would we have to be separated for weeks on end . . ."

". . . Are you there?"

"Yes." Her tone was poignant as she felt her entire being drawn into a vortex of emotions by this surreal twist of events.

"Imagine waking up to the sight of an emerald canvas painted with live, shiny, deep green tea bushes. We will float together on the flying carpet of weightless clouds, touching the zenith . . ."

Kamini opened her mouth to speak, but words eschewed her and she let out an inaudible plaintive whine.

Mani continued, blissfully ignorant of the inexorable impact his fanciful speech was having on Kamini.

"We will walk hand in hand through olive green forests of cedar, cypress and chestnut, in the gathering haze and dancing mist, and the dappled sunlight will dazzle our eyes by the confusion of light and shade. You will splash your soft feet in the crystal streams tumbling noisily from rocks to stones in picturesque hillsides."

Kamini spent the next week-and-a-half like a zombie, her life looming over her like a complex jigsaw puzzle whose irregular pieces did not seem to fit to produce any semblance of coherence. Her head heated up like a brick in a kiln as she spent all her waking hours envisioning a new life in Darjeeling. She pictured clearly a replacement for Mrs. Sinha and Mala, and other ladies at the club. Her *virtual* substitutes retained their personality traits, masked behind mongoloid features—characteristic of the hilly people. Only, she could not find a substitute for Nikhil. She would be jostled out of sleep in the wee hours of the mornings by menacing hallucinations of being forcefully taken away to Darjeeling.

She resolved to accost Mani to spurn his decision of relocating by using their only child Ankur as a pawn.

She would scrounge him, she determined, that Ankur's future would be marred forever if he was uprooted from the capital city of New Delhi. Afterall, education was far superior in Delhi as compared to Darjeeling. She would wheedle him, if all else failed, that she would go insane if taken so far from her parents. Mani was scheduled to return the day after, but it seemed like eternity to Kamini. For the first time in her seven married years had she waited so impatiently for her husband. She collapsed on the bed, exhausted from the motley of feelings whose tempo was invincible for her mind. That night, Kamini slept with the blithe and bliss of the mythical *Sleeping Beauty*, aroused only by the repeated doorbells of her prince.

As she closed the door behind her, a palm-sized wooden cuckoo pushed a small, intricately carved door of a beautiful darkwood clock and popped out to sing the hour. Kamini stared at the embraced hands of the clock, realizing how late it was in the day, and in her life.

Nikhil had come briefly to announce the news of his acceptance to Boston University, overjoyed at fulfilling his mother's most cherished dream.

He would come again he had said, if he could, to spend some time with her before flying to America day after tomorrow. Until this moment, she had revelled at the discovery that she was pregnant with his baby, though she hadn't the courage to tell him so.

Kamini shuddered to think that she had been standing in the same spot for an hour—one hand on her tummy—when the tiny wooden bird called again melodiously. She looked at the clock, staring fixedly at its separated hands. There was something about the clock that celebrated the separation of its hands, she realized ruefully. The cuckoo bird seemed more charming, its voice more cheerful, and the parade of forest animals circling the turning water wheel exuded unparalleled merriment and festivity. Her head spun like a top as she considered excuses to see Nikhil, *just one last time*, the same day that Mani was arriving. She winced at this cruel coincidence hurled at her by destiny. She sank in an ocean of timelessness, loathing to look at the clock that rejoiced every passing hour, while she yearned to hold time still.

Nikhil could not find time from his preparations to visit her. He scribbled his flight details on a scratch of paper and passed it along the parapet wall, when she beckoned him hysterically after hours of waiting. She could not sleep a wink that night, debating, amid a constant stream of tears, what she would say to him the following day.

The Indira Gandhi International Airport was abuzz with activity when Kamini parked her car at a vantage point that afforded her an unobstructed view of the assortment of people flocking it, while leaving her inconspicuous to anxious passengers and their sentimental well wishers.

Her quivering lips were pursed as her heavy-lidded eyes screened the crowd to catch a glimpse of Nikhil. Her swollen eyelids smarted each time they blinked over stinging eyeballs, barren of more tears and bleary from the strain of locating their soothing oasis. They persevered, flitting from harried travellers dragging cumbersome bags on screeching wheels, to debonair youth munching crisp potato chips, and inopportune taxi drivers honking raucously to attract commuters, thus breaking the idyllic bliss of couples smooching goodbyes.

Kamini summoned occult powers to fetter her fluttering heart from bursting out of the prison of her car and embracing Nikhil, who was surrounded by a canopy of people bending over him, leaving her to content with the sight of his short, wire-meshed hair.

Her entire existence pirouetted, making her nauseous with emptiness as she waited for his family and friends to disperse. A whimsical breeze was blowing outside as Kamini ejected from the car, her otherwise lithe body wobbly as if seized by paralysis.

She tottered to reach the entrance of the departure lounge, pushing and elbowing the waves of humanity that swept her like a massive undercurrent.

As she got jostled and shoved by an unruly crowd, Kamini's gaze did not lose sight of the wiry matted hair that seemed to be merging with uncountable heads. She ran to the small window with tinted glass and cupped her hands to her temples, pressing her face and gluing her eyes to the dark glass.

Within seconds, she singled out the rough curls belonging to Nikhil's head, before they blended with the surrounding hues and textures.

Back in the car, Kamini tenderly lifted from the dashboard, Nikhil's cap that he had forgotten on the day they had gone to *Dilli Haat*, and caressed it fondly. She stared long at a short strand of hair on its inside hem that had curled into a small zero. She pinched it gently and placed it on the ring finger of her left hand. The hair coiled around it, locking both ends evenly. With the same hand, she slowly pulled the cap from her bosom to her tummy, pressing it lightly and uniting all souvenirs.

Groom Bazaar

"Hurry up, Ma, or else we'll reach there at I.S.T!"
Sita smiled at her reflection in the mirror on
being chaffed by her son Rohan. She most
definitely did not want to reach the venue of her only son's
unofficial engagement dinner according to *Indian Standard Time*,
which signified late beyond acceptable limits. Yet, although she had
been facing the mirror for almost an hour, there was neither trace
of make-up on her face, nor effort in her dressing. Her soft oval
face was a cushioned setting for enormous, black liquid eyes that
wore a ubiquitous maternal expression which could be moved by
any earthly being's misery.

Her dark hair that hadn't been dyed for long, was parted in the
middle with roots shooting grey, and drawn simply behind her ears
to be tied in a non-fussy chignon low on the nape of her neck. Her
white sari was almost her uniform after her husband's demise two
years ago—only today, the texture was silk, in keeping with the
demand of the occasion. She nurtured views similar to widows of
her generation, who led a near ascetic life bereft of all epicurean
pleasures, to honour the soul of their departed spouse.

However, Sita wanted to look special today, to extend her first welcoming gesture to a family that would soon be bound to hers, after Rohan married his long-time girlfriend Ronnie.

"C'mon ma, let's go," Rohan said, garlanding his arms around Sita's neck like a double string by folding them one on top of the other. He pressed his mother's shoulders tenderly and moved his scarlet tie sideways before tightening its knot around the starched collars of his sky-blue shirt. His youth was staggering: it seemed like the Greek God Apollo had hand-carved his broad athletic body by embedding fine black eyes flecked with gold, around a classical aquiline nose arching over a soft mouth, left perennially open in an effortlessly engaging smile. His thick, black wavy hair shone with oil and was neatly brushed back from his forehead, adding to the radiance of his bronze complexion. When Sita rose from her dressing chair, her eyes met Rohan's in the mirror. A gleam of pride flickered through them at this rare combination of male beauty and moral excellence. Even though he had not taken after her physically, she had moulded his character in a way that could well be a force to reckon with.

The drive from their house to the Indian restaurant overlooking Central Park was treacherous, as New York was reeling under sub-zero temperatures, seasonal for mid January. As they reached the large red awning emblazoned with the name of the restaurant, Sita's heart pounded with apprehension that was tranquilized upon entering the sumptuous interior.

They had arrived before their guests, and a waiter courteously escorted them to their reserved banquet swathed in artistic patchwork of brown, yellow and orange. Clusters of red lanterns hung from the high ceilings, lending a warmth and colour contrasting sharply with the cold white snow outside. Rohan stood akimbo, looking out of the large glass windows at Central Park across the street that lay whitewashed, except the lake whose inky-black waters distinguished it readily.

Sita sat expectantly at the immaculately set corner table, bordered by a flaming red tapestry portraying the phoenix bird with its brilliant plumage, roosting in a nest engulfed by raging flames. She was glancing askance at patrons entering or leaving the premises when Rohan muttered suddenly, "Here she comes!" and pointed his chin towards a fair young blonde wearing a skimpy dress with spaghetti straps and pencil heels. The placid expression in Sita's eyes was unchanged as she looked intently at the western beauty. She was prepared to embrace any girl her son chose, as she believed she had instilled unwavering values in him to make wise decisions. Rohan laughed heartily at his lark and teased his mother by saying, "Ronnie will come with her parents." He wiped the corner of one eye and continued, "She'll wear more clothes for your first meeting!"

Even before he had finished, an elderly couple were seen inquiring from the waiter and regarding tables searchingly. Rohan nodded to his mother and dashed towards them. Shortly after, Ronnie entered and Rohan shook their proffered hands effusively. Sita stood up, joining her palms like a book in a traditional *Namaste* and gave Ronnie a gushy hug. She was enamoured by the pleasing frankness in her face, the centrepiece of her anatomy being her kind eyes with their gentle expression.

When everyone had settled into elegant chairs upholstered with smooth feather cushions draped in watered satin, Rohan caught the waiter's eye and signalled him by a subtle nod of his head.

"What would everybody like for drinks?" he asked with a joyous ring in his tone.

Sherry, Ronnie's mother, flashed her pearly-white smile as she spoke without referencing the green menu card shaped meticulously to resemble a banana leaf.

"Like my name suggests, I adore Sherry!"

The party burst into peals of laughter as the waiter inquired politely, "We have the delicate salty Manzanilla or the nutty flavoured Amontillado; which one would you prefer?"

"Bring the first one—the vanilla or whatever—for I can't afford to be nuttier than I am, when I discuss my daughter's wedding!" There were renewed outbursts of unbridled laughter, and sherry felt triumphant on setting the tone for an entertaining evening.

Her cheekbones daubed with rouge acquired a deeper red hue, though her chief asset was her infectious smile of even white teeth under thin lips smeared with magenta lipstick, much like strawberries on fresh cream.

"Sweet lime for ma," said Rohan confidently, peering into the waiter's elongated tablet.

"That takes care of all ladies but one." Ronnie's face flushed red as Rohan stared at her meditatively.

"Let's see; Chardonnay?"

"Margarita," she chuckled, as she corrected him amiably.

"Sir," yelled Rohan in typical army discipline as he urged Ronnie's father Chris to reveal his choice.

"We're made of tough stuff, boy!" bellowed Chris from under the folds of his double chin, snapping his black suspenders with his thumbs.

"I get it; gin and tonic then?"

"Neat whisky, my boy!"

"Watch out, sir, for inordinate levels of alcohol in the blood can lead one to blurt out one's mummified secrets that should best be left in undisclosed vaults."

"Soldiers fear nothing, my son; he who fears the fairer sex can guard his nation no better than he guards his zipper!"

Chris chortled at his own witty remark, and though his corpulent body abrogated any affiliation with active military service in the recent past, his small pugnacious eyes bore a look sharp as an axe, that could tell friend from foe instantly.

His stout rubicund face was sprayed randomly with craters—apparent tokens from his combat days—and his ravaged, even battered appearance lent him the distinction and verisimilitude worthy of nobility.

By this time the drinks had arrived, and the lively hum of conversation was as merry as a marriage bell.

"Did you hurt your leg in the army, or have you had a fall recently?" Sita had been meaning to ask after Chris' leg soon after she noticed him limp in his right foot. Rohan shifted uneasily in his chair, all while keeping his good-humoured smile, as, although he knew his mother could never rein in her maternal concern for everybody, he wasn't sure if this was an apt question for the occasion.

"Oh yeah, it got blown off during our action in the Vietnam War." The nonchalant way in which Chris answered, stroking his artificial leg, made one wonder whether he was referring to a vital body limb, or something as inconsequential as a lamp post blown away in a hurricane. Whatever it was, Chris' mien and his ability to make light of a horrific chapter in world history soothed Rohan, and he pined to steer the conversation to a gayer route.

"Let's everybody narrate how we met our lover or beloved," he suggested. "And remember—no omissions or commissions!"

"Boy, I see the alcohol working its magic on you already! Like I said, I fear nothing and no one and want to volunteer first."

No sooner had Chris unveiled his desire to relive the memorable moments of his love life, than a thunderous applause from the audience rent the air. He bowed theatrically in every direction and gulped his drink at one go, shaking the glass in his cavernous mouth to empty it of its last drops.

"Sherry's husband was my best buddy, and what he thought was a stupendous favour ever asked of a man, changed my life forever. He had lain in my lap in his last moments; well, you ought to remember that my lap was only a *half lap* as my leg was severed in the same explosion that cost my buddy his life."
Chris cleared his throat before it could choke up and clog his gallantry with the ardour of his emotions.

"He had clutched my hand with his trembling mass of blood and peeled skin, and looked into my eyes with an expression I'll take to my grave."
At this point, Chris glanced at Sherry, who was visibly moved and swallowing incessantly. Agonizing yet momentous memories flooded her mind by leaps and bounds, as she thought back of the cruel twist destiny had sprung on her when she was pregnant with Ronnie. From the time Chris called on her to break the news of her husband's demise, till the present day, they had mourned their losses together, smiled through their tears together, and been as inseparable as one's shadow. They compromised with life to feel complete again—he without his leg, she without her husband. As years rolled by, neither viewed their void as an impediment, but drew strength from it to laugh at life's ironic absurdities. She shuddered to think what her life might have been like if Chris hadn't made that unspoken promise to her husband on the altar of friendship.

"I say, words are more intoxicating than booze!" exclaimed Chris, looking around at pale faces and unblinking eyes.

"Well, I forgot to tell you how I proposed to her."

Sherry rolled up her eyes at Chris and her face turned sanguine with apprehension of what might follow.

"Ma chérie, give Chris a kiss!"

At this dramatic remark, Chris bowed again, blowing kisses at everyone as if he were leaving the podium after an impetuous speech.

Ronnie held up her glass and exulted, "Cheers to both my fathers—one gallant in death and the other gallant in life!"

An enormous clang of glasses resounded in the dining hall.

Rohan took his knife and cut the samosa into half from the spire, and poking his fork into it, advanced it to Ronnie who started nibbling at it.

"Madame, though our mike is deliciously edible, please use it as a microphone to make your speech."

Ronnie laughed so hard at Rohan's banter that the appetizing pastry burst open, spilling the lightly spiced potatoes and peas on her plate.

"Well, our story is the humdrum tale of two colleagues exhibiting disinterest in each other of so wide latitude that they end up falling in love eventually."

Her lilting speech brought instant smiles to all faces, and unconvinced that her love story was hackneyed, everybody looked at her eagerly to elicit more details.

"Journalism is an excessively insightful profession. It not only enlightens you on the events that shape the world on a daily basis, but also reflects the personalities and perspectives of the people you work with." Ronnie paused and mulled over some seemingly indelible incidents, smiling beatifically when she resumed her speech.

"It is sadly ironic that the outrageously horrific terrorist attacks of September 11, 2001, that were perpetrated by hatred, infused love into our souls by galvanizing us to act in solidarity towards the innocent victims. I would've gone without food the whole day when news first came in of the deadly strikes, had Rohan not brought me a sandwich and a reassuring smile, before scooting off to circulate in our newspaper office to collect funds for families who had lost earning members in the searing tragedy. As the hysteria settled and people grudgingly came to grips with this surreal incident, Rohan mobilized the entire office into small volunteer groups to assist the valiant firefighters with rescue and relief operations."

Ronnie's hatchet face was swept by a pinched expression, and her eyes became glazed as she ran her fingers through her silky auburn hair.

"Look at her making me a social martyr," interjected Rohan with an embarrassed smile, realizing Ronnie's inability to continue her speech.

"She conveniently obfuscated the uncountable instances when she championed the cause of single mothers and women subjected to domestic violence, by exposing their woes through her powerful articles."

Rohan paused, not revealing the quality about Ronnie that had touched his heart the most. She would often tear up and melt like soft wax while reporting on child abuse or infant mortality. This maternal streak in her character had likened her to his mother, winning him over many times.

There was almost a minute's silence, after which Sita looked at the children with an admiration that, if it could speak, would say, "Children, you've made us proud!"

"My boy, I know who the credit should go to."

Everybody turned their eyes to Chris as he scratched his shock of coarse tousled hair.

"You see this beautiful woman here?" He wrapped his stocky arm around Sherry as he spoke.

"She encouraged a lame man like me to pursue my passion for active army work. Do you want to know how?

Everybody nodded.

"Then say, *how* loudly!"

All voices echoed "how" in unison.

"Well, she showed me how rewarding and gratifying her work was as a counsellor with the Salvation Army. And voila, I'm back to the army, not living in barracks or operating rifles, but working in community kitchens and cooking meals for the homeless."

The waiter had cleared the table of appetizers, and stood waiting for instructions for the main course.

"Yes, sir, we're ready to order," Chris said, patting his well-rounded belly as he added, "So the moral of the story is that it's all in the genes, and thoughtful parents make generous children. So, ladies, what would you like to order for food? Mrs. Pundit?"

Sita started at being torn from her cocoon and blushed slightly as she answered Chris with downcast eyes.

"Just vegetable *biryani* should do for me."

"Ma, you'd better eat well, for it's your turn next to relate your love story."

Sita glared at her son with reproachful eyes as if warning him against his churlish demand.

"Good reminder, boy!" rumbled Chris, tapping his pudgy dimpled fingers on the table rhythmically.

"Foliage will not give you the energy you need to narrate your story, Mrs. Pundit; how about a meat dish?"

Sita was mortified at the insistence, but answered with an expression of resolute benignity on her sallow face.

"After Mr. Pundit's demise, I adopted vegetarianism."

A pall of solemnity fell over the party, and realizing the need to enliven the mood again, she added with a tardy smile, "Vegetable *biryani* is the delectable dish of fragrant *basmati* rice cooked with fresh vegetables and garnished with saffron and nuts. You would all vie for a taste of my dish when it arrives."

"If Mrs Pundit vouches so unequivocally for this rice dish, then let's order two of those so that we don't have to snoop around in her plate, and rob her of the calories she needs to sum up her love life."

Sherry's naive remark propelled Sita to a state of extreme consternation, and she felt her bones rattling at the prospect of reliving her lurid past.

At this moment, Ronnie interjected felicitously, shifting the spotlight from Sita to food, much to Sita's relief.

"I vote for ginger chicken; mom, we'd all share the extra rice dish, so what do you want as an accompaniment?"

Sherry leafed through the punctilious menu before quizzing the waiter who was standing, smiling patiently and awaiting complete orders from the group.

"This *tandoori* vegetable dish, is it purely vegetarian?"

"Yes, ma'am; this is our widely acclaimed signature dish prepared with marinated vegetables in a special clay oven."

"Excellent! Then Mrs. Pundit and I will soak in the heavenly juices of vegetables. What better time for me to kick start my long overdue diet plan?"

Sherry sighed in relief, and a self satisfactory smile lit up her face on her clever endeavour at assuaging Chris' unwitting suggestions of meat for Mrs. Pundit.

"Oh boy, dieting is the last thing this guy wants to hear about," said Chris, chuckling and caressing the contour of his belly bulging within the suspenders.

"Sir," he turned to the waiter with a mischievous but cordial smile dancing on his lips.

"Would you care to explain what *Jardaloo Ma Gosht* is, and if it is a distant cousin of voodoo the ghost?"

There was a hearty roar of laughter from everybody, and the waiter tried hard to maintain his composure amid uproarious giggles as he explained the ingredients of the succulent lamb dish.

"My turn," butted Rohan, and rattled off his dish by reading it verbatim from the menu.

"Mussels balchao with shrimp saag."

"Don't belch and sag so young in life, my boy!"

There was a renewed round of laughter and everybody, including the waiter, was enjoying Chris' entertaining humour, and the ambience around the table was uplifting and chirpy as a bird.

Shortly after, sundry aromas were frothing in the air, and the clatter of cutlery on fine bone china broke the concentrated silence of the group savouring the delicacies.

"Aunty, pardon my journalistic instinct, but I was wondering whether you had a love or arranged marriage."

The suave manner in which Ronnie addressed Sita in the spirit of pure curiosity unnerved her, as all others stared at her like a lynx, while she fought back the stand-offish expression in her eyes to replace it by her trademark smiling eyes.

"Mine's a rather rum story of falling in love while en route to having an arranged marriage."

Sita fell silent after this concise summary of her matrimony, innocently unaware of the monumental interest her paradoxical statement had aroused in her audience. She lowered her eyes and started spooning the *biryani* into her mouth, but when she raised her eyes again, everybody was looking at her with saucer-like eyes, imploring her to continue. She pretended not to take cue and busied herself by refilling empty glasses with water from a jug.

"Pray, continue," hazarded Chris when his eyes met Sita's.

"Well, I don't know where to start, and my speech will be more desultory than voluble," confessed Sita culpably, hoping to extinguish the spark of interest ignited by her brief exordium. There was no reaction to her self-proclaimed flaws of oration; on the contrary, expectant gazes and pindrop silence enveloped the atmosphere.

"It was in the summer of 1976 that my parents deemed the time was ripe to head back to our ancestral village of Madhubani district in Bihar to find an eligible groom for me. My father was a senior professor of Sanskrit at a government university in Delhi, and the spring semester had just finished in time for the protracted summer vacation. My mother, who was a housewife, prepared a bundle of rotis for our overnight train journey." Sita paused, and her face was a collage of conflicting memories crowding her mind and drumming its walls vociferously, to push open a door shut tight for uncountable long years.

"I didn't quite know what to make of it as I had just entered college, but knew it would be wanton to question the dictates of tradition. We squeezed into a yellow-roofed autorickshaw on a sultry Sunday morning, hardly able to breathe between the suitcases, rolled bedding, and a multi-layered steel tiffin carrier to whose handle mother tied the loose end of the muslin she had knotted on her rotis. Our bumpy ride came to an abrupt halt near the Jama

Masjid mosque, where thousands of protestors waved placards and yelled slogans amid brutal *lathicharge* by khaki-clad policemen."
Sita's ashen face reddened at the memory of bleeding heads, shrill horns, the dust, sweat and complete chaos that she didn't understand then.

"I cowered in my mother's lap as agonized wails deafened my senses, and I could no longer bear the sight of defenceless people falling to the fatal blows of police *lathis* without compunction."

Everybody's eyes were rolled up in their sockets and Sherry inquired subconsciously, "What had the people done to deserve this atrocity?" The rest of the party nodded as if they were too dazed to ask the same question Sherry now posed.

"Well, the then Prime Minister Indira Gandhi had proclaimed emergency rule, bestowing upon herself despotic power to rule by decree, thus bringing democracy in India to a grinding halt. It is said, her decision was dictated by political ambitions rather than welfare of the country. During this dark interlude in independent Indian history, civil liberties of citizens were suspended and scores of opposition leaders who threatened her political clout were forcibly jailed. The arbitrary destruction of the slum around Jama Masjid was one event in the exhaustive list of the government's crackdown that poor dwellers were protesting on the day we got stuck in the traffic jam. The slum dwellers vehemently opposed the razing of their settlements without any viable alternative, but were silenced by the iron fist police."

"Did you still make it to your home town, ma?" inquired Rohan with a heavy voice.

"Yes, we reached the railway station by crossing the historic ramparts of the Red Fort from which Pundit Nehru had addressed India on the eve of her independence. Thankfully, he didn't live to witness a day when poor Indians would be made homeless in a place he probably saw, while making his first speech emphasizing the need to '*build the noble mansion of free India where all her children may dwell.*'"

Chris scratched his dishevelled hair and asked with an incredulous expression in his eyes, "Why did the government want to demolish the slums?" He shook his head disbelievingly and continued, "We in America have inalienable rights, and nobody could land up one fine day and want to pull down our homes. I'm outraged that such heinous incidents can happen in independent and democratic countries."

Sita's face twisted to an anguished grimace and a deprecating smile broke on her mouth as she spoke.

"Well, the prime minister acted on advice from her son Sanjay Gandhi, who wanted to give a massive facelift to the national capital, modelled after sprawling western cities he had lived in."

"So aunty, how and when did you come to New York?" Ronnie's voice rang with breathless suspense.

Sita looked at Ronnie with deliberation as an avalanche of recollections flashed back into her memory. Her face wore an abstracted look and was as phlegmatic as the calm before the storm.

"We scrambled into our overcrowded second-class train compartment, and my parents protectively sandwiched me between themselves to avert unwelcome jostling or deliberate brushing of bodies by lecherous men towards me. So passed the afternoon, when the entire train seemed to reek of a commingling of odours like pickles, raw onions, curries and chutneys, among others. My mother served our lunch of rotis and roasted cumin potatoes on newspapers spread on our laps, covered by a small hand towel. After lunch, my mother, who was a massive woman with aristocratic features, dozed off, her mouth partly open and revealing the half-chewed areca nuts between her chipped teeth."

Sita broke off her narrative and lowered her head before confessing candidly, "I was embarrassed by my mother's enormous snoozing body, as her head hung over my neck, vibrating my eardrums with her intermittent snores. I wanted her to be as active as my father, who, although a shrivelled little man of sixty with a dome of a shiny bald head, pored intellectually over the local Hindi newspaper. Mother was jarred awake by the wailing airbrakes and squealing wheels of the train when it stopped at a station. More people with more luggage entered and squished into the remaining seats. Turbaned *chaiwallahs* peeked through the iron bars of the windows, yelling incessantly, "*chai garam—garam chai,*" as outstretched hands exchanged a few coins for thick orangey tea in clay cups. As our train rolled out of the station, jerking gradually before catching speed, my eyes fell upon a young man seated next to the window opposite me. When he showed his ticket to the controller, I noticed his gallant bearing and clean-cut strong features."

The contours of Sita's lips trembled as she bit it tentatively before resuming her narrative.

"At this moment, I was thankful to my mother for being half asleep and wished my father could have a siesta too, as I yearned to steal furtive glances at this fine, self-assured man."

A demure smile travelled from Sita's softly shining eyes and suffused her face with mirth and charm. She seemed to have been transported back in time by a sorcerer.

"At first, he didn't look at me, but towards evening our eyes met. Given the conservative traditions, we couldn't talk or even manifest the remotest interest in each other; and though I couldn't vouch for his feelings towards me, the longing yet helpless expression in his eyes seemed to reciprocate my ardour. The magic of love transfused us. No words issued from our lips. As night fell and people prepared to sleep, the pandemonium of the train calmed down—only to enter our hearts and shake them with its tempestuous ferocity. I lay on my berth wondering what my future husband would be like. A shiver travelled my spine when I saw his hairy, virile chest from the corner of one eye when he took off his *kurta* to sleep in his vest and pyjama."

Sita sighed, and a disquieting look crept into her eyes.

"What happened next?" prodded Sherry, while all others waited in rapt silence.

Sita tried to speak, but only her lips moved, and her enormous eyes were distraught with anguish. She finally pulled herself together and continued.

"I only slept in snatches, and was quickly awakened when a group of gruff looking presumptuous policemen entered the train in the dead of night and started rounding people up. They entered our compartment too and peered at people with frigid insolence, swooping on unsuspecting travellers, mostly young men. *My young man* held out his train ticket pertinaciously to resist the onslaught, but was boxed in the face and punched in the stomach before being forced out of the train amid a stream of invective and profanities. I was repulsed by the cowardice of fellow passengers who merely crouched in their berths at this brute spectacle. Soon there was a deathly silence in the train, broken only by hushed whispers. Stifled sobs could be heard from the adjoining compartment where a woman had been manhandled and her son forcibly taken away when she tried to expostulate."

There was discernible mockery in Sita's smile, and the tartness in her manner was evident as she spoke.

"I was livid with shock and totally bewildered, as I was unwilling for a somersault in my opinion about this young man. He seemed to have an unimpeachable character and dignity, and was the last person you could suspect of larceny or pilferage. Why, he had held out his legitimate train ticket with the tact and firmness of a gentleman! My head swam as we finally reached our village, and hard as I tried, I couldn't rid my mind of recurring images of this gracious, tall, spare and dignified young man.

Our ancestral house of Madhubani was in a state of disrepair from long years of neglect, and as my father busied himself with renovations for my marriage, mother started frenetic preparations for my trousseau. Before long, my father and some male relatives were ready to participate in the *Saurath Sabha Gachchhi*—the annual congregation of Maithil Brahmins organized to fix marriages. This really was a kind of an open-air *groom bazaar*, set in the lush mango orchards of Saurath—a village nearly six kilometres from Madhubani.

Women were not allowed in this traditional *groom shopping*, so I waited at home with my mother every single day of the fortnight that father went to negotiate, haggle and select my future husband. I lamented the irony of my name that comes from goddess Sita, whose *Swayamvara* was held in the same village. The goddess was privileged to garland the man of her choice from a long line of accomplished suitors, yet custom tightened its tentacles around this freedom of women, and since the fourteenth century, fathers and male relatives of prospective brides flock this village annually to purchase grooms."

Sita's distinguished features relaxed into a large, fond smile as she gestured everyone to continue eating while they listened. She herself chased a slippery pea from her *biryani* and pierced it with her fork with an air of triumph.

"The hot summer air had ripened the mangoes in the orchards under which young men dressed sprucely in lily-white *dhoti-kurta* sat on a *charpoy*, flanked by elder males of their family. The services of a reliable mediator or middle man, who is well-acquainted with the groom's family, are widely solicited by the prospective bride's family to shed light on the groom's resume. The *Panjikar's* stall is usually approached when a groom has been selected, at which time the *Panji* issues a mandatory certificate of genealogical record, attesting that there is no blood relationship between the bride and the groom.

Though father brought home a multitude of profiles scribbled complexly in his pocket diary, he couldn't seem to make up his mind. Some boys were to short, others hardly qualified, and most others demanded too much dowry. I found a certain relief in his frustration, and hoped we could return to Delhi without finalizing my marriage.

But this was not to be. Late one afternoon, father entered the house jubilantly with my two male cousins demanding sweets and spice tea. Mother rubbed the sleep off her eyes after a long afternoon siesta and stared speechlessly at my father. Before long, father was swamped by a deluge of questions from my mother, and I cocked up my ears for every word he uttered, even though on the outside I displayed an indifferent composure while preparing tea and snacks."

Sita's face blushed a deep crimson as she noticed the three waiters listening intently to her breathtaking tale, a little distance from their table. Most customers had left, and the restaurant wore a deserted look with its empty tables. Sita covered her face with her right hand that looked like the talon of an eagle, and the brilliant deep red glimmer of the ruby on her middle finger fused with her rosy cheeks.

"Mango ice cream?" Rohan asked mechanically and everybody nodded in a dream-like trance. All eyes were once again glued to Sita's face that mirrored changing emotions and fleeting expressions with the regularity of clockwork.

Groom Bazaar

"My father was brimming with joy and bursting with pride at a young man's courage to denounce the vice of dowry. He gave long and infinitesimal details of how a young doctor named Rameshwar contested his family's exorbitant price tag on him by giving his word to marry me, without even seeing my picture. My father equated him to lord Rama, who had descended from the heavens to claim his virtuous wife Sita."

Sita's eyes filled like pails of water and her voice rose and fell like waves in a choppy sea. She turned her face and contemplated the phoenix trapped in wild blazing flames until she regained her composure.

"I can't even begin to tell you the extent of my overjoyed perplexity when I came face to face with the young man of the train, on the night of my marriage. The endless wedding rituals had exhausted me, and though in the beginning of the ceremony I didn't lose any opportunity to glimpse his feet from my veil (I had only imagined his appearance by eavesdropping on my parents' conversations about him), when time came for our wedding night, my boundless curiosity was drained by unquestioned resignation. I remember freezing like a stone statue when he lifted my veil. I stared at him like you would stare at an extra terrestrial, and tried to comprehend this fortuitous turn of events. I had so many questions that I wanted to hurl at him with the speed of light, but words failed me. I was too overwhelmed to speak."

Sita stopped, and you could discern that she was as overwhelmed now, as she would've been then.

"You couldn't stop here, Mrs. Pundit," Chris cried out loud in an unrelenting tone.

"Why, I shan't sleep a wink in my life until I've unravelled the mystery of how Mr. Pundit, who was so brazenly scuffled out of the train that night, came to marry a woman who had an arranged marriage with a man picked up from a groom bazaar by her father." Chris smiled proudly at his recapitulation prowess, of events enough to befuddle a prodigy.

Sita grimaced as if her heartstrings had been twisted with a violent pang, and the look of her eyes beseeched to be spared the torment of further details.

Rohan regarded his mother with approbation and begged her to continue, utterly oblivious to what he was bargaining for by delving into the crevices of her heart.

Sita closed her eyes meditatively as if to steady the turbulent current of her thoughts, and let out a woeful sigh.

"The long arm of coincidence ordained that Mr. Pundit was travelling on the same train that fateful day, to participate in the same groom bazaar of Saurath to fix his marriage with the help of his family. Fortunately, my father hadn't made a decision until the concluding days of the bazaar, and when Mr. Pundit arrived late in the fair due to the train fiasco, he instantly recognized my father. Although he was flooded with offers of brides' parents willing to pay him a hefty amount in dowry, he prevailed upon his father to arrange his wedding with me, with whatever means my father could afford."

Sita folded and replaced the spotless white napkin beside her plate, signalling the end of her story, and probably, the end of their dinner.

"All's well that ends well!" cheered Chris feverishly.

"But ma, why had daddy been forced out of the train that night?"

"Good question, my boy! I'd have tossed and turned in bed had I gone without fitting this last piece of the puzzle in what I think was a roller coaster story."

Groom Bazaar

Sita turned a deathly pale and seemed to have aged by a few decades in a matter of seconds. Her lips were parched and cracked, her eyes sunk deep in their sockets, and her face sagged under the weight of its countless wrinkles.

"Pardon my folly, but I speak today of what I've never spoken. Yet, speak I must, for Mr. Pundit's honour is at stake."

Sita's jaw twitched spasmodically, for it moved long after she had finished speaking. Her words were garbled when she resumed talking, and her voice resounded with asperity.

"The same emergency rule of the government that bulldozed poor peoples' slums in Old Delhi, passed a draconian law to tackle the burgeoning population crisis of India. Unsuspecting innocent men were forcibly sterilized by the brute force of the police thirsting to fulfill bureaucratic targets. Mr. Pundit was one of the million or so people who fell prey to this inhuman government policy."

Sita broke into inconsolable sobs that she tried to muffle by pressing both hands against her face. Rohan sprung to his feet and rushed towards the restrooms. Ronnie followed close on his heels, but met him midway as he was turning and coming back. Sita had pulled herself together, and her disposition bore the dignity of Juno as she braced herself to endure the fury of her son's emotions. Rohan knelt beside her and gave her nervously clasped hands an affectionate squeeze before rising and embracing her ardently. He looked buoyed by the heartrending sacrifices and vicissitudes braved by his parents. The expression in his eyes synchronized perfectly with the surge of his emotions. He gazed reverentially into his mother's misty red eyes with a reassurance that his heart didn't grieve over the parents he never saw.

"You and daddy are the only parents I know—the paragons of virtue."

Rohan's eyes brimmed over with an involuntary stream of tears as he returned to his seat and was quickly hugged by Chris and Sherry. Ronnie wiped her eyes dry with her palms and Chris exclaimed, "Let's order straws to drink the mango shake that was once an ice cream!" Everybody laughed consumedly, and as the waiters came to clear the table, Sita motioned with her hand that she wanted to say something. The waiters replaced the plates, and once again there was complete silence as all eyes riveted on Sita's blissfully smiling face.

"This fine young man that you see here," she said, pointing to Rohan with opaque yet proud eyes, "he had outstretched his plump hands with curled fingers even when he was only a few months old in the orphanage Mr. Pundit and I were visiting, to adopt a baby before flying out to the United States to escape the barbaric oppression and atrocities perpetrated by the Indian government against its law-abiding citizens. Most babies were asleep; some regarded us impassively and I felt compelled to move on, debilitated by their innocent empty gazes. Rohan was different, and I knew as soon as I laid my eyes on him that he was cast in a unique mould. A mould that would fight the bleakest of moments, under the most insurmountable challenges to snatch light and joy from the jaws of darkness and gloom."

Sita looked at Ronnie reflectively and continued, "he will illuminate your life with gaiety and treat you like a *Rani*—an Indian empress, just as he has made every second of his parents' lives cherishable with his love and humanity."

Sita was looking out of the window, and everybody strained their ears to listen to her final words.

"When our steamer entered the New York Harbour on that dark, wet night, I had run to the deck with Rohan pressed to my bosom, and as Mr. Pundit and I, along with hundreds of other immigrants stared in awe at the majestic goddess of liberty with a halo around her head and an upheld shining torch beside the golden door, we knew instantly that our children would never live the nightmares of their parents."

There was a brief silence, and then, almost immediately, it was pierced by a deafening applause, and as Chris stood up to salute Sita, the waiters—reminiscent of their own murky struggles—chanted aloud in chorus, "Long Live America!"

The Package Deal

I cannot tell you the story of my marriage without narrating to you the extraordinary circumstances surrounding my brother's. I was a grade 12 student of science at Patna High School, India, when I befriended a meek, coy girl called Payal, one year my junior. It all started thus: everyday, after the final school bell rang—announcing our liberation for the day from bondage to voluminous books, ambiguous lessons and indefatigable teachers—we would run to our waiting vehicles of minibuses, tempos or rickshaws with the sole aim of "rocketing" a decent seat, lest we had to ride back home stooping or dangling uncomfortably on thin wooden benches placed in the centre of the vehicles, that sent its occupants piling on one another when the driver braked suddenly or turned a sharp corner.

That day, I had got delayed in class, scribbling in a hand that resembled a thorny wire mesh, crucial questions the biology teacher thought of dictating only after the home bell had rung merrily, drawing hundreds of students out of their classes like the Pied Piper's flute lured the rats out of Hamelin. I glanced at my watch gloomily, even though for the first time in my 12 years at school I had the company of a few classmates trudging along unhurriedly, as everybody was certain the good places of their transport would have been taken by now.

When I reached my minibus, I saw a row of school bags lining the seats, adjusted and readjusted, it appeared to me, by latecomers to squeeze in some space for themselves. Now, the owners of those bulging bags—front pockets soiled with grease of spilt curries from lunch boxes—queued up outside the school gates to buy spicy *churan* balls, sweet-and-sour dried mango candies or popsicles to enjoy on their way back home.

I stood waiting in front of the minibus, unwilling to occupy the innermost part of the wooden bench which would, when the bus was filled to capacity, be akin to a gas chamber—the mingled odours of students' snacks not exactly poisonous, but grossly suffocating all the same. Just then, a frail, pale-faced girl with two neatly oiled braids touching her thin shoulders entered the bus and sat in the front aisle seat, removing her bag and placing it on her lap. Seeing me standing outside the bus, she called out respectfully, "*Didi*, do you want to sit on my seat?" I was both surprised and impressed simultaneously, as it was rare for anybody to renounce so strategic a place, which not only afforded a bird's-eye view of the street in front, but also promised a hassle-free dismounting from the cramped bus when one's home came. I hadn't seen her in our bus before, so even while I debated whether to accept her munificent offer, she stood up and promptly sat on the bench, taking her bag with her. The sight of the empty blue seat—although torn in several places, with fetid spongy foam jutting out intermittently—was inexplicably inviting for me. We chatted all the way until the bus stopped outside her home in Kankarbagh, which, as she told me, was where they had rented recently, after being served notice by the previous landlord. It was her first day in our minibus, hence she had come early for fear of missing it altogether, as no one knew her yet to make the driver wait, according to the tradition for friends and acquaintances.

So started our friendship, with an unspoken promise of keeping a place for each other in the bus, urging the driver to wait if either one was running late, and chatting our way home. It was when I passed my half-yearly exams in flying colours, whereas she barely scraped through, that I offered to hand down my books and reference material to her next year for her critical final year of high school. She then confessed to me that her parents couldn't afford to buy enough reference books for her, nor send her to tutorials like other students attended: as her father, now retired prematurely due to health reasons from the position of clerk at the State Bank of India, was saving every penny to construct a modest home in the suburbs. Renting a place to live after their government accommodation was repossessed, had put a considerable strain on their resources—chief among them being her father's meagre pension. Her mother had recently started teaching Hindi to a few kids from the neighbourhood, in order to cover the spiralling expenses arising out of her older brother Karan's admission to Patna Law School in the fall.

Payal was fearful whether she would be able to attend college— her falling grades being reason enough for her parents to marry her off and save themselves the burden of paying for her higher education. So, when she confided in me that she had got a whiff of her parents' intentions to get her married in a simple ceremony with the little money they had rationed for the occasion, as soon as her high school results were out, I flew to her rescue. Our bus rides back home saw the chatting and giggling replaced by serious discussions about the human nervous system, with us both poking our sharpened pencils over the internal picture of the brain with such unbridled zeal as if its intricately coiled nerve cells were spaghetti we were relishing with chopsticks. Everyday, as the bus sped and swerved, I gave her mock quizzes on Newton's laws of motion, and we could never drop anything on the metal floor of the bus without dissecting the theory of gravity. Such became our obsession with science that we rechristened popsicles, "frozen H2O," sour mango candies, "vitamin C," and the salty *churan* balls, "NaCl"!

By now, Payal had developed an ease and appreciation for science, no longer viewing it as an encyclopaedic collection of complex formulae or tongue-twister jargon, but essential components intimately connected to everyday life. The only subject I couldn't help her out with, was mathematics. I confessed to her candidly that decimals decimated my sleep, logarithms chased the rhythm out of my life, and numbers simply made me go numb. She was the only one among all my friends to learn my best guarded secret that my older brother Gaurav—a math prodigy and a second-year computer science student at Patna Science College—was the reason I was able to demystify the concept of *pi* and guess the answers to complex trigonometry problems by looking at the triangle only once. Payal listened to my brother's prowess spellbound, comparing him—she later told me—to her own brother Karan, who, given his unyielding skill at argumentation on everything from the choice of channels on TV, to desert menu and the orientation of furniture at home, was encouraged by her parents to join law school so that his relentless arguments could one day start paying the family's bills.

With my 12th board exams barely a few months away, I offered Payal to come over to my house after school and join us when my brother coached me in the afternoon. She could hardly believe her good fortune and jumped at the offer—confirming it on the spot—dispelling my apprehensions of her parents' disapproval.

"They'll be only too glad if I can make a solid base to get decent marks next year," she enthused perkily, but her pale cheeks got even more pallid as she added in a low voice, "afterall, my mother says I won't get a good match if I don't pass the board exams in first class."

"To hell with the match!" I retaliated rather peevishly. "We'll make sure you do so well that your parents have no choice but to send you to college." So saying, I raised my right hand and, clapping it loudly on her left, promised to talk to my brother the same day.

The following day, instead of getting off at her own home, Payal rode all the way in the bus to mine, which was in the elite neighbourhood of Patliputra colony—far removed from the hullabaloo of the city center where she lived. She seemed overawed, even a little intimidated by the environs of the locality, and its generously spaced sprawling bungalows shaded by majestic fig and neem trees.

"How can you study in such surroundings?" she gushed, spinning around with her arms outstretched like a bird's wings.

"What do you mean?" I asked, opening our black iron gate inwards to let her in.

"I mean, this place is so romantic," she muttered almost inaudibly, feeling the glistening heart-shaped fig leaves arching over our driveway before entering after me.

"You'll soon find out," I laughed and rang the bell. My mother answered the door, and I could tell she had been napping, for she was in a loose-fitting polka dot nightie, and her eyelids were a little puffy.

"Ma, is *bhaiya* back from college?"

My mother just stared at us, nodding to acknowledge Payal's *Namaste* with folded hands.

The Package Deal

"Oh, I forgot; Ma, this is Payal—my junior at The House of Science in school; Payal, this is my mother."

"Gaurav came home a little early today," explained my mother, rubbing her eyes for a long time to use her arms to conceal her sagging breasts, as she avoided wearing a bra at home.

"Good! I'd told him yesterday that from today until our exams, Payal would also study math with us."

"You can both freshen up and have some snacks before you call him home. He's playing hockey in the field behind."

My mother entered the kitchen, and I tapped Payal lightly on her back to show her my room, as she stood inanimately in the parlour staring at our darkwood cabinets with neatly arranged china, and black genuine leather sofas contrasted with red-hot organza cushions.

We washed our faces and settled down to my mother's spicy *pakoras* and steaming *chai*.

When we had finished, I took her to my study, and placing our bloated bags on the floor, I started making space on the table for our math lesson.

"Now you know why there's nothing romantic when the inside of an idyllic house is full of books that teach you calculations and reasoning—none of which is required for romance!"

I hollered to my brother from the back window of my bedroom, and he arrived in a few minutes drenched in sweat; his t-shirt clinging to his chest as if he had showered with his clothes on. Payal shot up from her chair nervously as he entered the study, greeting us casually and excusing himself to change before the lesson could start.

All this while, Payal had been looking down, first at his white sports shoes, then at the matted curly hair of his lank legs.

Very soon, we were balancing equations, drawing spheres and angles, using the tips of our fingers for calculations as my brother forbade the use of a calculator, and laughing hysterically when he dismissed our ignorance of getting radically opposite answers to the same problem by calling it "a difference of opinion." All along, I noticed that Payal avoided eye contact with him, looking at his hairy knuckles as he explained theories and methods.

As our exams drew nearer, my brother split us in two separate groups to solve our individual questions and problems.

At first, I didn't sense anything between the two, but as weeks rolled by, my brother would ask me to study in my bedroom when he was teaching Payal, citing as reason the importance of concentration in my work for my decisive board exams.

The few times I entered the study to fetch a book or serve them tea, I observed the intimacy shared by them. Privacy had turned everything around. The previously demure Payal now gazed at him long, and didn't seem to crouch timidly when my brother rapped her wrist or head for a wrong cube root or a missed step in an algebraic problem.

My father used to arrive home late in the evening after closing the confectionery shop he ran, and hence, Payal never crossed his path.

It was only when he realized my brother was absconding from home until late hours that he grew suspicious. A few rounds of intensive interrogations with me revealed to him that most of Gaurav's after college activities revolved around Payal. Previously, Payal used to take the bus back home, but of late, my brother would give her a ride on his Hero Honda motorcycle, on pretext of browsing through some books at the Khudabaksh library close to her house on his way back.

The same Gaurav, who could never miss a spirited game of hockey with his friends after college, now started spending most of his time away from friends and family, coming home at dinner time. My father changed his schedule too, and it was plain to me that under his guileless bribes of pineapple pastries and chocolate fudges for me, was a mute offer from an inexorable sleuth to work as his undercover spy. Now, he used to return home before Payal and I got back from school, kept my sweet tooth flattered by delectable treats for spending more time in the study when Gaurav would be coaching Payal, and forcefully offered to drop Payal home in his car, insisting that my brother should study at home; and that he had to go out anyway to meet the bakery suppliers and stockists.

My brother felt trapped—as if his life was back to square one, with all the love and passion ruthlessly subtracted from it. My position in the quadrilateral wasn't any easier, and I felt everyone involved was tugging at my loyalties like hungry kids scramble to get a piece of the pie. So, I didn't disappoint anyone, and tried to play the perfect juggler by sneaking Payal's messages to my brother on weekends when she called to arrange clandestine meetings with him; covering up for my brother's long absence from home even on Sundays; all while religiously spying on the amorous couple after downing my father's bakery delights!

But the cat-and-mouse game came to a head, and the axe fell early one morning on the Sunday of March—barely two weeks before our annual exams were scheduled to begin. Gaurav sped away on his motorcycle on pretext of retrieving his notes from a friend. Immediately afterwards, my father dashed to his car and followed suit, like a bloodhound who has sniffed mischief and breaks into a frenzied run along the trail of crime. I sat on the couch, my biology text book in my lap, but my mind emulating the process of osmosis I was trying to learn, with all my weaker thoughts of exam results getting diffused to the more pertinent ones of what awaited my brother if he was caught red-handed.

Cell phones were unheard of back in the day, and my brother was going to get a pager as a gift from my father if he passed his final year in distinction. Unable to warn my brother or stop my father, I just waited—my heart in my mouth—for their return, while lingering over the chapter dealing with human reproduction, wondering why my father would oppose the natural union of a man and a woman, and reading in detail the biological fusion of the sperm cell with an ovum that resulted in my brother and myself, in the first place.

My mother went about her daily chores in the most unruffled manner, preparing *aloo parathas* for breakfast while watching the weekly episode of *Ramayana* on our living room television. "Go study in your room, choti," she recommended, as the serial gained momentum with the blowing of conches and trumpeting of elephants to mark the epic homecoming of the exiled king Rama with his wife Sita and brother Lakshman to Ayodhya.

"It's okay, ma," I replied, not wanting to budge, as I was deriving solace from the tearful reunion of father and son on TV, where each one forgave the other.

"This can only happen on TV," I mused, when I saw the rightful king Rama dressed humbly as an ascetic and touching his father's feet, who had banished him wrongfully to 14 long years in exile only to please his wife Kakayee, who wanted her biological son Bharat to accede to the throne. "No wonder lord Rama is worshipped as God," I concluded. "Surely Gaurav will not react in the same way if papa bans him from seeing Payal again."

After an agonizing hour-long wait, I heard a melange of heavy engine roar and a smooth zipping sound in the driveway, and held my breath as I knew my father had caught his prey and was bringing him back to the den. The two entered—one after the other—with faces flushed red as if they had been jogging together instead of riding separate motor vehicles.

"Breakfast is ready," announced my mother, settling the plate of tiered *parathas* in the centre of the rectangular teakwood table, next to a dated, framed family photograph of me sleeping in my mother's lap, and my father hunched on all fours with my brother riding him like a horse in our front lawn.

"Ask your son if he got the notes back," snapped my father waspishly, staring fiercely at my mother as if she was to blame for Gaurav's newly acquired wayward behaviour.

"We can talk while eating," my mother said, pacifying my father, and drew out a chair for him at the dining table. "Breakfast is getting cold," she reiterated, looking at me sternly, and I got up immediately to summon Gaurav from his room. Shortly after, we were all seated at the table, eating savoury *parathas* with whipped yogurt in perfect silence.

"Vidya, ask him who taught him to lie to his parents, and since when he's fooling around with that girl." My mother glanced at me, dumbfounded, and when I tried to intervene, my father silenced me with a vehement show of his hand.

"This is between Gaurav and his parents," he thundered, with a loud bang of his fist on the table, his curved beak-like nose inflating as the nostrils filled with air. He looked unrecognizable now—his usually tender eyes blazing with fury, and the trademark amicable smile of his face replaced by a cantankerous pout. Gaurav had stopped eating and was fidgeting with a concave wedge of green mango pickle, his head lowered over his plate as if in deep meditation for an accurate paraphrase of his feelings.

"I—I love Payal," he stuttered, raising his head slowly and gauging our reactions, while resting his imploring eyes on my mother's flustered face the longest to garner her support.

"You can love whoever you like," pronounced my father in the tone of a hardened magistrate, "but you'll marry the girl *we* choose for you."

"But papa, what's wrong with Payal?" appealed my brother, unwilling to accept the decree without arguing his case to the hilt.

"They don't even own a car, let alone owning a house!" exclaimed my father in a tone of sheer exasperation. "You should have drowned in the Ganges below before smooching that girl on Gandhi Setu bridge I caught you two on, after a 5 km chase; shame on you!"

"Your papa is right," interjected my mother in short staccato bursts, as if her voice was being tugged at from opposite sides by competing loyalties towards her husband and son.
"Afterall, your exams are just round the corner, and you have no right to waste his hard-earned money by squandering the time you should be spending studying."

"Ask him what's wrong if we expect him to marry a girl whose family can give a good dowry. Afterall, his education has cost us a fortune, and it's only natural that we get it back in his marriage—that's how society works."

It seemed to me that my father was having a conversation only with my mother, for he never once glanced at me, or addressed my brother directly.

"Tell him, Vidya," he boomed, once again venting his anger at my mother who was unquestioningly allowing herself to be used as his scapegoat in this entire drama. "Tell him how your dowry helped us set up the confectionery store when we couldn't pay for my college after my father's premature death from a stroke. Education came so easy to them that they don't value their blessings." My father's eyes were bloodshot now, and I could see he was panting hard, as a soft wheezing sound escaped his chest each time he exhaled.

The Package Deal

"You're no more a kid," observed my mother, her innocuous glance drifting from the toothless, pudgy face in the photo to my brother's drawn stubbled countenance, as if this fact had only now dawned on her. With her balanced intervention, she hoped to act as a buffer between the antagonistic camps represented by her husband and son. But unfortunately, it had quite the opposite effect.

Gaurav sat up straight and leapt at her remark, to use it as a missile he wanted to launch at his father, to annihilate his orthodox doctrine and pulverize all reasoning emanating from it.

"Exactly!" he spurted, as if vigorously shaken champagne had just been uncorked.

"I am an adult and should be treated like one, which means I must have the right to choose my own life partner." My father scowled at my mother as a fastidious captain would at an intern, for steering the ship in murky waters. However, he seemed to have grabbed the steering from my mother and endeavoured to veer the conversation away from its present rocky base to smooth territory, single-handedly.

"Young man," he said tartly, sizing up my brother's face across the dining table as minutely as a painter regards his model for a portrait. "At your age, I was already working as a handyman in a small catering company of Varanasi, several hundred miles from my ancestral village of Kalyanpur. One evening, after I returned to my quarters from a hard day's work of rolling *puris* and washing dishes for a huge wedding dinner, I learnt of my own marriage through a telegram from my father placed on my *charpoy* with the words: COME HOME SOON. MARRIAGE THIS SUNDAY.

I placed the telegram back on the bed without ascribing much importance to it, as matrimony was a common occurrence in our large family. It was only when the high carbohydrate dinner of leftover *puris* and *kheer* rekindled my tired brain that I jumped up with a start. Being the youngest sibling out of six, marriage so far had only meant slaving in the makeshift camp to feed the entire village, and a dozen or so rituals that I had learnt to perform robotically to bless the newly-weds from the other side of the *pandal.* Now, the full intent of the telegram struck me with the force of a hurricane: blowing away my senses and uprooting my freedom. It was indeed *my* marriage father was alluding to, and the immediacy of it left me feeling as defenceless as a chicken before it is slaughtered. So, my son," my father sang in a sermonizing tone, moving his forefinger back and forth as if he were going to arrive at the moral of this surreal story as we both listened disbelievingly, for my mother was nodding her head in affirmation at every word my father uttered.

"When a girl chosen by *my* father can be as virtuous as your own mother, and the dowry brought with her lead to our astonishing prosperity, in a wedding performed in less than a week, how can *we* go wrong with you? And don't you now throw at me the argument of a generation gap," forewarned my father, sharpening his glare at my brother.

"We will not expect you to see your bride for the first time on the day of your marriage, as was the case with Vidya and me."

At this point, my father broke off into a throaty rolling laughter amid bouts of loud coughing and wheezing. I started smiling too, reminded of a related anecdote he had narrated to us in the past of how his friends had convinced him that his bride-to-be was cockeyed, and my father had tried to peek into my mother's long veil several times in vain during the wedding ceremony, to confirm the rumour.

My brother failed to appreciate the humour associated with so grave a life decision, and he cornered my father with the analytical precision mathematics had taught him, the disgruntled look never leaving his agitated face.

"So, as long as you get the dowry, it's okay for me to marry whoever I like—is that correct?"

My father grimaced by pursing his lips so tightly that it made his eyeballs jut out like an owl's, for this objective-type question deserved a better explanation than a mere yes/no response.

After a studied pause (in which my father scratched the tuft of hair in the centre of his balding scalp several times, looked out of the window at the spring blossoms of pansies and wild chrysanthemums blooming in our garden, and examined the half dozen rings on the fingers of his hands), he steadied his gaze at my brother's perturbed face and said, "the highest bidder of a worthy, well-bred girl will win our son's hand in marriage."

He banged his fist once again on the table like an auctioneer who strikes the hammer to close a deal, and walked off peremptorily to his room.

The following weeks brought renewed cheer to my father and he resumed his original schedule, for life in our household seemed to be back to how it had been, before the Payal saga began.

Both Gaurav and I were busy with our exams, spending most of our time indoors poring over books, colouring notes with fluorescent highlighters, and pacing up and down our rooms to memorize answers to sure-fire exam questions.

Payal had stopped coming too, and it was evident that my father credited himself with my brother's change of heart—or so he thought.

I was completely bowled over when Gaurav let me into the conspiracy he had been hatching, all while devouring books like a hungry demon, and filling out forms faster than a printing press.

Infact, he had been studying hard to excel in his exams, so that the two dozen or so job applications he had sent off to top-notch American software companies would land him a lucrative contract abroad.

His plan was to earn in dollars, save hard, and benefitting from the exchange rate between currencies, collect enough rupees to then hand over to Payal's parents, which they in turn would offer my father as dowry for their daughter's marriage!

Whether it was his rigorous training in mathematics, or simply his unequivocal love for Payal that led him to formulate this foolproof strategy—I don't know. All I know is that I joined their ranks as a trusted confidante and aide, calming Payal's apprehensions in hushed telephone conversations, striking the postman like thunderbolt to prevent him from handing over the unusually increased volume of overseas mail to our parents, and mitigating my brother's disappointment while sifting through the piles of polite rejection letters from companies.

Weeks passed by, and my brother's hopes of going abroad were beginning to fade, so he started cudgeling his brains to look for an alternative solution. The local employment paper at home used to be red with circles he drew on job offers: within every circle a number—like the marks teachers give after correcting exam papers with red ink. Only, those numbers in my brother's case indicated the years it would take him to collect a sufficient dowry for his own wedding, according to the salary offered by the company.

Then, one day, on a scorching June afternoon, Gaurav and I were playing cards on the living room couch while mother snoozed in her bedroom, as part of her routine afternoon siesta. We were starting a new game of *bridge*, with slightly altered rules to suit two players instead of the customary four, using just one deck of cards in place of two. Gaurav shuffled the deck and I cut it promptly, but just as he had dealt the cards, I caught sight of the khaki-clad postman pulling up in our driveway on his black bicycle. I gave a little start, and replacing my fan of cards facedown on the coffee table, darted to the door. "At least say the trump," screamed my brother rather petulantly, to which I looked back at him and yelled, "hearts!"

I returned with a spring in my feet, looking contentedly at the stiff bright envelopes addressed to me from friends who had sent birthday greetings to wish me, as most of them were away for the summer vacation.

My brother was staring at his cards dejectedly as it seemed trump cards had eluded him, or was it that he had run out of luck with "hearts" altogether? Well, as we found out moments later, neither was his case. Sealed in a nondescript white envelope, with a series of miniature US flags sprawled across its top and smudged with black wavy postmark blotches, was a brief offer letter from a reputed software company of Seattle.

"Would Mr. Gaurav Kashyap be interested in the position of technical support consultant in their organization?"

My brother beamed with joy, reading and re-reading the succinct letter, before finally folding it back into the envelope and hurling it conclusively on the scattered cards with a shout, "Queen of hearts!"

The pandemonium woke my mother, and soon she was busy in the kitchen frying *pakoras* and *gulab jamuns* to celebrate the news.

My father received the news with more jubilation than we had expected, bragging over mouthfuls of *gulab jamuns* during dinner that a foreign-returned boy commanded the handsomest dowry in the marriage market. I could tell from the complacent expression in his eyes and the smug smile that lit up his triumphant face that a big measure of his contentment came from the fact that the phenomenal distance between the two countries would extinguish any flicker of emotion still igniting the young hearts. He was to be proven wrong once again, for my brother had pledged to justify the proverb, "Distance makes the hearts grow fonder."

The two intervening months that lay between my brother's departure to the United States, seemed to engorge all the time and attention of our household. So much so, that my passing the board exams in high first division was dwarfed in magnitude compared to my brother's heroic achievement. Now, my mother had no more time for relaxed afternoon siestas, and she could be seen bargaining for linen and towels in crowded markets, head covered by the *pallu* of her sari under sweltering skies, and shopping bags serving as umbrellas during pouring rain.

Even my father never accosted Gaurav for remaining outdoors most of the time, telling him he understood how exacting preparations could be when going overseas, and even encouraging him to make the most of his time with friends, as he was going to be lonely initially in a new country. So, when my brother showed me the seemingly infinite photographs of himself with his only close friend Payal—that he intended to take with him to combat the separation pangs in Seattle—I understood what had kept him away from home all these weeks. There was no place in Patna the two didn't visit together: licking ice cream cones in Gandhi Maidan, eating *litti-chokha* from roadside vendors, prostrating with covered heads in the Patna Sahab gurdwara and uncountable temples to seek blessings for a future together.

They even went to Patna museum, posing alongside antiquated statues of Buddha and Mahavira in bronze and terracotta. The photograph that arrested my attention most was that of Payal standing next to the third century sandstone sculpture of Yakshini, her bashful eyes averted from the camera lens due to the goddess' nude voluptuous breasts. I anticipated—from Payal's enjoined fingers raised to her chin—that she was mentally imploring this goddess of wealth to bestow enough fortune on Gaurav in his new mission, so that the barriers standing in way of their marriage could be surmounted. Gaurav, contrarily, looked steadfast, staring into the camera with a resolute smile tempered with affection, as Payal froze him in time against the background of a 16-metre long gigantic tree that had become fossilized into a mammoth stone over millions of years. The unflinching expression in his eyes seemed to challenge any worldly force from standing in the way of his eventual union with Payal.

As his flight was in the wee hours of a cool September morning, there was not much fanfare involved in Gaurav's departure. My parents could barely sleep that night: my father worried about driving him to the airport on time, while my mother rose early to shower and pray before preparing fresh *ladoos* that she intended to pack for her son, in the event he should find the airplane food unpalatable. As for me, I slept unruffled, confident that the hoopla in the house would rouse me in time to bid farewell to my brother.

Gaurav departed amid tearful chanting of mantras by my mother as she feverishly circulated the silver plate of *aarti* around his face, filling the morning air with camphor scent and circles of smoke. I hugged him tightly, pointing both thumbs up as he bent forward to touch my mother's feet. With one look at me—as if in confirmation to seal our secret in a deep trench until his return—he marched to the car with the tenacity of a warrior confident of winning the battle, and didn't look back.

After receiving a sleepy call from him in a voice sodden with jetlag, amid a chaotic buzz of activity and announcements at the Sea-Tac International Airport the following day, the wait to hear from him again seemed interminable. Within this time, I had been accepted at Patna Science College for a major in microbiology, while Payal resumed her visits to our house, albeit her zeal to coach with me in place of Gaurav for her board exams was infinitesimal, to say the least. Her waning desire, however, assumed robust proportions when one afternoon, while I was trying to trace for her the history of aviation from the Wright brothers' humble invention to the present day supersonic aircrafts (as part of her physics presentation the following day), the mailman brought along a spectacular postcard of scintillating skyscrapers forming the backdrop of what appeared to be a very long-legged tripod with a flying saucer atop, piercing the night sky. Payal and I promptly closed our textbooks detailing the drab theories of aviation, in favour of marvelling over the practical snapshot from across the oceans that had made a successful landing after a long haul flight, PAR AVION.

As she blushed over Gaurav's familiar handwriting that resembled the curly hair on his legs and knuckles, I read it aloud with varying emotions of awe over his majestic descriptions of America, and humour on his complaints of a staple diet of scrambled eggs and toasts, as his stock of *ladoos* packed by my mother had run out, forcing him to try his hand at cooking.

"Couldn't we open an e-mail account?" he asked, implicating Payal in the adventure right away. "Here, everybody has a personal computer," he wrote, "and my American friends wonder how I majored in computer science without owning one!"

The high-tech boom was yet to hit India with full force, and cybercafés were few and far between. Still, Payal and I embarked upon a hunt in my neighbourhood to locate one. After walking through a maze of winding streets and crowded bazaars, we came upon a multifaceted shop offering STD/PCO, Xerox, fax and internet services all squeezed into a single room the size of a big closet. When our turn came after a half-hour wait to use one of the two bulky computers, we were at a complete loss to manipulate the intelligent machine. Although neither Payal nor I could remember the steps followed by the owner of the shop to open our electronic account on Yahoo!, we spent the next hour perfecting our practice of accessing, composing and sending a new e-mail. We couldn't send one to Gaurav right away, as we had forgotten to carry his postcard along, which had his e-mail address on it.

Once home, we revelled over our accomplishment, and the newfound power of passwords and instant messaging was as intoxicating as sitting in a time machine and racing past archaic eons towards a futuristic world.

No longer would we have to wait three weeks to hear from Gaurav! Needless to mention, Payal's visits to my place more than doubled in frequency, and in between memorizing molecular formulae for organic and inorganic compounds, we brainstormed for a catchy e-mail address.

A personalized option of chotipayal @ yahoo.com was agreed upon to replace the present uninspiring one of indianews, which sounded more like a tabloid website than an e-mail account.

As if his regular messages were not distraction enough, Payal started printing Gaurav's photographs he sent as attachments using his roommate's digital camera.

One afternoon, when Payal started arguing irrevocably that the diagram of a frog's viscera was that of a fish's, I decided time had come to limit our hi-tech conversations with my brother over the internet. It was imperative for her to pass high school with respectable marks to get admission to college, which would stave off her parents' ambition to find a groom for her, thus allowing enough legroom to Gaurav to save for the dowry.

And saving he was! All the photographs he sent would show him keeping a safe distance from paid excursions and entertainment. Thus, while his friends entered the renowned Seattle Art Museum in downtown, Gaurav was content posing in front of it, next to the embodiment of labour—the hammering man—drawing inspiration from the toiling metal sculpture. In pictures of the colourful and animated *Pike Place Market* at the waterfront, it was obvious that Gaurav was only quenching his appetite by taking in the mesmerizing views of a panoply of boats bobbing over the sparkling blue waters of Eliott Bay. All his friends—Americans and Indians alike—had bags full of fresh farm produce, in addition to heaping plates of crunchy fish and chips in pier restaurants.

As my brother explained in his subsequent e-mails, he had concocted innovative excuses to avoid spending, while keeping the real reason for his frugality strictly confidential. Although he never refused going out with friends to restaurants or bars, when time came to place orders, he would politely count himself out, ducking behind obligatory fasts and religious reasons. He also made it a point to leave early, so that he could get home in time to cook a quick meal of eggs or vegetable rice before his roommate arrived.

Gaurav confessed that his favourite hideout was the naturally lit reading room of the Seattle central library on Fourth Avenue, for which he walked almost four miles from his room to save monorail fare. The sight of the hammering man pounding away silently—right across the street from the library—would ensure that the embers of desire to fulfill his mission in America were always smouldering in his heart. Payal was moved to tears when she read that Gaurav had gone to attend a meditation workshop in Nalanda west to overcome homesickness, when ironically, he had never found time to visit the age-old ruins of the original famed Buddhist university in his very state of Bihar.

Weeks rolled into months, and my parents never suspected any mischief when Payal and I would play truant for hours after studying together in the afternoon. My mother was happy writing long letters to Gaurav on traditional sky-blue aerograms, chiding me gently for my refusal to add a few lines to my brother. "We communicate everyday through a world wide web of advanced technology," I would joke, knowing fully well that technology was to my mother what opera is to a hearing impaired; she would just shake her head incredulously and busy herself with the familiar domain of housekeeping.

All seemed to be falling in line with the plan, and my brother was overjoyed with his steadily increasing stockpile of savings. The snapshots he sent of his room mirrored the extreme parsimony with which he was leading his life in Seattle. Living out of a suitcase for paucity of closet space, clothes were strewn around the hard single beds facing each other in a congested attic room. The only low desk and chair seemed to have been bought at a thrift store, the chair being higher than the cracked glass table. In the far corner of the room—next to the door for the shared bath—was installed a two-plate electric stove. The very sight of his dwelling made me claustrophobic, and I was glad he didn't have to spend whole days cooped up in that hole: the job and library providing spacious respites.

It had been a little over a year since Gaurav's departure, and he would have stayed on longer, had an unprecedented event not forced him to request an emergency leave at work, pack his bags, and rush back home.

Payal had failed her high school exams, passing only in English and Hindi, thanks to the freedom of expressing thoughts openly in the languages, without the rigours of memorizing or practising rules and theories of science.

I felt a little culpable in this unwelcome turn of events, powerless to go back in time and erase the internet adventures that siphoned off precious time we should have spent studying. Payal's visits to my house whittled, and our communication dwindled to occasional phone calls where she informed me in fits of tearful discomposure that her parents had started inviting prospective grooms' families to the house, her mother forcing her to don saris and parade in them with trays full of tea and snacks. She was trying everything in her power to repel the families from approving of her, right from attempting to look ugly by applying the make-up provided by her mother rather shabbily, besides pretending to be insolent by having prolonged eye contact with her potential in-laws, and never touching their feet.

"Would I tell Gaurav to return immediately before all is lost?" she pleaded with me in a voice shaking with foreboding. "Gaurav has already applied for emergency leave," I assured her, "and will be back as soon as it can be approved." My parents were obviously kept out of this dramatic unfolding of events, and when Gaurav showed up with bag and baggage early one chilly December Sunday morning, my father smelt a rat. My mother was ecstatic at the surprise and couldn't stop hugging my brother, repeating like a parrot how thin he had become and wiping her tears with the free end of her sari. "Go make tea for your brother," she commanded. "He must be cold after such a long journey." My father, however, sat quietly at the dining table, sipping dark orange pekoe from a fine china tea cup. Gaurav touched his feet and was about to disappear into his room when my father called out, "Young man, were you missing us so much that you didn't even have time to give us a quick call informing us about your arrival?" Then, measuring up my brother from bottom to top like a cop looks at a hardened criminal, he mocked, "unless the cause of your unannounced visit lies outside the walls of this house." My brother regarded my father with a startled expression, staring dubiously at the weekend edition of *The Times of India* lying open on the table, as if wondering whether his top secret had been splashed in national newspapers.

"How long have you come for?" demanded my father, poking Gaurav's reverie with his autocratic voice. "One month," he squeaked, pouring out the tea I had made for him into his saucer, to finish it fast and hibernate in his room.

"Good!" beamed my father in exhilaration.

Replacing his reading glasses on the bridge of his curved nose, he pulled out the classified matrimonial section from the assortment of special Sunday inserts of the newspaper, and started circling advertisements with a blunt pencil stub.

Meanwhile, my brother slurped his tea in hurried mouthfuls, blowing the surface of his saucer with trembling hands. There was a loud clank as he replaced his empty cup on the saucer, and just as he was about to run into hiding, my father spoke out, looking at him sternly over his spectacles with a wry smile.

"Listen to this: Wanted tall, handsome Kashyap boy working with top MNC in India or abroad for fair, slim, homely graduate girl fluent in English. We are affluent, traditional Hindu business family settled in south Bihar, and will host a lavish wedding for our only daughter. For full details contact Box no. 3025." As if to answer the questions raised by Gaurav's frowning eyes, my father continued, "this is just one example of the thousands of people craving to marry their daughters to boys working abroad. We were deluged by photographs and resumes of girls from prosperous families when we posted an ad for you." Setting his glasses down on the table, my father pierced my brother's eyes with a razor-sharp glare and concluded, "one month is enough time for us to get you married before you return to America."

Gaurav slept off his jetlag the entire day, waking only for my mother's diligently prepared elaborate meals and snacks. Even a blind could tell that my father had summoned all his faculties for surveillance on our activities: his ears pricking at every ring of the phone or doorbell, his eyes scrutinizing our every move even if we stepped out of the house only to bask in the winter sun, and his touch scanning every object that came out of Gaurav's suitcase.

Notwithstanding this heightened security, Gaurav and I snuck out of the house early next morning in my father's car, on pretext of attending the morning prayers at Hanuman temple. It was as if the owner of the vehicle had himself handed over its keys to car thieves. We sped away, Gaurav feeling like a Hollywood action hero behind the wheel, while I anticipated the various reactions Payal's family could have at our unexpected visit.

Contrary to our apprehensions, we were both well received in the modest Joshi household, Payal's mother busying herself almost immediately to prepare breakfast for us, while Mr. Joshi ushered us into a small drawing-cum-dining room. We sat upright on hardwood chairs, while Mrs. Joshi filled the tight space with strong aromas of *puris, aloo bhaji* and lemon pickles—a typical brunch in traditional Brahmin households. My brother and I had only to walk a few steps in the same room to sit at a wicker dining table flanked by four cane chairs. We made ourselves comfortable on the patio furniture of their drawing room, and Gaurav hunted for an opportunity to table the proposal he had been working so hard on, for the past several months.

"It's not your fault," Mr. Joshi was saying, urging us with his hand to start eating as Mrs. Joshi looked on. "Payal just doesn't have the knack for science."

"He's right," concurred Mrs. Joshi, refilling our plates with hot *puris*. She looked exactly like Payal, only older and haggard due to the many stresses life had dealt her family. Although her forehead was creased with anxiety, she forced a smile to her thin lips and said, "You tried your best, and even though it's not easy to find a match for a high school failed, we're doing our best."

My brother saw his opportunity in this desperate remark made by Mrs. Joshi, and nosedived into his proposal without prelude.

"Uncle," he said, with the aplomb of a banker who is trying to convince an investor; only, in this peculiar case, the banker was to provide all the funding for the deal!

"I would like to marry Payal, and will even give you the money my father is asking for dowry." Silence gripped the room, and suddenly, the flesh-and-blood humans in it seemed to have been transformed into lifeless stone statues. Unable to endure the suspense, my brother stammered, "Do you agree?"

Mrs. Joshi was trying hard to maintain her composure, and even though her face glowed with a gratified smile like someone who had stumbled upon an oasis in the middle of a parched desert, her eyes welled up with tears, unable to contain this unforeseen bounty of fortune.

"We could never have dreamt of a home like yours for Payal," she sighed pensively, wiping her glistening eyes with the back of her hands. Then, looking at Gaurav's earnest face, she continued, "I knew Payal liked you, but when she described to me the layout of your bungalow, with its exquisite interiors in the posh Patliputra colony, I discouraged her from nurturing false hopes."

Mr. Joshi stared at his wife disconcertedly, shaking his balding head in disbelief that his wife had kept him out of his own daughter's emotional quagmire. The glint in his eye suggested that he now understood why Payal was perpetually quiet and disinterested in the proposals they were considering for her. Although Gaurav's offer was potent enough to relegate his most significant worry of settling his only daughter, Mr. Joshi did not betray any sign of alacrity yet.

"Marriages must have the consent of parents," he opined meditatively. "Will your parents agree to welcome as daughter-in-law, a girl who has failed high school, even if you take care of the financial aspect?"

"Don't worry about that, uncle," reassured Gaurav spiritedly, dubbing the family's reticence as approval. "I'll take care of everything."

As we prepared to leave, Mrs. Joshi became sentimental once again. "God has been very generous to us," she acknowledged, pushing back tears and swallowing repeatedly. "Karan recently got accepted as legal counsel with the reputed ICICI bank, and now Payal—"

"Did she know about this?" interrupted Mr. Joshi, confronting his wife facetiously, a jocular grin stretching across his face.

"I swear, I know nothing," confessed Mrs. Joshi, turning beetroot with embarrassment.

"I thought it all finished between them when Gaurav went to Seattle."

Growing suspicious herself, and staring questioningly from my brother to me, Mrs. Joshi asked, "Was she aware you were coming today? They told me they were going to Hanuman temple to offer prayers of gratitude for Karan's new job."

"Hanuman temple?" echoed Gaurav and I in unison, bursting into peals of laughter.

"Oh, you kids!" exclaimed Mr. Joshi jovially, escorting us to our car.

Coincidentally enough, in our entire drive back home, we didn't encounter a single red light: the "Stop" signal changing to "Go ahead" as soon as our car approached the traffic lights.

"What's up with the Hanuman temple story?" I quizzed my brother, nudging him lightly with my elbow.

"I don't know!" he gushed elatedly. "Seems like it's our day of coincidences today—here comes another green light!"

"What about Papa?" I asked, sobering up.

"What about him?" imitated Gaurav in a grave, husky voice, hurling my question back at me.

"I mean, *he* could be the red light in this love story."

"Do you know how much I've saved?"

"No."

"15 lakhs!"

"What! Really?"

As per Gaurav's meticulous plan, three days later, Mr. Joshi fixed a meeting at our place after a punctiliously scripted telephonic conversation with my father—all while keeping his credentials of being Payal's father, incognito.

On the appointed day, my father went into a tizzy, decorating the crystal flower vase on the dining table with fresh rose shrubs ensconced in a fan of cypress leaves from our garden. "The highest bidder has made his offer!" he enthused perkily, wiping the glass of the framed photograph beside it, with the edge of his shirt. Gazing fondly at the young Gaurav saddled on his back, my father smiled at the picture with the pride of a horse whose rider has just won the Derby race.

He poked his head in the kitchen door with the regularity of a cuckoo in a cuckoo clock, ensuring the cashews were crunchy, the raisins not soggy, the sugar in the *ladoos* "just right," and the dough of the samosas fluffy enough. "Afterall," he philosophised, "the temper of rich people is intricately connected to their palate, and as unpredictable as the monsoon sunshine!"

Gaurav and I played *scrabble* in the study while waiting for the Joshis to show up—he in his crisp, navy-blue tuxedo, I in a pink crepe salwar-kameez. He was winning, sweeping up a whopping number of triple word scores on simple entries like "love," "marriage," and "life," to name a few; whereas I struggled painfully even with impressive formations of "unpredictable," "apprehension," "disclosure," etc. I resolved to abandon my habit of solving crossword puzzles in the newspaper everyday, if I had to suffer such a humiliating defeat after all the practice.

Suddenly, the doorbell rang, and in his haste to adjust his crimson tie, Gaurav struck the *scrabble* board with his elbow, sending my words in a wavy shiver; while his held firm, as if the tiles were glued to the surface with some sort of invisible magnetism. He followed my father in the drawing room at a galloping trot, while I joined my mother in the kitchen to fry the samosas that were to be served "piping hot".

A sprightly blend of voices wafted through the air, the loudest being my father's—not his habitual overbearing tone, but the atypical melodious notes of obedience and consent, like a musician following a maestro.

A few minutes later, my father poked a nervous head into the kitchen door and commanded, "Hot tea and snacks, quick!"

The Package Deal

My mother emptied the last lot of oil-dripping samosas into the metal colander set on a thick pile of newspapers to allow the excess oil to drain off through the perforations. Then, untucking the *pallu* of her silk sari wrapped around her waist, she decorated the samosas on a big floral plate with a small glass bowl of tamarind chutney in between. Tea and other snacks were already placed on a silver tray.

"Bring them in one by one," my mother commissioned, looking satisfactorily at the tray and the plate of samosas, and left for the drawing room. I remained standing alone, regarding the golden-brown pyramids of samosas and wondering whether the trivial looking snack had the power of swaying opinions, or whether it would just symbolize a tomb in our household, reminiscent of Gaurav's love for Payal.

When I entered the drawing room balancing the tray, my father was engrossed in an intensive interview with Karan, like an HR manager conducting background checks. When he saw me, he motioned me to start serving anti-clockwise, starting with Mrs. Joshi. Upon exchanging pleasantries with her, I noticed how make-up had transformed Payal's mother to the extent that she no longer looked related to Payal at first glance: the daub of rouge on her sallow cheeks having imparted a warm glow to her gaunt face. In addition, her temporarily crimped hair had lent her a fuller appearance.

It was not merely Payal's mother who defied any resemblance to Payal. Her brother Karan—who I saw for the first time—looked entirely unrelated too. Unlike Payal, he was tall, well-built and athletic; his wool-like bushy hair completing the description of a sports champion. Had he not been wearing a creased black suit with a starched white shirt—the buttoned collars of which were tightly secured by a black bow tie—it would have been a marathon to guess his profession of a lawyer. Yet, it wasn't before long that his personality traits spilled the beans. I had already served the samosas, and was going around the table with the plate of *ladoos*, when Karan spoke out as soon as I bent forward to offer the sweets to Mr. Joshi.

"Papa, you're not allowed any sweets."

"Once in a while is okay," protested Mr. Joshi, helping himself to a *ladoo* anyway.

"Your diabetes caused you to retire early from your job. We don't want you to retire early from life." The argument was conclusive, and Mr. Joshi excused himself as he replaced the sweet awkwardly from his plate, back into its rightful serving dish.

"Give *him* the extra *ladoo*," jested my father, pointing at Karan. "Afterall, he got a job with the famous ICICI bank!"

I rose from the couch and lifted the plate of *ladoos* once again, to offer Karan. He promptly picked up the same piece that his father had renounced, while I looked at the metallic lustre of his black leather shoes in embarrassment.

"Now, the math adds up to my satisfaction," quipped Gaurav wittily. "The number of sweets consumed should be equal to or greater than the number of people in the room!"

Despite the effervescent ambience pervading the atmosphere, the Joshis exhibited a certain discomfiture, akin to the apprehension of fishermen in the deceptive calm before the fatal storm.

Mrs. Joshi had twice reached for her white resin purse with mournful sighs, but had lacked the courage to pull out of it Payal's life-size picture clad in a sari. Mr. Joshi, on the other hand, eyed the tan Samsonite briefcase lying at his feet intermittently, without a grain of ownership.

The Package Deal

After two rounds of tea and several helpings of snacks, the conversation around the coffee table was pruned to a tumultuous buzz of desultory voices coming from two distinct groups. My father was still interviewing Karan, while my mother was animatedly enumerating the ingredients that went into the tender stuffing of samosas at Mrs. Joshi's polite behest.

Sitting next to my brother on the couch, I kept pressing his toe with my pumps, urging him in hushed whispers to help Mr. Joshi seal the marriage deal.

Gaurav had tried everything in his power to propel Payal's father into action, to no avail. Mr. Joshi would just smile helplessly when Gaurav stared at him meaningfully, squinting his eyeballs towards the briefcase. Finally, realizing that spurring Mr. Joshi to action was as challenging as expecting an imperturbable mountain to explode into volcanic eruption, Gaurav took the reins of the situation in his own hands.

"That's a lovely bag you have, uncle," he bursted humorously, in a stentorian voice that calmed the chattering groups like a pail of water thrown on a bonfire.

"Oh!" exclaimed Mr. Joshi, flinching, as if something had stung him from under his seat.

"This is for your father," he stuttered incoherently, advancing the briefcase to my father.

An angelic smile lit up my father's face.
"What's the hurry, Mr. Joshi?" he asked with an amused laugh. "Afterall, the boy and girl need to meet first."

"Your decision is my law," riposted Gaurav quickly, without losing even a second. "Didn't you and mummy meet on your wedding day?"

My father regarded Gaurav with the wonderment of a child who has just witnessed a magician pull a rabbit out of a hat.

Flummoxed by my father's reluctance, Mr. Joshi once again held out the briefcase across the table to him. Without touching the bag, my father got up, and going around the coffee table with a notorious glint in his eye, came and sat on the empty seat next to Mr. Joshi on the couch. Relieved, Mr. Joshi laid the briefcase in my father's lap, which made my father convulse as if he was being electrocuted.

"But this is *your* money, Kashyap sahib," pleaded Payal's father pressing the briefcase forcefully in my father's lap, beseeching Gaurav to intervene with pitiful eyes. But even before my brother could weigh in, my father hurled a bombshell that left me brain-dead for an instant. Shifting to the edge of the couch in a semicircle—a contrite expression overpowering his calculative eyes—he spoke to Mr. Joshi in a tone of unsurpassed filial duty.

"I really like Karan."

Mr. Joshi frowned questioningly at my father.

"I mean, for my daughter Choti."

By and by, I revived from my temporary coma with a beehive around my brain, and stole a diffident glance at Karan. There was a mild flutter of astonishment on his serene face, like soft ripples in an otherwise placid sea. This picture of youth and poise enamoured me, with Cupid's arrow striking at the dormant recesses of my heart.

The tussle over the briefcase was still continuing when Gaurav intervened decisively.

"But, Mr. Joshi," my father was trying to elucidate.

"Now there is no question of dowry—we both give a daughter and get a son. It's equal."

Math was certainly something my brother understood better than everybody else.

"Keep the money, uncle," he said pertly to Payal's father.

The Package Deal

Less than a year after my marriage to Karan, we all moved out of the rented accommodation to a comfortable double-storeyed house in the suburbs, bought with Gaurav's spartan savings in Seattle. However, the monetary details of this *package deal* remain tightly sewed in our hearts, even though my father often wonders how the Joshis hit a jackpot after years of financial inadequacy.

The Inseparables

Chanda had not a care in the world. At twelve years, she didn't have to be taught in her grade seven junior school that monkeys were the ancestors of man to anneal her bond with nature. She lived with her parents in the *temple village* of Madhuban, so christened, for in the course of thousands of years, a bevy of magnificent milk-white Jain temples had sprouted on the undulating hills of the deeply forested Chotanagpur Plateau to commemorate the Tirthankars who attained salvation there. These religious shrines attracted Jain pilgrims from world over like a magnet, permeating the atmosphere of the tiny village with chaste spirituality.

Although Chanda didn't cover her mouth with a cloth or walk barefoot like the Jain *sadhus* did, to avoid ingesting or hurting insects, her prodigal heart bore an affinity toward everything living—big or small. Thus, on her way to school every morning through the meandering routes of the dense jungle, Chanda greeted birds by chirruping after their jumbled dawn excitement, ran after butterflies breakfasting on blazingly coloured flowers by batting her hands up and down like their wings, and skipped in a zig-zag over long trails of ants trotting in a disciplined queue. She would bend over vibrant magnolias and daisies and wild roses just as they were opening up their petals to the sun's first auriferous touch.

Her snacks, too, were drawn from the multiferous bounty of nature. Being short and squat, she was not physically endowed to reach the fruits of her desire hanging enticingly from tall trees, but years of practice had transformed her stocky fingers into nimble catapults to fell pods of tamarind and clusters of berries with a single stone.

The school being a long three-kilometre trek from her home, Chanda often napped under the umbrageous banyan tree at a midway point, after swinging with its thick dangling shoots that eventually take root in the soil to support the massive branches.

It was during one such trek when Chanda was flouncing behind a bushy brown squirrel, balancing the school bag slung on her left shoulder as she munched a raw guava with her right hand, that a bright green fledgling parrot hopped onto her shoulder from the trees above. She froze, not wanting to scare the little bird away by her bouncy jumps. Turning her head slowly to the parrot, she noticed that it was a baby, as its feathers hadn't yet attained their full adult colouring. Guessing the reason for its unannounced visit by the constant wiggling of its small pink tongue, Chanda advanced the uneaten portion of her guava to her guest. The parrot gawked at it with circumspect eyes that contracted and dilated a few times, and then, convinced of no perceived danger, scooped a small bite from the fruit with its curved red beak. Thrilled by the adventure, Chanda started chatting with her new friend, alternating the fruit between her mouth and that of her friend's.

"Mithoo! Yes, I'll call you Mithoo!" she exuberated, as the parrot flopped from her shoulder onto the thrush below and waddled clumsily in front of her, fanning and flipping its tail contentedly.

"Talk to me Mithoo; tell me where you live," demanded Chanda, bending to offer more guava to the parrot. When all she got for a reply was a wild shriek from the bird, she sighed reflectively.

"They say parrots like you who have a black ring around their necks can talk. But I think that's only a myth. Why, you don't have to go through the drudgery of school to learn how to read and write and become civilized. Nevertheless, you are my friend—*my best friend*," announced Chanda, stroking Mithoo lightly on the woolly feathers of its head.

"Who are you talking to?" panted Bablu, running to where Chanda was standing, thereby threatening the parrot into a lopsided dash for the thicket.

"Nobody," replied Chanda wistfully, parrying the question and tossing the remaining guava in the direction of the bushes where her new avian friend had escaped.

As the two walked to school together, Bablu's incoherent prattle about homework, cricket, lunch-box, marbles and bicycles drifted around Chanda like the buzz of a swarm of bees. Her thoughts were consumed by her tiny friend of the morning and whether they would ever meet again.

On her way back home in the evening, Chanda scanned the landscape with telescopic eyes—she examined the trees above and called out, "Mithoo!" with unfailing regularity, cupping both hands around her mouth to produce an echo effect. Padding as gently as a cat on the undergrowth, she peered hopefully behind boulders and tree trunks, yet there was no trace of the parrot.

The following day was Sunday, usually Chanda's favourite day of the week, but not this time. For the first time in all her school years, she yearned for the school to be open so that she could scour the jungle for her missing friend.

The Inseparables

"Don't you want to eat at the Kothi today?" quizzed her mother in a stumped tone when she saw Chanda sitting in her night clothes on the cemented steps of their neglected backyard. One of the highlights for Chanda on Sunday afternoons was to lunch at the imposing Jain Guest House called *Shwetambhar Kothi*, across from their nondescript two bedroom concrete house. The Guest House served as lodging for the scores of Jain pilgrims that thronged the village of Madhuban, and although free vegetarian meals were served there everyday, Chanda could only savour the traditional food on Sundays.

"They don't use onions, garlic, or potatoes, yet their food is tastier than yours," she would often complain to her mother.

"It's the change that you like," her mother would reply fondly, explaining to Chanda the reasons behind the Jains' refusal to eat certain types of vegetables, especially roots.

"So, they don't even want to kill insects they can't see?" Chanda argued culpably, examining the ground below her feet. Then, remembering something, she suddenly sprang up and darted towards the kitchen.

"I know, I know, you're hungry," chanted her mother, following her daughter close on her heels. Chanda dashed out of the kitchen, sprinted to her bedroom, and pinching some fifty paise coins from a jumble of bobby pins, rubber bands and bindis in an old aluminium biscuit box, leapt out of the house.

"At least change your night clothes," shouted her mother, running to the courtyard through the open door. But Chanda had already crossed the street and was marching steadily towards the village bazaar. For Sarla and Rishikesh Purohit, Chanda was the light of their lives—their raison d'être.

Rishikesh worked long hours in hazardously profound depths of the earth in one of the city's mica mines to provide a comfortable life to his small family. He would quickly forget his perilous hours spent in obscure dungeons of the mine—foraging metals and minerals—when Chanda narrated her adventures at school and gifted him handfuls of vivid wild flowers she gathered from the jungle. As Sarla latched the door behind her, she wondered what had possessed Chanda to run to the bazaar in such frenzied precipitation, without even caring about lunch.

Chanda had now reached the fruit vendors after crossing a maze of street stalls selling everything required to lead a modest village life, from clay pots to cotton linen and rubber flip-flops. She skipped happily homewards, swinging her small plastic bag full of raw green guavas. "Now Mithoo can't hide from me," she gushed victoriously, her chubby face lighting up with a broad smile.

The following day on her way to school, Chanda carried two guavas from her cache and resolved to trace Mithoo with their inviting smell. Biting into one of them, she called out in warning tones, "Come fast Mithoo, wherever you are—I'm not going to save this for you too long." Flocks of birds panicked into flight as Chanda approached them in search of Mithoo. Finally, she abandoned her half-eaten fruit under the same bushes where Mithoo had disappeared after endearing himself to her in their maiden introduction.

Days rolled into weeks and weeks into months, but Chanda did not relinquish the hope of finding her friend one day.
She continued discarding a half-eaten fruit of her morning breakfast under the same bushes, sometimes with an angry warning, other times with conciliatory wheedling to coax her friend out of its

inconspicuous hiding. Seasons came and went, but nothing changed Chanda's routine of talking to overgrown bushes a little distance from the expansive banyan tree of her midway repose from the school. But, on this torrid June afternoon, she stood a long time contemplating the weed infested overgrown grass and ferns that had been rendered pale by the intense rays of the sun. "If he were anywhere near, I'd spot him," she reflected optimistically, grateful to nature for stripping the parrot of its surrounding camouflage.

"Listen, Mithoo," she began, walking over blotches of hay. "From tomorrow my school closes for our two month annual summer vacation. I will not be bringing you fruit anymore, but if you come out of your hiding, I can show you my house and you can visit me during my holidays." Chanda waited a few minutes—attentive to every subtle sound—her bulbous eyes strained to scrutinize every modicum of her surroundings under the potent light of the sun. As she walked home dejected, she threw small stones and pebbles aimlessly in the thicket around her, causing cautious rustling of leaves where small burrowing animals and reptiles lay hidden.

In her two month hiatus from school, Chanda got busy with holiday homework and class projects, besides playing kho-kho with village children in her free time. She would often think about her lost friend Mithoo while eating fruits, and wondered whether he waited for his share every morning. Yet, she refrained from sharing her unique experience with anybody in her entourage.

By the time her school reopened, she had given up all hope of ever finding her friend again. However, she couldn't stop herself from throwing cursory glances in the direction of the same thicket, twice everyday, on her way to and from school.

Monsoons lashed Madhuban with unprecedented ferocity, flooding the village and wreaking havoc on the paddy fields. Chanda's journey to school became increasingly treacherous as dangerous reptiles lurked everywhere—their holes having been filled with rain water. On one such August afternoon, Chanda was returning from school when huge mushroom shaped black clouds gathered over the sky, strangling the sun into oblivion under their dense embrace. Rain fell in torrents as Chanda ran towards the shelter of her familiar banyan tree. The hardbound Hindi text book she had used to cover her head was soaked and reeking of moulding paper as rain pattered over it from all directions.

Throwing her bag on the ground, she huddled close to the broad trunk of the massive tree and looked up at its dripping leaves. At first, she dismissed what she saw as an illusion. But when she looked hard, she could scarcely believe her eyes. Perched atop one of the branches was a lone parrot with a black ring around its neck! Chanda stopped breathing momentarily and could clearly hear the loud thumping of her heart. Then, very cautiously, she bent over her drenched school bag and retrieved a soggy, crumpled paper cone containing sprouted gram which she had forgotten to finish after her physical exercise class of the morning. Tiptoeing back to the trunk, she raised a fistful of the snack to the branch of the tree housing the bird.

The parrot took no notice and continued to peck at the wood with its sharp beak.

"I know you're hungry, Mithoo," began Chanda in a reassuring voice.

"But wood is no food when you have delicious sprouts waiting for you!"

Whistling softly, she repeated tenderly, "Mithoo, come on now; come down." The whistling attracted the parrot's attention and it eyed the gram with some interest. Soon, it hopped down to a lower branch and Chanda could hear the clicking of its beak distinctively.

"Good boy!" she encouraged, and raised her palm as high as she could stretch her hand. Taking cue, the parrot flew down the tree and walked excitedly around Chanda's belongings.

"Upon my word!" she exclaimed disbelievingly. "You're a big boy now—all grown and walking confidently."

Even though she couldn't be certain, Chanda's instinct said she had finally found her Mithoo. The parrot, for its part, ate effortlessly from her palm and raised its head at the word "Mithoo."

By now the downpour had eased to a light drizzle, and Chanda gathered her belongings to leave, but not before arranging a tryst with her friend for the following day.

"Should we say, same time, same place tomorrow, Mithoo?" she demanded, emptying the contents of her paper bag close to the parrot's clawed feet.

The bird bobbed its head as if in consent, and scooping some water from an upturned leaf in its lower beak, tipped its head back to let it run down its throat. Smiling contentedly to herself, Chanda walked away slowly, looking back occasionally at Mithoo, until she tripped on a pointed rock and landed into a swirling puddle almost knee-deep.

"What a mess the rains made of you!" lamented Sarla, taking her daughter's squelching shoes and drenched bag when she reached home. Chanda looked unruffled, incapable of suppressing her bursting joy at rediscovering Mithoo.

"It's nothing, ma," she protested. "I'll be sparkling and dry as the moon after a bath," she joked, giving her mother a tight wet hug.

"I don't know anything," argued Sarla. "The flooding is expected to get worse; don't go to school tomorrow." But Chanda wouldn't hear of it. For nothing in the world could she break her appointment with Mithoo. Little did she know that she wouldn't have to wait until the following day to meet her extraordinary friend.

After a well scrubbed bath had erased all traces of her slushy trek from school, Chanda sat on the narrow wooden bed of her sparse room overlooking the courtyard. In front of her lay the sodden text book that had served as her umbrella in the afternoon deluge.

She was opening every page of it cautiously and drying it with a small floral handkerchief when she heard a soft hooting sound from the courtyard. Looking out of the vertical iron bars of her bedroom window, Chanda saw globules of rain drops shining like beads of pearls on the trees and grass under the milk-white light of the crescent moon. She got up from her bed, and clutching the cold iron rods, peered into the spangled gauze of peepul and neem trees in her courtyard. She was about to retreat when she heard the hooting again. Mystified, she ran out of her room barefoot to discern the source of the bird call. She walked the entire length and breadth of her courtyard several times, her feet splashing on small puddles of water, when a soft grinding sound arrested her attention. Looking up at the thick arching neem tree, she clearly perceived the silhouette of a bird in the opal haze of the night sky. She approached the tree with some trepidation as its sweeping branches cast eerie shadows on the ground around her, dwarfing her frame under its walloping stature.

"Mithoo!" she called out in soothing tones to calm her frayed nerves. When she got no answer, Chanda was ready to break into a run to her room when she heard a familiar whistle.

"It's indeed you, Mithoo!" she jubilated, circling the neem tree in excitement as all fear left her instantly.

The Inseparables

The following morning, Chanda awoke with the glare of the sun streaming its dusty beam in a slant through her open window. She was rubbing her eyes sleepily when the hoarse raucous cawing of crows made her spring to her feet and scoot out into the courtyard.

The breeze outside was crisp even though the warmth of the sun promised to evaporate the dew drops from the night, unless the storm clouds drifting steadily towards it were to shroud this mighty ball of light and heat. Spotting Mithoo effortlessly in the daylight—perched on the same neem tree as the night before—Chanda gestured to him feverishly.

"Wait right there, Mithoo," she urged, with a show of her palm as she rushed back to her room. In less than half an hour, Chanda stumbled out of the house, her mother helping her mount the canvas school bag on her shoulders.

"Don't eat all the guavas or you'll get a tummy ache," cautioned Sarla, as she saw her daughter talking to the neem tree. But it was as if Chanda was becoming impervious to the human world as her bond with Mithoo intensified. Now they went to school together, playing peek-a-boo, and Mithoo often got distracted in the jungle by the buds and berries, until Chanda coaxed him out of his foraging to be content with her guavas.

Chanda didn't see the time passing as swiftly as sand slips down one's fingers. She was soon going to turn sixteen, and even though everything conceivable around and about her had been practically transformed beyond recognition, the only thing that remained immutable was her friendship with Mithoo.

Sarla and Rishikesh spent long hours after dinner talking in muted voices about Chanda's marriage, the need for her to finish her last year in school with good marks, and ways to instill in her childish heart, a desire to transition into womanhood.

But Chanda, although perplexed by ostensible upheavals in her body due to hormonal perturbations, failed to comprehend her parents' anxiety in her every move. And even though Mithoo had only learnt the word *Chanda* in the course of their protracted friendship, she felt at peace by sharing her worldly worries with her trusted avian friend.

"How lucky you are," she sighed, as she sat under her banyan tree retreat one afternoon on her way back from school. "You don't have to learn about countries, or past rulers, or the solar system to find a boy to marry you.

"I know, I know, my talk makes you sleepy," she chided Mithoo when she saw him resting on one foot atop a branch particularly shaded from the sun, his beak tucked into his back feathers.

"Yet, I confide in you, as I know you will never give away my secrets or betray me."

"Why do ma and baba fret over my marriage?" She asked Mithoo as they resumed their walk back home. Mithoo listened attentively, flying from one tree to the next in reflective meditation, but eventually raised his nape feathers as if shrugging his shoulders in perplexity.

"Even if they send me far from them," continued Chanda in a visibly moved and agitated tone, "you'll come with me, won't you, Mithoo?"

Chanda squatted on the grass and held her rotund face in her hands, tears flowing copiously over her stocky fingers. Mithoo flew around her in circles, drumming his wings on her covered face until she got up, wiped her tears and continued her homeward journey.

The Inseparables

Her dreaded day of departure from Madhuban arrived soon after Chanda passed her matriculation exams in first class. When her stellar school results led to a precipitation in matrimonial arrangements with a proposal received through the village barber, Chanda cried her heart out to Mithoo in despair.

"I wish I hadn't crammed the capitals of countries by heart, or the grammar rules of English, or balancing equations in mathematics."

Mithoo's tiny head was lowered in concentration, and he stared at his sharp claws helplessly. Chanda rattled on, without caring if Mithoo needed explanations or clarifications for her desultory wayward train of thought.

"I love studies, but they only seem to doom a girl to marriage." She looked up at the scintillating night sky pensively. The soothing white full moon appeared to her like a serene planet, surrounded by countless twinkling diamonds.

"It's false, total nonsense!" spat Chanda vexedly. "Earth is *not* the most habitable planet in the universe due to its optimal distance from the sun!" Her angry eyes were welling with tears. "How can a planet be habitable when you have to leave your parents and friends to live the rest of your life with absolute strangers?" Mithoo looked up at her outburst, but hung his head again as if ashamed at his inability to help solve his friend's quandary.

"Tell me, Mithoo—" Chanda coaxed the parrot to make eye contact with her, which he did, with unfocussed button eyes.

"You fly to faraway lands; surely you know of better places than earth?" The perplexity in Mithoo's eyes deepened and he raised his head high for lack of answer. Chanda noticed the moon race feverishly through the stifling night clouds and sighed, "It moves so fast, you couldn't get there even if you wanted."

The marriage was solemnised in a traditional ceremony enjoyed by the entire village, except Chanda. She seemed to be suffocating under the weight of rituals, never holding her face still when women forced make-up on her round obtuse features. The child in her still wanted to chase impulsive squirrels, or run for the vanquished kite after a stiff duel of paper and thread in the skies. But the cumbersome sari, together with the weight of jewellery and tradition arrested her liberty. She sat statued for long stiff hours, watching the exhilarated dances of guests, wondering why they were rejoicing her departure from the village.

Sarla and Rishikesh were relieved at settling their daughter. Chanda's only respite was the assurance that Mithoo would come with her. Which he did. Flying all the way from Madhuban to Bengabad, never leaving sight of the car in which Chanda was being taken away to start her new life.

The intricate henna pattern was still deep orange on her palms when Chanda was quickly shown the exhaustive household chores she was expected to accomplish daily at her in-laws' place. From dawn to dusk, she slaved tirelessly, putting three meals together on time, beating clothes in the courtyard before rising, wringing and drying them. Any extra time would be spent brooming and scrubbing floors. Yet, she saved some energy for the night, as that was the time she would pour her heart out to Mithoo.

"I hate my parents," she confessed to Mithoo one night, when they met at their designated place of the neem tree shade just outside the house.

"They never call me home without my husband, and there's nowhere I can go with him around—not even to eat my favourite tamarind from trees."

Chanda's droopy eyes had a faraway look, and Mithoo was picking his feathers in anxiety. "Baba looked so stressed when he came here last time," she frowned, as if trying to remember hard. "The fridge he brought with him looked like our fridge at home."

Their nightly tête-à-tête was terminated brusquely with a shrill call from Hari, her husband. Chanda winced at the prospect of another painful duty she was forced to carry out every other night.

"I'm so tired," she lamented, getting up. "I hope he's not as wild with my body tonight, as he always is."

Weeks rolled by, and Chanda started feeling the intensifying brunt of verbal abuse by her mother-in-law. A tall, thin woman, as sparse as a cane stick in physical attributes, she spared no opportunity to ridicule Chanda.

"We would never have married our handsome son to this short, fat and ugly . . ." she paused theatrically, hand still raised menacingly at Chanda.

"Why, I don't even see a woman in her," she mocked her demeaningly.

Chanda was about to sit down to her afternoon meal, but the blizzard of expletives rained on her by her mother-in-law blew her appetite to shreds. She grabbed a handful of green chillies from her plate and ran out, crying bitterly.

"Go, go, princess of Madhuban," the old woman shouted sarcastically. "Your royal family is thrusting used, second-hand goods on us after promising a hefty dowry."

Out under the neem tree, Chanda's muffled cries woke Mithoo from his afternoon siesta. Hopping next to her with small somnolent eyes, Mithoo nudged his head comfortingly against Chanda's fleshy arm. This gesture of affection by her non-human friend perked Chanda slightly. She gently poked the green chillies under Mithoo's red beak as he sat, grasping her wrist tightly with his clawed feet.

"Isn't this world bizarre?" Chanda questioned philosophically, biting one end of the green chilly hungrily. "Humans are sometimes so *in-human*, and you—my non-human friend—so incredibly *humane*."

Mithoo, for his part, was just happy Chanda wasn't crying anymore, and as if to celebrate this fact, he kept feasting on the green chillies without making an effort to understand her steadily maturing perceptions of the world. He had succeeded in cheering Chanda's dampened spirits by hanging upside down from a branch, and using his beak to climb up and down the tree trunk.

Chanda was engaged in an animated game of peek-a-boo with Mithoo, the latter giving shrill calls each time Chanda found his hiding. Suddenly, a wretched face peeped out of the gate, red with anger.

"Birdbrain!" swore Chanda's mother-in-law and slammed the gate shut behind her. Not caring to enter the house anyway, Chanda continued her lively play until an old car came hooting down the dirt path, leaving in its trail an explosion of static sand clouds.

Chanda was overjoyed when she saw her father dismount from the car. Rishikesh hugged his daughter ardently, but soon noticed a disconcerting fact about her.

"You've grown thin, my baby," he remarked, unsure whether Chanda was adjusting well to her dramatically changed life.

"Your mother's the same," he commented a little more jovially, regarding his daughter with misty eyes as she resumed her game with Mithoo.

"She misses her baby girl, and has lost a few pounds worrying about you." Rishikesh choked with emotion and busied himself by giving instructions to a few men emptying the boot of the car.

"Then why doesn't she come see me?" questioned Chanda with a voice that sounded rather cross.

"She'll come after I can get some unfinished business done," Rishikesh murmured in such low tones that only he knew the urgency of his mission. The gate had been opened wide to allow the men to carry in cardboard boxes of appliances, kitchenware and some wooden sidetables.

From the other side of the gate, Chanda heard her mother-in-law's taunting voice. "We're not beggars Mr. Purohit, so stop bringing us alms."

Rishikesh was already out of the front gate when Chanda heard the old woman's ultimatum to her father: "Don't show your face again until you can bring the air-conditioned Maruti Suzuki 800 car you promised at the time of the wedding—and remember, it better be brand new, not used like your fridge."

A month passed by, and there was no news from Chanda's family—neither visit nor phone call. "The scoundrel has no intention of bringing the car," the old woman whined gripely on the night her daughter Renu came home ahead of her delivery. Renu eyed Chanda sceptically and remarked, "It all looks like a plan of her family to tie this black milkless buffalo to Hari's neck for free." Renu maliciously dropped a glass tumbler of sherbet Chanda was offering to everybody. Blood red liquid oozed away from its shattered glass body, seeping into the right-angled veins of the tiled floor.

"Who could tell those fat hands are so weak, they can't even balance a tray?" The old woman shot an accusing glare at Chanda as the latter busied herself by gathering sharp glass pieces with her bare hands. Chanda often wondered whether her fate would've been different, had the garlanded man in the framed photo that hung in the drawing room not watched over the proceedings of this house mutely. Her late father-in-law's benign wrinkled face seemed to ordain "Overrule" for every act of misconduct or injustice perpetrated in the house, but his voice left an insignificant vapour behind the thick glass that sealed his views from escaping. It seemed as if his stubbled lips were slightly parted in disdain at what his waning eyes witnessed on a daily basis. He appeared as incapacitated as a gagged and handcuffed judge, forced to comply with pronouncements by serial offenders.

A few weeks later, the family was gathered for dinner on the courtyard floor after a massive power cut steeped the entire town in darkness.

Hari swore loudly at the inopportune interruption during a heated cricket match between arch rivals India and Pakistan. Renu grumbled her rice pudding in the fridge would go sour. But Chanda was accustomed to the frequent power outages. Her routine never changed—rain or shine, light or dark. She stirred huge casseroles of curried vegetables while supervising rotis in the confined light of an oil lamp. Her mother-in-law kept barging into the kitchen with strict instructions to add *this* ingredient or sprinkle *that* masala, sending Chanda to a tizzying hunt for them, the iron ring of the lamp looped around her wrist like a bangle weighed down by a heavy stone. She was sure she wouldn't be able to meet Mithoo tonight, as the family slept in the open during power failures.

Loud cricket commentary belting from a portable radio broke the still night silence of the house. Hari didn't work at the government electricity department as they had boasted at the time of his marriage to Chanda. "Where's the electricity to provide?" he would laugh scornfully when Rishikesh asked him if he was home early from work. Hence, the pressure on Chanda's family to cough up a staggering dowry, as the paltry amount of pension received from the tile manufacturing company Hari's father worked in, barely met the family's growing needs.

Chanda had already made half-dozen trips to the courtyard, bringing hot rotis for the family when Renu grabbed her wrist and wrenched it. Chanda bit her lip until the stinging sensation weakened.

"She's conspiring to kill my unborn baby," yelled Renu, passing the incriminating evidence of Chanda's machination to the old woman's seasoned hands, who examined the roti scrupulously, dusting it from both sides on her palm. Her wizened eyes narrowed, creating three deep furrows on her forehead. She pinched the slightly uncooked sides of the roti with her tough yellow nails and hurled them at chanda's face. "Uncooked flour can not only lead to miscarriage, it can also cause infertility, you bitch!" Chanda walked back to the kitchen, only to discover that the one on the stove had already been burnt. She yearned to talk to Mithoo, to vent her feelings and forget her perpetual pain, even if momentarily. But she knew it was impossible tonight. Suddenly, the animated cricket commentary was interrupted to relay some breaking news.

"Bastards!" lashed out Hari spitefully. "We had almost struck a sixer when these mother fuckers—" Hari stopped short of completing his curse on seeing his mother's hand wave in front of his face anxiously. In the silence of the moment, the newsreader's voice delivered a sharp message to its audience.

"This is All India Radio, and I am Deepak Bhaskar with urgent breaking news. There are confirmed reports of the mica mine collapse in Madhuban district after the roof caved in, trapping all 50 miners who were heading out of the mine after finishing their shift. Relief and rescue operations have been hampered due to the massive power cut in most regions of the area. Sources say that the trapped miners had access to little or no safety equipment. We will bring you the latest on this story as new developments become available."

The cricket commentary had resumed with its concomitant fervour when Chanda brought hot rotis to the courtyard on her next round. Her mother-in-law snatched the plate from her shaking hands and ordered viciously, "Go phone your family to ask when the car is coming. Looks like your father planned his own death!"

Stubby coarse fingers powdered white with flour covered Chanda's plump lips as she uttered a muffled cry and ran towards the house.

"At least turn the gas off, princess," hollered Renu acridly. "Your father won't buy us a new house if you burn this one down!"

Chanda shot back into the kitchen to obey the last instruction before dashing back into the house.

She couldn't sleep a wink that night; bitter wails of her mother swirled in her ears despite the loud snorting and snoring around her in the courtyard. Chanda had never shared her grief with her parents, and now her heart ached from the burden of unspoken agony.

"Mithoo must be asleep," she rationalised, trying to lull her exhausted body to rest by humming a faint tune. But her mother's anguished cries came swooshing back in her ears, stealing the repose from her searing hot eyeballs. When she did drift into a state of fluid semi-consciousness before dawn, Chanda saw vivid pictures of her father trapped within the dark, dank folds of the earth where no light from outside could break in, nor any voice of comfort reach him from the world above. She pictured herself shouting to her father from the mouth of the fateful mine, but it was as if the ill-fated mine had shut its monstrous mouth with gigantic piles of debris and rubble, just like massive sharks snap their sharp serrated jaws tight after swallowing their prey. Suddenly, she was jolted awake by repeated blunt blows of shoes. Hari was beating her vexedly, mouthing loud obscenities.

"Stop shouting early in the morning, you whore!" Chanda ducked behind her pillow but the beatings continued.

"You sleep like a princess, but shout as if we are torturing you here."

Chanda wept silently and wiped the tears and snot off her face with her palms.

"Now go prepare food; we're not your servants," commanded Hari, dropping the heavy rubber boot and warning her with a wagging index finger. From the corner of her eye, Chanda noticed Renu and her mother-in-law snigger smugly.

Quietly, like a prisoner, she filled a small brass pot with water from the courtyard tap and went outside for ablutions. She had barely splashed a handful of water on her aching eyes when an idyllic sight soothed her pain and suffering magically. Mithoo was perched on a high branch of the neem tree, his wings raised above his back like an eagle's. Chanda watched this blissful spectacle as Mithoo continued to preen and fan his feathers, oblivious to his friend's presence below the tree. When she could wait no longer, she called out softly, "Mithoo, I know you're angry I didn't meet you yesterday . . ." She choked up. "I have a lot to share with you, my friend; please don't turn your back at me," she supplicated.

Mithoo instantly turned around, closed his feathers and gave an alarmed whistle. In no time he had flown down and was eyeing Chanda's brass pot curiously.

"Even this big pot can't contain all the tears my small eyes hold back," confessed Chanda, stroking Mithoo's back gently. "They want a new air-conditioned car," she lamented, throwing up her hands in despair, entirely unaware of her sudden high-pitched voice laced with anger. She bent low and faced Mithoo's confused bead-eyed glare. By now he had brought one leg up and behind his wings to scratch his head in bewilderment.

"I know you don't understand," Chanda empathized with Mithoo's conundrum. "I don't either." She scratched her head on cue. "I mean, they have no money to buy gas to run a car, but they force my parents to give them one."

"Aiyeee—!!!" Chanda shrieked hoarsely as a brute force yanked her from behind, pulling her thick plait of hair mercilessly.

"I'll tell you who doesn't have money, you untouchable bitch!" Chanda's mother-in-law was dragging her by her hair to the courtyard where Hari and Renu stood in aggressive postures as if to tackle a wayward buffalo. Mithoo flew into the courtyard, snorting air through his nose in anger at the old woman who refused to let go of Chanda. The very sight of Mithoo agitated the old woman, who tried to chase the bird out of the courtyard with a broomstick, all while pulling Chanda by her hair in every direction.

"This jungly whore is completely deranged! She was talking to this stray bird that we don't have money for gas!" The old woman thrashed Chanda with the broomstick in frustration as Mithoo flew in her face menacingly.

"She said we force her parents to give us money!"

"You said *that*?" Hari grabbed Chanda firmly by the shoulders and repeated his question. She struggled to free herself, but he punched her mouth so hard, the cleft of her upper lip split and bloodied her front teeth.

"She better be taught a lesson!" fumed Renu, seizing the opportunity to slap Chanda's badly bruised face. Chanda's loud wails muted Mithoo's shrill screams, who was drumming his feathers relentlessly in the faces of her aggressors. In deep throes of his emotional overload, Mithoo nicked and bit Renu and Hari in a vain attempt to prevent them from flailing Chanda.

Unfortunately, it was too late. The old woman hobbled out of the kitchen excitedly, gripping a plastic jar of kerosene in one hand, and the kitchen lighter in another. Rushed furtive glances were exchanged between the accomplices who undertook to neutralize the victim for a smooth execution of the crime to follow. Hari had pinned Chanda face down to the ground, pressing her neck by the full force of his heavy-booted leg. Renu had put her entire body weight on Chanda's back so that she had no recourse to struggle. The old woman undid the lid of the plastic jar with sinewy fingers trembling with excitement. Within seconds, the air grew thick with the pungent smell of kerosene that was liberally dousing Chanda's crouched squat frame, coiling like a deer firmly under the tiger's incisive jaw.

The old woman struck the lighter.

Nothing happened.

Not a spark.

Like a pistol that just clicks when its trigger is pulled if its first chamber is empty.

But the second is loaded.

With a bullet.

In this case, with a spark.

That deadly spark snowballed into a mass of fire whose legs took it in frenzied directions. Until the wobbly legs couldn't move. Under the weight of melting skin and burning hair. The mass of fire still held its voice. A voice of agonized, gut-wrenching wails—of help—of desperation—and finally—of resignation.

And amongst it all, a lone parrot circled the thick, impenetrable fumes: drawn by the familiar voice, but unable to find the innocent eyes that had befriended him, the stocky hands that had fed him, the benevolent heart that had transcended borders of *speciesism*. A presence that had refused to discriminate between *human brain* and *bird brain*.

But a presence that was going up in smoke, pore by pore, its blood evaporating quicker than water in a steam kettle. Sharp orange flames singed Mithoo's feathers as he got dangerously close to the screaming mass of fire, bobbing his tail vigorously as breathing became arduous. Eyes cloudy and voice almost lost due to excessive smoke inhalation, Mithoo dropped to the ground and fell unconscious in a corner of the courtyard.

When he awoke several hours later, he gaped at the scene with an open beak. A charred, unrecognizable body lay motionless on the floor, covered upto its neck by a stark white cotton sheet. Mithoo threw his head back in horror. Surrounding the black-and-white corpse were solemnly dressed women wiping their eyes dry with the loose end of their white saris—the traditional colour of mourning.

Every few minutes, a thin woman let out heartening groans of *"Hai meri beti!"* (O, my daughter!) and passed the loose end of her white sari over her dry eyes. This coordinated outburst lead one lady or another from the crowd to console the thin woman by pressing her shoulders reassuringly, or patting her back. The comforting gestures invariably made the thin woman stare blankly at the dimming evening sky and question God in a remarkably injured tone, "Why did you kill her father? The grief drove my beautiful daughter-in-law to suicide . . ."

Soon after, preparations were underway for a procession worthy of a celebrity. Hari had brought dozens of marigold garlands, bags full of scented rose petals, packets of sandalwood incense and saffron.

The Inseparables

Renu had dressed the coal black skeleton in her wedding sari—red silk with gold *zari* borders. Thick layers of foundation caked the black featureless face, lips forced into a shapely smile by blood-red lipstick.

Like a clown's. Both mocking the superficial world with their twisted cynical smiles that force them to conceal their unfathomable grief behind greasepaint. In death and life alike. As if both existed simultaneously: dying everyday while living, and alive in death. And smiling. Like Chanda. At the hordes of mourners who were conspicuously absent when she was fighting for life, but who were now praying for her peace in death. Chanting, *"Ram Naam Satya Hai,"* (only God's name is the ultimate truth).

Carrying her like a sacred goddess on a wooden shaft in death, while despising her as a monster when she lived. Raining fragrant flowers on her corpse, while inundating her with humiliation in life. Until they reached the site of her funeral pyre by the banks of a river, where they would take a holy dip after consigning her already burnt body to flames. To wash away their sins of burning her *twice*—once in life, once in death—until all that remained of her innocent eyes, stocky hands and benevolent heart were ashes and obstinate bones. And those too, would be immersed in the same river so that sins and virtue, evil and good commingle to perpetuate life on earth.

Large orange-yellow flames leapt to the sky after generous quantities of clarified butter were fed to them. Engulfing the red setting sun. And the blood-red smiling lips.

Long after the flames had subsided and the sun set below the horizon, another procession approached the river banks. Jain *sadhus* swathed in white unstitched robes marched past the smoking funeral pyre in single file. Barefoot, to not crush insects under their feet. Mouths bandaged to not ingest invisible insects while breathing. Chanting, "*Ahimsa Parmo Dharma*" (non-violence is one's utmost duty). The last of the *sadhus* noticed a subtle flutter on the smouldering remains of the funeral pyre. Approaching it cautiously, he extricated a badly burnt parrot with his bare hands from a pile of fuming burnt rubble. It regarded the *sadhu* with glazed eyes and wriggled out of his hands to land back on the smouldering pyre. The *sadhu* stared long at the parrot after its swollen eyelids were pasted shut. He couldn't help remarking the peace on the little bird's face despite its agonizing end.

Pavitra in Paris

"**L**adies and gentlemen: Air France, flight number 359 from New Delhi to Paris is ready for boarding. All passengers are requested to queue up at gate number 1. Please have your boarding passes and identification ready."

The short bursts of announcement made Pavitra jump in his new and supremely uncomfortable rubber shoes. Shifting his weight from one leg to the other, he gaped at his surroundings in wonderment.

Anil was waving at him frantically, flapping stiff paper documents while balancing a fidgety toddler in his arms.

Pavitra bolted towards him, halting a respectable distance away and threw his hands together, palms joined nervously in anticipation of impending orders.

He knew no better. In his living memory, and in the memory of his father and forefathers, all his ancestors had been loyal servants to the *zamindars*—the rich land owners. Although deemed *untouchable* and not allowed inside the house, they received two square meals in exchange for back-breaking work at the fields.

"Stand in line," commanded Anil tersely, ironing out the creases from his rumpled ivory silk shirt with the back of his hand, as he bent down to put his three-year-old daughter on her feet.

Pavitra obeyed, moving systematically behind people, whose backs he used as shields to screen himself from disapproving eyes. Five-year-old Sahil, Anil's older son, pranced towards him and advanced his unlaced shoe dangling over his toe. As Pavitra sat on his haunches to tie the loose ends of impeccably polished genuine leather shoes, a proud smile lit up his weathered face sagging under decades of hard labour. Touching his master's child was a rare privilege. Even more singular was accompanying them to a foreign land abounding in opportunity and wealth.

The lush orchards in his remote Indian village of Belsandi had been teeming with ripe mangoes and juicy litchis, yet he had slept on empty stomach for nights on end, unable to find work feasible for his six decade old wasting frame. Beaten ruthlessly several times by adolescents guarding the coveted produce, whom his failing vision always overlooked, attempts at stealing a few fruits for dinner were invariably foiled brutally.

As he had lain on the floor of his mud hut in the middle of a ghetto, miles away from upper caste concrete houses, images of his dead wife beckoning him had flashed across his delirious mind. He still loved her, he thought, wincing in pain from the bruises, although she had eloped with a more prosperous man much younger than himself.

Alas, he lamented, if he would have also had half-a-dozen children like his older brother Bhola, he would have been equally successful, with more bodies to work the landlords' fields. Yet, he didn't want to blame his only son Kishori for his misfortunes. Afterall, he had a family of his own to feed before worrying about an old and ailing father.

He was positive he was hallucinating when he saw Anil, upright and trim in his plum suit, tinted sunglasses inverted on his head to perceive clearly in Pavitra's obscure dwelling. Every bone in his skeletal body twinged as he had laboured to draw himself up out of respect for his master, who had done the unthinkable by coming to his humble abode.

"You're going with me to Paris." Anil's laconic instructions were met with an unblinking vacant stare, punctuated with a question mark. For a man whose world gravitated around mundane gestures in a daily struggle for survival, the destination was trivial compared to what he might be able to accomplish there.

"Sahib, are there fields in Paris?" he had asked naively in a Hindi contorted by a distinct village accent, every word spread out over agonizing sighs. Anil's intellectual features, accentuated by bespectacled scholarly eyes and a receding hairline, had betrayed a cynical amusement at this ignorant inquiry. "You will help Tania with household chores."

"Move on!" came a gruff voice surveying Pavitra scornfully and breaking his reverie abruptly. He inched towards the counter where people took off jackets, handed over bottles, and raised their hands to allow uniformed men and women to pass a metal object over their bodies, he thought, to help with measurements for their new garments. Afterall, when he had reluctantly accompanied Anil to the gigantic mall the size of his village settlement—bustling with shops selling detergent and tomatoes under the same roof—a boy with a badge had got him to raise his arms before giving him the blue blazer. As he bid farewell to his tattered khaki shirt with missing buttons and a grimy dhoti, to trade it for creased trousers, starched cotton shirt and a casual blazer, his personality did not seem to synchronize with the transformation. The blazer hung loose on an arched back, and the trousers felt unseemly over emaciated legs. The universal self-conscious expression he wore—as if begging apology for his presence, and his sheer existence from passers-by— made spiteful people hostile, indifferent people curious and courteous people proud. He cowered under beeping gates with flashing lights, oscillating back and forth amid smirks from security personnel. Tania maintained a calculated distance from him, burying her nose in an English-French dictionary. As onlookers scrutinized him from head to toe with the amusement of regarding a chimpanzee perched on all fours on a zoo tree, she looked away, disowning the savage being.

The arrogance of being the wife of a flourishing software engineer, invited to tour the world to impart his skills to technology giants of the west, added to her demeanour, superiority of a borrowed character. At twenty-eight, she could boast of nothing more than two kids, excessive make-up and extreme attention to her choice of clothes. Although discernibly overweight owing to lack of exercise after childbirth, she had an inexplicable penchant for figure-hugging clothes. Her disproportionately heavy hips that swelled under a slender waist were draped in skin-tight grey denim jeans that tapered down tree trunk like thighs before flaring over skinny legs. The matching cleavage-flattering t-shirt she wore, didn't seem to be doing justice to a voluptuous bosom drooping under layers of adipose.

Middle-aged men travelling alone stole lustful glances at her, while Pavitra kept his eyes glued to her glossy black stiletto heels. As passengers poured into the departure lobby, scattering to occupy immovable burgundy plastic seats stuck to each other with horizontal black beams, Pavitra shuffled in his feet, floundering over unattended bags and belongings. His body was stiff, its muscles smarting at the joints from standing in footwear for long hours. Upon close inspection of the lounge, he spotted a quiet corner at the end of the horizontal rows of seats, away from burgeoning queues facing two glass-enclosed telephone cabins. He slunk away, peering behind him surreptitiously and tripping occasionally on unlevelled carpet edges. As he reached his inconspicuous hideout, he smiled self satisfactorily and slumped on the ground, exhausted. Looking around, he stretched his legs in front of him, letting out a muffled whine as he rested his bent back against vibrantly papered wall. The relief on his shrivelled face was similar to a bird flying out of its cage after long captivity, as he unstrapped his shoes and pressed his frosted feet lightly.

"Where's Pavitra?" Anil's tone was plagued with apprehension and ire. Tania raised her mascara-coated brushy eyebrows complacently. "I thought he was with you." She looked around condescendingly before covering her face with a book displaying the title *French Made Easy* on a white vertical band, sandwiched between a blue and a red, signifying the French tricolour. Anil stood transfixed while his eyeballs moved searchingly through the room, pausing on groups from behind an auburn rectangular plastic frame. Suddenly, he quickened his pace, stumbling over unfolded newspapers and plastic cups, jerking his hand free from Sahil's grip, who started wailing loudly. Tania picked him up impassively and plunged him into the seat adjoining her own, without closing her book.

"Who told you to sit on the ground like this?" reproached Anil, making some heads turn. Pavitra was smiling beatifically, honoured by his master's concern, though not fully comprehending the reason behind his admonition.

"Come with me right away!" He took Pavitra's rawboned arm and dragged him to a seat on the last row, at the rear end of the lounge. Pavitra crouched, huddling within himself like a horse dreading to be flogged. His face was damp with sweat as he shrank himself to avoid touching his neighbours. An executively dressed young woman, typing rhythmically at her laptop, moved to the next seat after looking at his bare feet—black and leathery, and spotted with raisin-like blisters. Nobody, he thought pensively, would believe in his village that an untouchable like him had been touched by his master and other affluent people. He regarded his shoes, still lying at the spot he had left them, their flaps swaying mildly in the breeze of ceiling fans.

"Business class passengers are requested to line up in front of gate 1, thank you." Pavitra craned his neck to identify the source of this message, but got distracted by massive black televisions suspended precariously from the ceiling. He wondered why there were no advertisements of soap cakes, or basmati rice, or even flashily dressed gods and goddesses, as he had glimpsed occasionally while mopping the floors in his master's bedroom.

"Economy class passengers can please start lining up at gate number 2." Oblivious to yet another unidentifiable speaker, Pavitra stood up to allow people to pass him, holding his breath the whole time.

"It's our turn to go!" Anil looked exasperated, yet his voice was placid like the waters of a tideless sea. Tania and the kids had already entered the tunnel-like tube connecting the waiting lounge to the designated aircraft.

Pavitra pressed his lips tightly together while he manoeuvred the shaky floor leading to the plane. As Anil peeked into aisles, tip-toeing through co-passengers and excusing himself for brushing past women, an oblong handbag landed on Pavitra's head from a sleek overhead storage compartment. "What are you doing with *my* bag?" came a vexed voice belonging to a robust elderly man eyeing him with suspicion, his silver Santa Claus beard merging with the spotless white free-flowing *kurta* he was wearing. Perplexed, Pavitra dropped the bag and stood culpably with downcast eyes imploring, "I'm not a thief, sahib; I didn't touch your bag—"

He now froze with fear, his gaunt body trembling lightly, as he recalled the events of the fateful night he had been beaten black and blue by the villagers. Vanquished by poverty, jaded by a squalid life, and desperate to turn his fate around, he had pledged allegiance to a local gang of robbers, accepting the unskilled work of carting the booty. After what had seemed an impressive maiden attempt, Pavitra had bundled the valuables in a coarse bed sheet, and had leapt down the window to scurry off to a pre-decided meeting place. One of the robbers had stabbed the owner and left him to bleed, without realizing that the latter possessed a country made pistol. Far from being agile and nimble at sixty, Pavitra was shot in the foot by the owner of the house, and handed over to the police after being squashed to pulp by infuriated villagers. He had wanted to commit suicide then, having tarnished the flawless reputation of his ancestors who could lay their lives happily to protect their masters, if need be.

"He's with me, sir; sorry about the inconvenience." Anil's glare pierced Pavitra's soul as their eyes met accidentally. "This is your seat," he signalled wearily. "Come to me if you need anything; I'm across from you, near the window."

As Pavitra saw his master's figure disappear among diversely coloured crop of heads, he muttered a silent prayer of gratitude to one of his many gods. After the government abolished *Zamindari* from independent India, scores of peasants starved—their landlords having migrated to metropolitan cities in quest of a livelihood. "May God bless Anil and his family," he prayed earnestly, looking at the roof of the plane. He would no longer go without medicine when his feet burned with fever, or walk barefoot on scorching sand, or even pull his own tooth out with heated tongs when it pained excruciatingly.

"Monsieur, voulez-vous du vin?"

Pavitra convulsed involuntarily at this unexpected intrusion. He stared fixedly at an elegant face, fresh peaches and cream in complexion, bowing with a tray carrying blood coloured liquid in stick like glasses. Unable to decipher his garble sprayed with fervent gesticulation and fitful folding of hands, the stewardess pulled out a stowed slim table stuck to the back of the seat facing him. He sucked his stomach in and stopped breathing as a half-filled wine glass was arranged neatly on it, with two varieties of crackers packed in transparent cellophane. She replicated her actions for his neighbour, and was about to wheel her trolley warily through the narrow aircraft alley as her gauzy eyes fell on Pavitra's unfastened seatbelt. Confident that verbal communication was impossible with this client, she replaced her tray on the top tier of her trolley, and bent gracefully to reach for the buckle to strap his belt. Pavitra squeezed his eyes shut so tightly that a tear escaped from the corner of one eye and sat obstinately on a welt on his cheek. The man whose very name signified chasteness and purity in his native language, sat paralyzed, meditating feverishly to be pardoned for his unmindful tactile encounters.

As the intoxicating beverage took effect, Pavitra felt himself splashing his feet in the muddy waters of his village pond with soaking wet buffaloes. He awoke to tantalizing odours of food lying meticulously covered in disposable boxes on the table in front of him. He punctured the plastic covering of the food with the spikes of a fork, but his face contorted strangely as he began to shovel it down his throat. He rose partially from his seat, only to be pulled back by the belt wrapped around his waist. He wrestled with it, frustrated, until it snapped open, rudely awaking his taciturn neighbour.

Anil was watching the personal television tucked away in his armrest when Pavitra stood beside his seat noiselessly. Tania had apparently dozed off after reading a few pages from a glossy fashion magazine, which now covered her chest at the page she had left off. Unsure of how, yet Pavitra was desperate to get Anil's attention. The monotonous refrain of "Sahib, Anil sahib," seemed to fall on deaf ears, as Anil had plugged ear phones to listen to the dialogues of the film he was watching. Pavitra finally shook his arm vigorously, making him shriek in alarm.

"What's the matter?" he asked rather crossly, extracting the wired buttons from his ears.

"Sahib, jungle!" was all Pavitra could put together.

"Oh, come, I'll show you the men's washroom."

Pavitra stood immobilized, his reflexes numbed. He yearned to defecate, like he always did, in strictly demarcated forested spaces for his caste. The days he forgot to carry a dusty bottle for his morning rituals, he would stop by the pond to enter it, wearing his dhoti, and cleanse himself prudishly under modestly lowered eyes of half-drenched women, working lather on their clothes. The banal sand of his village was like precious gold dust he could not find to wash his hands in the sophisticated aircraft lavatory. He had barely reached his seat, feeling utterly unholy, when a passenger complained furiously to a stewardess, "Your washroom is a big mess! What do you charge all the money for?"

Pavitra stared helplessly at the foam-like pieces of cheese-filled spinach ravioli, flanked by sautéed potatoes and green beans. He dare not eat anything, he pledged, for fear of using the toilet again. He tilted his head in both directions, inspecting the prawn-shaped croissant, expecting it to move anytime.

"Ladies and gentlemen, this is your pilot speaking. We are now flying over Paris, and expect to land at Charles de Gaulle airport in approximately fifteen minutes at 10:30 p.m. local time. The temperature outside is a mild twenty degrees Celsius under cloudy skies. Please fasten your seatbelts to ensure a smooth landing. We hope you enjoyed your flight aboard Air France, and look forward to serving you again in the future. Thank you!"

As Pavitra looked back after descending the steep aircraft stairs—clinging to the banister the whole time—he recognized the winged steel animal behind him. Packets of food and bottled water had rained from its belly, making villagers run amuck, after the perennial floods had washed everything in their fury. He had hurled stones at it, maddened with rage, wading through knee-deep waters, unable to compete with brisk youngsters fighting for limited rations.

"Sit there with the kids while Pavitra and I bring the luggage," Anil said to Tania, pointing at some unoccupied seats in the airport lobby. "This way, Pavitra."

Pavitra's head spun as he looked, stupefied, at the steep escalators resembling the cascades of his village. The only difference, he thought, was that instead of gushing the colourless, life-sustaining liquid, these imposing machines were awash with a riot of rainbow colours.

"I'm talking to you, Pavitra." Anil stood right in front of him, both hands on his waist forming two inverted triangles. He had walked ahead in the hope that Pavitra was following him, but retraced his steps to find him glued to the same spot he had left him. It seemed to Anil that Pavitra had neither moved nor blinked, probably not even breathed. He seemed to be frozen in time like the extinct dinosaurs.

Pavitra fell behind Anil as if under a hypnotic spell, following him, dazed. His head moved curiously along with suitcases—big and small—bearing security tags and rotating on conveyor belts. He jumped back in fear when Anil grabbed two luggage bags and threw them violently on the ground.

"Put these on the cart while I get the others."

Tania was re-touching her make-up, blissfully oblivious to the hoopla around her, and did not notice the two men join her. She peered into the round palm-sized mirror of her compact powder, squinting, as she drew outlines on the contours of her lips with a blunt cherry pencil. Thereafter, she unzipped the side pocket of her satchel and produced a brush that she coated with lipstick the colour of blood. With strokes akin to an experienced painter, she filled her pout with the cosmetic, pressing her lips a few times to spread the colour evenly. She looked striking, even seductive, when she was done.

"Mr. Leblanc should be here," said Anil, stroking Sahil's hair that covered his forehead in a fringe. Tania sighed, looking at her daughter attentively, who was playing with her satchel. She snatched her bag back as the child threw out the lipstick that was jutting out of its half-zipped side pocket.

"Did you call him?" she asked, bending forward to grasp the lipstick rolling under her neighbour's seat, and in the process, revealing her crescent-like breasts bulging over a leopard skin brassiere.

"The line-up for public phones is crazy. Let's go towards the exit and find out if he's here."

Tania rose, pulling up the edges of her jeans on her waist, and hoping Anil would take care of the kids, as he always did uncomplainingly, for everything. The placard screaming *Anil Jha* in bold black lettering caught her attention, and nudging Anil, she pointed her forefinger at a stocky man with slit eyes and a smug smile.

"Enchanté!" Mr. Leblanc shook their hands and ruffled the kids' hair as Pavitra stood behind, merging in the background with a cab driver unloading bags from a cart.

"I'll drive you to the hotel tonight, as your train to Marseille is late in the evening tomorrow," Mr. Leblanc offered, guiding everyone out of the airport, and into the parking lot.

"Pretty nice of the site manager to allow me a day off to tour Paris with my family," Anil said, looking at the overcast night sky through his window in the car. "There isn't a great deal you can see at this time—"

"Well, the cherry on the icing is that I am at your disposal tomorrow as your tour guide!" Mr. Leblanc flashed a yellow-toothed smile that made his eyes look like two pencil lines drawn with the precision of a ruler. He was exhilarated at the idea of trading a sedentary day at an enclosed office, for one packed with sightseeing.

At the hotel, as he helped Pavitra empty the boot of his car, he exclaimed, "That's our company's way of saying, *Bienvenue en France!*"

Tania's ears pricked and she whispered "Merci," after mentally translating the words she had memorized from her book.

Left to the privacy of a spectacular room at the hotel, Pavitra touched everything culpably, wiping it after, with the edge of his shirt. He resembled Mr. Bean—a child trapped in an adult's body—as he ran his fingers over the three-branched brass candelabrum, which he believed was a modification of *Nataraja*, the Hindu god Shiva, engaged in his cosmic dance. He stroked the tassels knotted to curtains on his stubbled cheek, remembering barbers shaving beards of clients seated on wooden chairs under shady trees. He played with the switch of a night lamp, flicking it on and off repeatedly, wondering why his village was always plunged in darkness when it was so easy to bring light.

Next morning, Anil entered his room to find him lying flat on the chestnut carpet, deep in slumber, his blazer bunched under his head as pillow.

The family was at breakfast when Mr. Leblanc arrived. He looked rather casual and relaxed in golf apparel and sported an exuberant smile, through which gleamed the silver coating the crevices of his lower jaw. "What do I see here?" he exclaimed cheerily, bowing to the family and hovering over the table cluttered with a golden-brown stick of crusty baguette, a large transparent glass pot of dark coffee with some bowls, wrapped butter cubes and a small jar of apricot jam. Seeing the empty plates, he surmised they had not yet begun breakfast.

"Good timing!" he chirped, ripping the dark brown pointed edge of the baguette and squeezing a cube of butter between its soft gaping cavity. Tania licked her copper glossed lips hungrily, unsure if anything displayed across the table was even edible. She silently mocked at the absentmindedness of the waiter as her kohl rimmed eyes rested on the enormous coffee pot. "Did he expect us to drink directly from the pot?" Her eyes roamed the exquisite dining hall brimming with laughter and excited chatter of tourists bending over colourful maps, in the shadow of silk lampshades fringed with bell-shaped metal beads of a darker hue.

Mr. Leblanc poured some coffee into a small bowl and dipped an oblong piece of baguette into it, before thrusting the dripping moist morsel into his mouth. "You folks not hungry?" he asked thoughtfully.

"This is very different for us," replied Anil, referring to the served food with a circular movement of his gleaming eyeballs. "We are accustomed to omelettes on buttered toasts, vegetable fritters or stuffed *parathas* for breakfast, washed down by very sweet chai."

It appeared to Mr. Leblanc that this description of their preferred breakfast generated saliva in their mouths, as Anil swallowed after touching the tip of his tongue to the corners of his mouth. Tania was no longer distracted by neighbours, having pardoned the waiter for not bringing coffee mugs. She contemplated Anil, as if he were ordering the delicacies he had just enumerated.

"Oh là là!" ejaculated Mr. Leblanc, as though he had just balanced a complex algebraic equation. "I fully understand now. Why don't we proceed with our sightseeing? We can stop on the way for an early lunch." As he spoke, his half-visible eyeballs darted left and right through its gashes. "I don't see the gentleman who was with us last night?"

Anil paused briefly before his brain could associate the word *gentleman* to Pavitra. "He's our servant." He did not feel the necessity of telling his name—the occupation being Pavitra's all-encompassing identity.

"Aren't you lucky to have someone to cook for you, or clean up after you, or even look after your kids?" Mr. Leblanc gazed at Sahil, who was engrossed in a long, hardback comic book of Tintin, as he stared at the chubby boy-scout with his hair cropped like a blonde plume in the centre of his head, and a snow-white dog by his side. "In France, everybody became equal after the French Revolution of 1789," he concluded somberly.

Pavitra was happy to eat in the seclusion of his room at his masters' behest, who were too ashamed to let him be a public spectacle in the dining room. He wolfed down the baguette without breaking it into smaller pieces, famished after renouncing his in-flight meal. He then scooped the jam with the curve of his four fingers and licked it voraciously. He stared at the butter knife, not knowing its utility, as there was no plastic or cellophane to be ripped from the food. He lifted the lid from the coffee pot, and inserting his index finger in the deep brown liquid, moved it backwards and forward before exiting it completely from the receptacle. He replaced the lid and pushed the pot away after deciding it was too hot to drink.

"Our first stop is the spectacular gothic cathedral of Notre Dame," announced Mr. Leblanc, as his twentieth century vintage Citroën glided through busy streets bordered with European architectural marvels and open air cafés.

Pavitra sat in the navigator seat adjacent to Mr. Leblanc, flabbergasted by all that crossed his vision: huge multicoloured umbrellas with scalloped edges shading effervescent people from the nippy autumn breeze and the oblique sun rays; an endless black tunnel with luxury cars zipping past, blocking his eardrums; a river with giant boats oozing with people taking photographs. And so much more he had never seen before, and didn't know existed.

"Antique car," complimented Anil, as the party exited the parking lot to merge with a steady stream of zealous tourists wearing cameras in their necks.

"Yes, I like to call it a cross between a golf cart and a jelly bean!" Anil flashed a concurring smile as he turned around to glimpse the hybrid machine described by his host. He was struck by its unusually small tyres, and shook his head, grinning, to dismiss the idea that should one of its tyres be flattened, Mr. Leblanc would put the car in his pocket and walk away.

As Mr. Leblanc pointed interesting photo angles to his guests strolling between the two arms of the river Seine, Pavitra looked heavenwards, mesmerized by the miracle of harmony, equilibrium and proportion that lay exposed in front of him. He awed at the architectural marvel of the cathedral with the reverence and dread of facing an invincible extraterrestrial superpower.

Tania watched the kids distractedly, while Anil knelt, tilted, and closed one eye, zooming and focussing his lens sedulously on the stupendous façade of arcaded entrances depicting saints leading the worshipper and tourist alike. He bent backwards to capture the massive arched entrance teeming with saints carved in stone, wearing wings and looking up with folded hands or one hand on the chest, as if blinded by the halo surrounding the bearded man supporting a tiara of thorns.

Tania ogled at slender European women, femininely dressed in revealing off-shoulder knee-length dresses of finely embroidered crepe in ocean colours, accentuating their pale complexion and lending them an unspeakable sensuality. Some had coiled a matching cashmere scarf around their neck, while others slung a silk jersey on their shoulder. She envied a young woman, tall and pencil thin, whose ochre-yellow pleated skirt contrasted daringly with an aubergine boat-neck silk top. Her wavy golden hair was secured carelessly with a butterfly shaped clasp, exposing a pronounced spine flanked by shining shoulder blades. Her ensemble flowed fluidly around her minimal curves. On impulse, Tania drew back her arm to touch her spine with the pads of her fingers, but excess loose flesh had almost obliterated its existence. She suddenly loathed her designer *salwar-kameez* which drowned the last remnants of her body shape, lending her the appearance of a moving mound of sequined coarse fabric.

Anil beckoned Pavitra to join them as they were ready to enter the church. Pavitra advanced at a deliberately slow pace, hoping to be abandoned and left behind. Anil waited impatiently, tapping each finger consecutively on the closed shutter of his camera while the others walked through the imposing entrance.

"What is inside, sahib?" Pavitra demanded meekly.

"This is a place of worship for these white people." Anil looked demeaned at inventing such a simplistic description of a historical monument.

Pavitra looked around, as if attempting to find a place to flee, and bore on his face a phobia of being lynched for coming so close to a place of worship. He remembered the detour he had to make every single day to avoid his village temple nestled in the cavern of a massive tree trunk. The modest terracotta statue of the elephant God *Ganesha* smeared in fiery orange, blessed all but his untouchable caste people. He recalled with goose flesh the stern warning by the village elders of being ostracized, when his son Kishori had dared to bend his head in prayer from his bicycle facing the temple, at a time when his wife was sprawled on the ground, screaming in pain during childbirth. The pariah had since hung a cut-out from a calendar, of goddess *Lakshmi* to pray to, whose four hands lifted him in succor, whose lotus eyes healed him with benevolence, and whose opulence diminished his misery.

Following his master like a prisoner follows the jailer, Pavitra was resigned and acquiescent. With his limited powers of reasoning, he convinced himself that his true salvation lay in obeying his master's every command. His precept seemed to bear fruit, for with every footstep, he felt he was entering the precincts of heaven. The oppressive height of the vault made him giddy; the kaleidoscope of iconographic splendour etched on stained glasses brought him face-to-face with angels and saints. Belittled as Quasimodo of Victor Hugo's *Notre Dame*, his feet froze to boulders, unwilling to face GOD HIMSELF behind the high altar.

He fell to his feet, weeping bitterly and praying, "O God of whites and blacks, may I be reincarnated in this very land where people touch each other without qualm; where your house is open to all who care to enter; and where the bane of hunger and destitution does not haunt!"

Tania strolled alone, charmed by the medallions of stained glass, which she thought resembled her custom-made blue pottery choker pendant. She looked up and marvelled at a scene that imitated her matching block printed navy-blue sari.

"This is precisely where the semi-blind composer *Louis Vierne* had collapsed, his left foot coming to rest on the low C pedal of the organ." Anil lowered his head, nodding occasionally as a sign of profound interest and concentration in Mr. Leblanc's recounts about the emotionally charged symphonies of the French legend.

"I know a cosy Indian restaurant off the avenue of Champs Elysées." This pleasantly dramatic change of subject by Mr. Leblanc made Anil straighten his back and grin sedately in an effort to quell his surging delight at a hearty Indian meal, afterall. He lingered aimlessly, awaiting an opportunity to whisper the exhilarating news in Tania's ears, who, by now, looked dreadfully bored of gazing up the ornately sculpted ceiling, or admiring the refractive qualities of stained windows. Every now and again she yawned wide, without placing a hand on her gaping mouth, sometimes staring fixedly at the graceful breezy movements of elegantly dressed French women.

Back in the car, she squeezed her tumid hips to make space for frazzled kids drooping over her and Anil. As they drove through the swanky promenade of Champs Elysées, lined with trees bearing bronze leaves swaying in the balmy autumn air, Pavitra peered out of his window at the concentration of luxury boutiques and haute couture showrooms in rapt awe. He reiterated a mute litany, fortified by closed eyes and folded palms lying in his lap. He beseeched the Almighty to never sever him from Anil, with whose grace he had vanquished all privations. His maudlin sentiments reached a dramatic crescendo when a mustached, tan-complexioned durwan, dressed royally in a beige Jodhpuri suit and scarlet turban flung the door open, bowing respectfully to usher them into the restaurant. The musical chimes above the door blended effortlessly with the soul-stirring notes of the duet between Indian classical instruments of the tabla and the sitar, creating a range of effects: the roar of a fighting army, the ripple of water and the rustling of leaves.

The interior of the restaurant was stately yet functional. Walls and ceilings were painted in ostentatious magenta—lacquered, gilded and decorated with mosaics, etched glass and inlaid mirrors to indulge the elite South Asian clientele. Alternating vertical panels of dark and light wood, rose-pink banquettes, chairs covered in pearly-gold leather, tall partitions and a central pillar created intimate spaces to appeal to the westerners.

Pavitra was instantly struck by a male marionette decorated on a ledge by the entrance. Its wooden face painted in red hot, along with large protruding eyes resting curiously over sharply defined features, seemed to ogle hungrily at patrons, as if they belonged to another planet than himself. Its body of stuffed cloth was draped with a bright spangled robe, and a turban with a glittering plume rested on its head. For a split second, Pavitra thought he personified it: though richly dressed, he too was invariably manipulated by his masters—gyrating and dancing to their tunes when they pulled his invisible strings of obeisance and servitude. Like the wooden doll, he betrayed neither sentiment nor desire.

"What part of India are you from?" Mr. Leblanc quizzed the bashful waiter who was staring fixedly into his slender white tablet for noting orders, hoping the party would settle for lunch buffet instead of a custom meal.

"I'm from Pakistan, sir—from Karachi." He was still penetrating the blank white paper with his incisive glare, as if mortified by the discord between his country of origin and the name of his restaurant.

"Business runs better if we use names of Indian legends like *Gandhi* or *Taj Mahal*," he ruminated, with a disoriented expression of yearning in his melancholic eyes. He regarded Pavitra subconsciously and added, "When I first came to France aboard a cargo ship, I was penniless and never wanted to return home. Now I have in abundance of my needs, yet I crave to be reunited to my soil."

Everybody took turns to heap their plates with a delectable array of perfumed rice, topping it with steaming silky curries seasoned artistically with onion rings and diced chillies.

Tania looked at Pavitra's plate, fazed, as he balanced an overloaded stack of a mountain of rice, drilled into a pit on top to pour curries, now indistinguishable, like the myriad molten rocks and sediments composing the lava gushing out of a conical volcano. "I wish Anil had coached him on etiquette," she mourned petulantly, scowling at the golden-brown *gulab jamuns* sitting precariously on the edge of his now invisible plate, ready to topple over. "Only if he knew he could serve himself as many times he wanted; and that there is a separate plate for sweets after the main course!" She exhaled helplessly, examining Mr. Leblanc's face sceptically—though minutely—for traces of sardonic repulsion at Pavitra's brute comportment. But he was smiling, his face cocked towards Anil, as the latter fed the kids one by one.

Pavitra settled at the far end of the table, celestial joy radiating his face at the sight of copious food. A rare indecision swept his face as he popped a succulent sweet *gulab jamun* in his mouth. Never before was he faced with a choice so vast, a platter so generous! Unruffled by the elitist rules of fine dining, he gobbled pickles after sweets, licking his fingers relishingly, as if soaking in verbal orgasm. For a man who ate *rats* for survival, this newfound romance with life was almost a mirage.

"En route to the tourist Mecca of the prodigious web of iron," quipped Mr. Leblanc, chuckling, as the car penetrated the rose coloured evening mist that markedly enhanced the romantic ambience of the city.

"I had to take infinite precautions to avoid seeing the perfect antenna!" he jested, turning back and looping one hand around his seat, while contemplating his company with gusto. Anil looked fatigued, and still jetlagged; however, he forced a plastic smile and pressed the delicate arms of his kids sitting squished on either side, as if posing for Mr. Leblanc's camera. Tania was deftly wiping the bristles of her lipstick brush with a small cotton swab that looked as if it was soaked in blood.

"Voilà!" exclaimed Mr. Leblanc euphorically, as the silhouette of the Eiffel Tower soared like a pure line despite its complex geometry, against the Paris skyline. "He was right when he remarked that the only place in Paris from which he could *not* see the Eiffel Tower was when he lunched atop one of *its* restaurants! Oh, I mean, *Maupassant*, the famous French author," Mr. Leblanc quickly added, solving the conundrum responsible for his audience's tepid response to his witticism.

As Pavitra ascended the tangle of iron plates, girders and bolts of the world's best loved tower in an oblique elevator, the panorama below him emancipated his spirit. He loomed over the crowds, envisioning himself as a king attired in purple robes, wearing a gem-studded crown and watching over his commonplace subjects with an ingratiating smile. His visage exemplified a calming perspective to the chaos of the world below—a world rife with disparities, and rancour, and want, and much more. As his spirit triumphed atop the lofty structure, he felt weightless, and flawless. For the first time in his sixty odd years, he had conquered inferiority and subjugation.

The therapeutic effect of the delicate lines, the dense heavy metal, and the staggering height—all left him inebriated with ethereal prowess. Back on the ground, he followed the others like a somnambulist. As the party halted at a traffic light, his eyes fell on a carousel on the opposite side of the street. Young and old were clinging to poles, bobbing on wooden horses that rotated on a platform.

His trance broke after he had stared long at the horses rotating on the same axis—round and round—without galloping away into a land of their choice. He suddenly realized that he was returning to be the horse his masters would ride, rotating ceaselessly till the end of his life. He stood still in the middle of the road, ecstatic at his resolve to return to the dizzying height of the tower where he had savoured his first taste of liberation.

She looked majestic: her graceful legs shining like a blanket of stars, uniting the earth to the divine, all while keeping a maternal vigil over the mundane life below; her eyes lost in the sky.

He ran across the road, thirsting to embrace as if his *mother*, in all her splendour.

A few minutes later, Anil stood electrified, sunk in a sea of flashing lights and strident sirens hollering *emergency*. He looked up at the enigmatic structure shooting a light bulb-sized elevator to its peak, as if transporting Pavitra's soul to heaven.

Splash!

“**M**y son, it is God's will. That's the way God tests you. Suffering ennobles you—makes you a better person.” Bheem Ojha's reverie was broken by complete silence: odd—very odd—as one would expect silence to encourage reveries, even nurture them.

“*Bhery good! Neksht, continue.*”

As the next boy took over to read from where the previous one had left off, the class of forty-five tenth graders stared into their thin, grease-stained English text books, yawning, sketching cartoons and scribbling messages to each other. All but one seemed to follow the abysmal rendition of Dr. Christian Barnard's speech, by his neighbour, nervous about his turn to read at the end of two paragraphs. Bheem Ojha had heard the *same* lines from the *same* lessons thirty-eight times in his long career as the English teacher at Pusa High School for boys.

His was an enviable job. In the confines of his compact, poorly ventilated classroom, he was the unchallenged king. With forty-five submissive pupils to rule over from his throne of a rickety wooden chair with a single armrest, Bheem Ojha had presided over uncountable grievously flawed elocutions. He was well-liked by his pupils, mostly since his classes passed without incident. Nobody was ever corrected for mispronunciations (which occurred almost every word per sentence!); no punishments were doled out for skipping full lines (as the teacher himself was never on the same page as his students!) and no questions or debates were encouraged or entertained.

As the soiled wall clock struck 4, a raucous bell sounded in the already noisy corridors. Students from all classes bundled out into the courtyard like sardines spilling out of cans. This classroom was no exception. Bheem Ojha was no longer the king in command. Chaos had replaced his authority even as the student reciting the prose in a monotonous sing-song lullaby sharpened his voice over the hullabaloo and scrambled to finish his last lines: "It opened my eyes to the fact that I was missing something in all my thinking about suffering—something basic that was full of solace for me."

Bheem Ojha inadvertently blurted out, "*Neksht, continue,*" anxious to be reminded of that "something basic" about suffering that would be full of solace for him.

Silence—one more time silence broke his reverie, but this time not without leaving him infuriated. He much preferred the silence to come from forty-five mute puppets arranged horizontally in front of him, who could be manipulated like battery operated toys: speak, stop, continue—

The sight of dozens of disobedient desks and chairs strewn haphazardly across the room invoked his ire. He slammed the text book close, but the title of the lesson swam indolently across his head, pinching his temples with a pricking pain as he repeated it mockingly, "*In Celebration of Being Alive*—indeed!"

It was a quarter past four when he stole away to the bicycle stand: an act totally alien to his extrovert self; a deliberate attempt to flee

Splash!

his colleagues, some of whom had jokingly reminded him this morning of his impending retirement exactly one year from today. He glanced frequently at the scratched glass of his HMT watch—as old as his career itself—in a bid to show he was in some sort of a hurry, even though his mind pictured the animated revelry in the staffroom. He pined to scrape away the leftovers from lunch boxes that filled the staffroom religiously after school everyday with an overbearing, yet inviting odour. He missed the sweet masala chai prepared ritualistically by Mrs. Farooqui, whose coy beauty he had never ceased to admire silently, despite her loose-fitting *kaftan* that covered everything but her lotus-pink hands that carried the tray clattering with small ceramic cups—from teacher to teacher.

Drinking her thick, orangey concoction was, for him, in an unexplained, indirect way, equivalent to touching her. Often its first wary sip had stung his upper lip with the heat of its steam and spices, even as the sugar from it caressed and soothed it. He would look both ways before licking his lips culpably.

But not today. Today something just wasn't right. The guard bowed to him as his bicycle glided down the cemented slope leading out of the enormous rusted gate of the school. He instinctively picked the dirt path to avoid the road riddled with potholes, and, despite the extra energy he had to expend in navigating the slippery gravel crunching under his tyres, it appeared as if the bicycle rode Bheem Ojha just like waves ride surfers out in the sea. Even though he was not on a surfboard in the middle of crashing waves, his mind was consumed by a turbulent storm of emotions no less in ferocity than a violent sea storm.

Only this morning, before he left for school, his younger son Ganesh had broken the unthinkable and grossly reprehensible news of his love affair with a *Chamar* caste girl, whose ancestors skinned dead animals for a living. "And the fool expects that woman to cook in our kitchen and contaminate our lineage?" Just then, he was thrown into the air with a rude jerk as the back tyre of his bicycle exploded with a deafening blast. "The bastards!" he cursed out loud while muttering the more obscene curses under his breath. This scenario played out with the regularity of clockwork, as the over-zealous youth who ran the cycle repair shack in the bazaar by the crossroad, took it upon themselves to diligently scatter nails along the route to ensure a steady flow of customers! The repertoire was much too familiar: the diagnosis of a puncture, the 15-minute wait killed by a forced stroll in the bazaar soaking passersby with enticing smells of steaming sweet *jalebis*, succulent *gulab jamuns* and crusty *pakoras*. But Alas! He was diabetic. Yet, today he stood commandingly in front of the deep black *karahi* sizzling with golden pipes of *jalebis* fried together into a tempting maze with no escape exit.

"All of these except those two in the corner," he instructed the fat sweet-maker who was wiping the sweat from his face with a small grimy towel placed for the purpose on his shoulder.

No, Bheem Ojha was not indulging himself because he had avoided Mrs. Farooqui's sweet chai today, and could afford to compensate the saccharine here, instead. Infact, he didn't care about dietary restrictions anymore. "Don't eat *this*, don't eat *that*," he scowled angrily. "I'll eat everything! My sons should work after I retire and take over the responsibility of running the household. How long will I fend for everybody?"

For the first time in almost four decades, Bheem Ojha didn't sulk while dishing out the 10 rupee bill to the disreputable looking youth who fixed the puncture, after he returned to collect his bicycle from the shack.

Splash!

No, the change of heart wasn't because he was heady from the sugar rush supplied by his prohibited food binge. Infact, he suddenly realized that he respected those young men (his son's age), despite their bedraggled appearance and uncouth faces smeared callously with black grease akin to tribals. And this, inspite of the fact that it was hard to tell with complete certainty whether the nails on the dirt path outnumbered the potholes on the roads!

Even as he walked his bicycle gently to avoid encountering more flat tyres until he reached the relatively smooth bridge over Kosi river, he sighed to himself, "at least those lads are earning a living—by hook or crook." He stepped on the left pedal with his weathered leather slipper—whose loop over his big toe had tripled in size over the years—and propelling the cycle forward with some racing steps with his right foot, he mounted the pointed seat with ease and grace despite his unwieldy flowing *dhoti*.

The river that he was so used to crossing twice everyday without as much as a thought or a glance, arrested his imagination, as if demanding its rightful admiration today.

"Even Kosi has changed its course," he groaned, allured by the shining sparkles dancing on its waves to the whimsical tune of the setting sun which was throwing sporadic beams of glittering shimmer while playing hide-and-seek with clouds.

"My sons have stayed stagnant like the pond water of our village infested with algae . . ."

"But how can they move on—flow like Kosi—when there are hardly any jobs or opportunities?" he mused. "Why, mend bicycles, scooters, rickshaws—anything."

Bheem Ojha didn't wish to debate the subject beyond this point, as he couldn't accept that he had been aggressively unwilling to stake his life savings in helping his sons start up a small business.

The piercing calls from a farmers market, of vendors desperate for last-minute bargains before closing was a welcome distraction for Bheem. He once again dismounted from his bicycle, unable to manoeuvre it amid surging crowds walking in complete defiance to his persistent bell, barely audible over the commotion and din enveloping the market.

He seemed to have been transported into an altogether different world by the magical powers of a genie, when he turned a corner across the dirt path and entered a mustard field dazzling with bright yellow flowers under the dying light of the sun.

As he sat on his haunches to urinate—duly coiling his holy thread around his ear for the unchaste task—a burly black buffalo appeared out of the thicket, looking like an island in the vast sea of yellow flowers.

Bheem Ojha was a trifle abashed when the buffalo continued to stare at him with big, curious watery eyes, hindering the privacy of his habitual open-air toilet with mute impudence.

"Shoo, Shoo!" he screamed indignantly, waving a broken twig at it, his *janeo* still looped behind his ear.

The buffalo stood planted, unruffled by the warning, and, as if in crude retaliation, emptied its bladder in a continuous stream of running water. Bheem Ojha backed off, uncoiling the holy thread from his ear, while his bovine intruder still stared at him quizzically as if demanding from him an explanation for all the fuss surrounding the simple act of answering nature's call.

He rode along unconsciously, until he was shaken back to his senses like the surfer who is flung into the air unexpectedly when a gigantic wave knocks him from behind. But unlike the surfer, Bheem Ojha's object of consternation lay in front of him: an unruly mob of middle school children who were blocking the road leading to his house in Malinagar village.

Splash!

He was determined not to accept defeat by the two-dozen "parasites" as he often referred to them, crowding the street in animated and fiercely contested games of marbles, tic-tac-toe and cricket.

"Grow up and suck your parents' blood like leeches, or land up in my school in the false hope of getting a job!" he snapped peevishly, glaring condescendingly at the *untouchable* kids mingling freely with the crowd. He rang the bell on his handlebars furiously, and within seconds, the road was cleared of everything save a few marbles rolling aimlessly, while three uneven pieces of wood secured in the pits of the street to serve as wickets, stood tilted and desolate. Bheem Ojha rode along triumphantly, the wheels of his bicycle stamping under them the chalk lines drawn by the kids. The impact of his presence was like the strike of lightning: sudden, fearful and debilitating.

The kids dreaded the "Master Sahib," with his six-foot tall frame dwarfing the bicycle he rode, and whose whim could permanently change futures by passing or failing students in English. They crawled back to their abandoned games, keeping the noise level to a bare minimum until the robust cyclist bearing the sternest eyes behind thick glasses was safely out of view.

Bheem Ojha had by now broken off the main road and was riding along the thin treacherous lane of caked mud until he reached his village temple adjoining the pond. There was a flurry of activity both inside and outside this Ram temple indicating that the time for evening prayers was drawing near. Village women, young and old, made a beeline outside its unassuming small gate, their faces covered till their noses with the *pallu* of their saris, and hands bearing a plate full of flowers, sweets, coins, sandalwood paste and an oil lamp. A group of men were huddled in a close circle a little distance from the gate, smoking *bidis* while waiting to enter the temple after the women.

Bheem Ojha paused under a tree across from it, trying hard to focus his thoughts in the cacophony of loud temple bells and unrestrained excitement flowing from the devotees, who assembled at the premises every evening to catch up on village gossip and socialize—a definite highlight in their mundane, uneventful life. He parked his bicycle by resting it against the tree trunk and closed his eyes in silent meditation.

After 20 long years, Bheem Ojha was conversing with the god he had apathetically renounced when lower caste people from his village were allowed to enter the precincts of the temple. "What has happened to the world?" he questioned, standing on his toes to catch a glimpse of his addressee, his keen unforgiving eyes cutting through the layers of obstacles that stopped him from having eye contact with the statue of lord Rama. When his eyes did meet the benevolent blue stone eyes of the god after penetrating scores of heads that stood in between, he poured out his heart with the same fury with which black storm clouds pour torrents of rain on the earth.

"My father and ancestors would never have believed that Hindu dharma would one day come to such irreparable disrepute. Those lower caste people who couldn't even dare to stand next to us—the Brahmins—not only play with our kids and defile temples, but also dream of marrying into our families! And all this because the government cares more about strengthening its vote bank with profane disregard to religious sanctity. The politicians have reserved most jobs for these people, and our kids—whose families have dedicated their entire lives to the service of god—are sitting at home twiddling their thumbs due to unemployment!"

Splash!

Bheem Ojha pounced on his bicycle and rode away like a whiff of wind, pedalling as fast as he could. When he reached the cowshed of his humble dwelling, he was drenched in sweat and panting hard. Mohan, his elder son, was tending to the cow—the family's most prized possession.

Upon seeing his father, he rushed to grab his bicycle and park it, but Bheem just dropped it on a stack of hay and left without a word.

His grandchildren, Chotu and Guddi, who were propelling with a stick an old bicycle tyre perforated across its entire body due to the numerous punctures suffered by it, tumbled over Bheem fondly, caring little about the tyre that glided off in the open drain of the house. Bheem brushed them off coldly, making straight for the farthest wooden chair in the verandah, without acknowledging the presence of his younger son Ganesh who was still sulking in a corner from the morning altercation.

"Don't bother to prepare any supper for me, *Patna wali*," Bheem called out loud to his daughter-in-law. Radha came rushing out instantly, hands white with the wheat flour she was kneading for the rotis to go with dinner. Hailing from the city of Patna, her marital name automatically changed to "Patna Wali" (the one from Patna).

"Did you eat outside?" she questioned, wiping her forehead with the free end of her sari.

Upon no response she added, "You will lose your health if you skip meals." She entered the dark interior of the house hastily and came out again with a small towel and a pitcher.

"I won't die if I don't eat one day," responded Bheem finally, taking the things from Radha's proffered hands.

After his ablutions at the well, he entered his bedroom from the rear and lay on his bed after barring entry of bugs into it by erecting a mosquito net all around. Bheem Ojha's room was pitch dark when Radha entered, and with the modest light of a kerosene lamp, placed a covered plate of food on the table—the only other furniture in the room besides the bed. She then gathered the clothes piled on its side and headed to the refrigerator in the lobby to hang them inside it! Yes, the fridge that was so zealously given to her in dowry, had been serving as an almirah from the time she came as a young gullible bride. The city she belonged to was blessed with intermittent supply of electricity—a rare privilege in the dark and poor state of Bihar—even though the filament in the bulbs shone out like a dim flickering candle. But here, in her married home, light bulbs were more a plaything for the kids, who had delighted in turning them like tops until they smashed to pieces, and now, empty sockets jutted out of the walls.

A massive splash accompanied by a gigantic thud jolted the Ojha household out of slumber in the middle of the night. Everybody sprang out of bed when Mohan screamed, "Earthquake, rush out!" Almost immediately, both the kids began to cry in shrill voices, adding to the pandemonium.

In the tumult that followed, there was a mad race for the door, with everybody fumbling, groping and tripping over each other in the dark to find it. It was in this commotion that Ganesh mistakenly grabbed Radha's breasts as she stood next to the door, wrapping her sari somehow, before leaving the room. He clambered out, his hands quivering with embarrassment and fear. Radha, on the other hand, blushed whilst a tingling frisson travelled her body with the speed of light.

Once outside, everybody discovered to their utmost relief that the ground under their feet wasn't shaking, afterall. No signs of seismic upheaval could be found either, under the serene surroundings lit dimly by the milky white light of the half moon. The mildly blowing

Splash!

breeze threw eerie shadows of dappled light on the marigold flowerbed, the well and the forested thicket beyond. A grasshopper jumped on Guddi's tiny barefoot, and she clung to her mother in horror. Chotu, for his part, was quite enjoying the midnight confusion, and strolled leisurely to the well, dragging a stick behind him that dug a zig-zag line in the mud, marking his trajectory. Upon reaching the well, he suddenly shrieked, "*Daddaji*'s slippers!"

Everybody rushed to the well in a flash and made another blood-curdling discovery. Strewn around the tall well wall were Bheem Ojha's *dhoti* and vest. Total panic seized the family while nervous incoherent outbursts pierced the deathly silence of the night.

"*Babuji*!" screamed Radha. "Where's *babuji*?"

"Bring a flashlight, fast!" hollered Mohan, blowing his lungs hollow with the strength of his command. Ganesh bolted towards the house with an unsteady gait as if his feet had been suddenly paralyzed with fear. When he entered his father's room, he froze like an iceberg and stood still: pale with apprehension and cold with remorse. Then, gradually, the reality of his surroundings thawed his frozen frame, and he could feel the heat of blood rushing to his head. By now, Ganesh was trembling like a wilted dry leaf as he replaced the cover of the untouched food on the table, weakly clasped the flashlight from near the pillow of the empty bed, and dragged himself out of the half-open rear door of his father's bedroom.

Outside, some neighbours had gathered after hearing the turmoil, and Mohan was peering down the well crying loudly, "*Babuji! Babuji!* Where are you?" Ganesh approached him quietly from behind and handed over the flashlight with quivering fingers.

"It's all your fault!" lambasted Mohan, snatching the flashlight from this brother and switching it on and off amid violent jerks to make it shine brighter. When the overused batteries of the flashlight failed to cast more light than a few dull yellow orbs on the murky black waters of the well, Mohan hurled it angrily on the ground and threw up his hands, sobbing bitterly.

"Damn this wretched tree!" he swore indignantly, striking the massive trunk of the jackfruit tree with his fists, that spread majestically over the well, not allowing any moonlight to penetrate its thick foliage.

"Isn't there a decent source of light in this household?" bawled Mohan, sitting on the ground with his wet face in his hands.

The neighbours looked on: some unsure of how to help, others doubtful if they should interfere in another's family matters, and yet others gossiping and speculating over Bheem Ojha's reasons for suicide in hushed tones.

Just then, Radha came running out of the front door, struggling with the rusted knob of her old kerosene lamp as she ran, even though her vigorous efforts yielded a modest haloed light from the handmade cotton wick. Ganesh ran towards her, and, meeting her midway, snatched the lamp from her hands. He then rushed back to the well, pleading beseechingly as he lowered the lamp as far down in the well as he could. "*Babuji*, please come back; please, I beg you!"

"He'll never come back, you fool!" rebuked Mohan, his face red with fury. "Had you not fought with him this morning over that girl, nothing would have happened."

The whispering and gossiping among the neighbours grew more intense on hearing this latest garnish to an already spicy curry of events, and the semicircle of spectators drew closer to exchange notes.

"Stop blaming me!" retorted Ganesh hotly, still gaping down the well until a few bats flew into his face, attracted by the light of the lantern. He waived them aside with a frantic swing of his hand, and replacing the lantern noisily on the cemented floor surrounding the well, advanced to retaliate against his brother.

"It wasn't my affair with Sujata that drove *Babuji* to jump in the well. Infact, you are 37 and still unemployed, and *that's* what ticked him off!" Mohan shot up from the grass like an arrow, and hands on his waist, marched intimidatingly towards Ganesh.

"Do *you* have to pay for my expenses, or for those of my family, you idiot?" He raised his younger brother's chin with his forefinger, and was about to slap him hard when Radha came running as fast as a protective tigress, and clenched her husband's raised hand.

"Don't you dare hit him!" she commanded her husband until he was forced to drop his hand, and also the idea of chastising his brother.

"We are one family," she appealed in the soothing tone of a mediator. "Instead of fighting amongst yourselves and wasting precious time, try to find *Babuji* as soon as possible," she urged.

"We don't know how to swim," lamented Mohan, rushing imploringly towards the gathered neighbours, who too shook their heads regretfully.

But out of that group, an elderly man—and a good friend of Bheem Ojha's—by the name of Narayan Singh stepped out of the semicircle with a bright idea.

"Rush to the temple and summon the villagers who are conducting night-long prayers there. Not only do they have powerful lights, but some of them are good swimmers too."

Ganesh didn't lose a second after hearing this sound advice and, not caring about his undressed appearance, ran out of the house in his striped long underwear and slippers. Two other villagers from the semicircle ran after him.

Mohan was pacing up and down the well in a state of frenetic anxiety, clenching and unclenching his fists behind his back as helplessly as a prisoner who is handcuffed around his wrists, and can do no more than wrestle with his restraint. It is then that Narayan Singh approached him with, what according to him was, yet another seasoned counsel.

"Don't be so perturbed, son," he began in a comforting tone when Mohan was gazing inconsolably at the demonic waters of the well that had swallowed his father alive.

"You should thank your lucky stars for this perfect timing coordinated by God."

Narayan Singh looked up at the sky and continued, "It's a blessing from the heavens above that Bheem committed suicide *before* retiring. Now, at least *you* can get *his* job on compassionate grounds and support your family." Narayan Singh gazed into Mohan's fiery wet eyes and said with a reminiscent sigh, "You won't regret it at all. Bheem used to tell me that no job could be better than his, for, who pays you these days to daydream in class and still get respect and obedience in return?" Narayan Singh's unbridled laughter was hijacked by Mohan's sharp reprisal.

"How dare you say that?" he shot back in complete disbelief. "I want my father, not his job!"

Radha had stopped a few yards from the duo: the veil of her georgette sari covered her nose, yet her eyes issued stern orders through its sheen to her husband not to argue with village elders in keeping with the norms of the society. With great difficulty, Mohan suppressed his anger from boiling over and burning Narayan Singh for his insensitive and inopportune remarks.

Meanwhile, Ganesh had reached the village temple, sweating profusely in the nippy autumn air. Inside the temple, the ambience was eclectic. A small group of entranced people were sitting around

Splash!

a holy fire, chanting mantras and singing *bhajans* in front of richly ornamented statues of Ram and Sita.

So engrossed were they in their fitful singing and simultaneous playing of the tabla, harmonium, percussions and other musical instruments, that they failed to heed Ganesh's whirlwind entry and frantic gestures. It was only when he jolted the priest that the music stopped abruptly. Vinayakji—as he was called—was the head priest of the temple, and not only did his name come from one of the many names of the elephant god Ganesh himself, his rounded pot belly resembled that of the god, along with their common sweet tooth for *ladoos*.

Vinayakji's benevolent brown eyes displayed a trace of chagrin upon being interrupted so unceremoniously in the middle of his sacred duties. It was probably because the intruder shared the same divine source of nomenclature with him that Vinayakji prevented himself from venting his brewing anger at Ganesh. But when Ganesh related the reason for his uncomely intrusion in a series of breathless blabber, everybody present—including Vinayakji—was overcome with compassion for the plaintiff. Vinayakji raised the enormous conch to his forehead, closed his eyes in a brief silent prayer, and blowing the conch hard, signalled everybody to rise and accompany Ganesh to his house.

Twelve men marched grimly through the dark village streets and alleys, bearing powerful *petromax* lights on their shoulders. By now, the number of villagers gathered at the Ojha household had swelled like flood waters, bringing massive new waves as the sensational news criss-crossed the entire village.

Layers of crowds gathered around the well moved away as the dozen men were spotted approaching it. Mohan dashed to join them, and within no time, sturdy ropes had been tied to the base of the imposing tree adjacent to the well. Vinayakji supervised the rescue operation and blessed the valiant divers—Lakhiram, Sujata's brother and Binod, the veteran fisherman—who held their noses and dived into the well, one by one, after securing the loop of the rope around their waists.

Unrestrained jostling broke out as the crowds surged towards the well to witness the heroic action in progress. The dozen or so men in-charge of pulling the ropes were pushed and thrown about in the melee. Tension ran high as innumerable onlookers waited for results with bated breath.

After ten minutes of acute suspense, Lakhiram and Binod were pulled out of the well by relentless tugging of the ropes. The soaking-wet, breathless men just gestured with their hands that they didn't find Bheem Ojha and collapsed on the ground to regain their breath. The ominous silence that followed was only broken by Vinayakji's fervent chanting of mantras. When he stopped, he ordered Mohan to prepare immediately for *Mahayajna* (grand prayers) on the premises to ward off the ghost that was now Bheem Ojha's bodyless soul.

"*Bhoot!*" screamed some villagers in petrified voices and ran away in the direction of their homes. Others consulted with village elders and decided to stay until the ghost was exorcised, lest it should follow them and haunt their houses.

Mohan and Radha moved like zombies: preparing for firewood, clarified butter, incense and other imperatives needed to perform the ritual; while Ganesh, despite his dazed state, set about locating Bheem Ojha's horoscope as per the priest's advice to summon the spirit first, before forcing it to retreat into its black world.

Soon, a solemn white bedsheet was spread on the grass between the tree and the well, with Mohan, Radha, Chotu and Guddi sitting cross-legged on it facing Vinayakji, who was feeding generous ladles of *ghee* to the flame that leapt up dangerously upon each offering. Ardent humming of unintelligible Vedic mantras in Sanskrit permeated the air as villagers huddled into small groups and looked on circumspectly from a distance. Ganesh was leaning against the tree trunk, feeling very restless by the uncanny turn of events, and faint by the choking black fumes, the hypnotizing effect of the chanting, and the overbearing sweet smell of sandalwood incense.

"Now, bring me the horoscope of the deceased." Mohan turned back and nodded at Ganesh to bring over their father's horoscope for Vinayakji.

Ganesh just stood incapacitated: staring at the red flames with glazed eyes that did not blink even after they got clouded like a smoke screen with its thick fumes. Mohan got up, walked towards him, and took the crumpled paper from his fist with an angry shake of this head.

Vinayakji opened its torn creases carefully, placed it next to the fire, and after bending over it laboriously for a few seconds, surveyed his apprehensive audience minutely.

"Nobody could have stopped it!" he announced with the intuitiveness of a clairvoyant, tapping the horoscope with his ostentatiously ringed fingers.

"Nobody has ever escaped it—neither the mighty emperors, nor the invincible warriors, not even the unchallenged ascetics. No mortal can overcome the juggernaut influence of a triple conjunction: Mercury, Venus and Mars all in the same house! And to top it all, the moon is exacerbating the already perilous planetary alignment."

Vinayakji untied the pencil stub hanging from the holy thread slanting on his chest, and drew out some complex charts and crosses on a scratch paper that was tucked behind his ear. He finally looked up at Mohan and ordered him with the authority of god's envoy: "You must donate me a cow if you want your father's soul to rest in peace. Without *Gaudaan,* it will keep wandering the cosmos without ever attaining Moksha."

Mohan received the command with resignation, for he knew he had to do everything to allow his father's soul to reach its destination of ultimate peace and rest, even if it meant condemning his family to the throes of poverty after relinquishing their only family wealth.

Ganesh was overcome with emotion and remorse upon hearing this devastating news of a double loss, and ran around the gigantic tree trunk to hide himself from his brother's razor-sharp glares. Once away from censuring vicious glances, he slipped into a loud, involuntary self-introspection of his perturbed feelings by rebuking himself severely for his callousness.

"I wish I hadn't argued with *babuji* over Sujata," he sobbed bitterly, hugging the rough jagged tree trunk for solace as far as his arms could stretch. "Afterall, I have loved *babuji* for three decades, and Sujata only entered my life last year." Ganesh wiped his eyes and nose with his bare arms and slumped to the ground, letting his back hit the trunk with a severity that sent a few spiky dry scales poking his unrobed back.

"Don't cry, my son!" came a mellow soft whisper that sounded like Bheem Ojha, and Ganesh shot up from the ground like a bullet. He looked around to confirm if he was hallucinating, or whether his father's ghost was really consoling him.

"Don't be afraid," came the voice again, this time a little louder and more authoritative, but distinctly his father's! Ganesh stood still while his bulging eyes scanned the surroundings nervously.

"I'm here, on the tree," persisted the voice, a little vexed at not being treated seriously. Ganesh broke into a cold sweat and was about to run when the voice came nearer, cajoling him to listen.

Splash!

Tightening his fists and clenching his teeth to steel himself for the apparition, Ganesh looked up at the branch right over his head. Sitting perched on it was none other than Bheem Ojha—his father!

Ganesh's jaw dropped in bewilderment, and he touched the foot dangling from the thick branch to make sure what he saw was a tangible being, and not an airy mirage. He felt cold flesh and hard bones indeed! Too baffled to pose questions, he just gaped open mouthedly for answers.

"I didn't commit suicide; no, I just threw a jackfruit into the well to test you all," confessed Bheem in a subdued voice, surveying as if his classroom at Pusa High School. Only here, there was no "complete silence" and obedient students, but a domineering priest, gossipy onlookers and repentant sons. But above all, the most repugnant result of his *test* was the talk of giving up their only cow!

As Ganesh's trance broke, and he gradually understood how the priest had manipulated the peculiar situation in his own favour by corroborating his father's death with hollow astrological arguments, even though the body was never found, Ganesh held his father's feet and put them to his forehead. Bheem Ojha jumped down from the branch and patted his son's back affectionately.

"Sujata will make a worthy addition to our family," he announced proudly, grinning with gratitude. Ganesh could hardly believe his ears when Bheem added, "afterall, her brother Lakhiram had dived into the well to rescue me." The father-son duo stood silently for a few minutes, both as if taking the time to rejoice over their good fortunes.

Bheem Ojha, for his part, was sure that this was the *best test* he had ever administered in his entire career as a teacher, for all his prejudices had melted away as easily as fat burns in the sun. He put his arm around Ganesh's fleshy shoulders, urging him to walk towards the front of the tree, while he envisioned the shy, forgiving face of Mrs. Farooqui in his mind. As the burning fire drew closer, he could feel love transcending all inconsequential barriers of caste and creed, race and religion in its heat. He finally felt at peace with himself for allowing his son to follow his heart's call: for heart recognizes love, and only love—whether that love is for a low caste girl like Sujata, or for a Muslim woman like Mrs. Farooqui. *"In Celebration of Being Alive*—of course!" he laughed out loud.

Wild shrieks of *"Bhoot!"* from the villagers rent the air as Ganesh and Bheem Ojha came in full view of everyone. Vinayakji's eyes bulged like saucers and he blinked hard, wondering whether he had suddenly acquired the elusive art of reviving the dead, or whether his worst fears had come true and Bheem Ojha was not dead, afterall. He was confident that the latter reasoning was true, as his priesthood had only been a fortunate legacy—conferred on him by his accidental birth into a Brahmin family—where lifelong privileges and luxuries were guaranteed just by the cramming of a few Sanskrit *shlokas*.

The remaining villagers galloped away, petrified by the spooky family reunion when Radha, Chotu and Guddi hugged Bheem Ojha tearfully. Only Vinayakji sat still—in shock and grief—as he turned to look at the cow left behind when Mohan ran towards them from the cowshed.

The Perfect Match

Lovely looked unfazed as the sea of moving heads around her swelled, bringing in its rising tide more pushing and jostling, until finally an overwhelming wave of humanity surged from behind, sweeping her and numerous other unsuspecting souls like useless shells and molluscs on the beach.

But Lovely was not going to give up so easily. She readjusted her starched cotton *dupatta* to form a V over her nubile chest, and tightening her clutch over a betel-stained 20 rupee bill, charged through protesting tight crowds. She kept firm when *bidi*-smelling men rubbed against her deliberately, and fought back viciously when sweat-soaked people tried to prevent her from regaining her lost place with force.

"I was the first one to arrive at the counter!" she yelled, exasperated, as a turbaned man and his family made a human chain to block her advance to the front of the queue.

"Everybody says that," retorted the Sikh virulently, clenching his fist and pointing it towards Lovely's jaw.

Destiny decided the winner and vanquished in this heated war of words, as a massive push from behind propelled Lovely to the very front of the counter, just as the Sikh family got separated in the sudden commotion.

"How many?" roared the bearded man, twisting his wrist to form a question mark with his fingers. Lovely regarded the face that seemed to be sliced uniformly by the thin cylindrical metal rods separating him from the mob behind her.

"Just one," she blurted, as the pressure of human bodies pressed her slender frame against the wall. She saw the sliced hand scribble something on a papery blue ticket and tear it off a thick pack. Lovely instantly dropped the crumpled bill through the bars, and saw the sliced hand iron it out with a wry smile, as he noticed a blood-red betel spit dot forming a bindi on Mahatma Gandhi's broad forehead. She had barely snatched her change back when she got forcefully pushed away from the ticket counter.

Thrilled at her success, Lovely started wading through the sardined compound with the glee of a fisherman who has just made a prized catch. The din around her was hallucinating. Cautious sales calls of black marketeers were silenced abruptly by shrill wailing of infants. Lovely had now reached the gate from where she could read PRINCE CINEMA in red paint over a jaundiced yellow wall. The unimposing structure seemed inadequate to house the vast outpouring of humanity sprawled in its exterior. Young kids swung on the low, rusted gate of the cinema in a game to cross with its help, the broad, stinking drain whose green-black slush attracted swarms of mosquitoes and houseflies. Along the drain—right where the gate ended—was pitched a makeshift *chaat* shop under the whimsical shelter of a tarpaulin roof. Hordes of people crowded around this stall, as a dark-faced man wearing a sooty vest and dhoti served crispy, plump, deep-fried balls by cracking one end open with his black nailed finger. He was robotically dipping the cracked *puris* into a steel bucket containing algae-coloured water before serving them onto the insatiable appetites of leaf-plate stretching hands.

The drain behind was clogged with scattered leaf plates. The street was streaked with meandering streams of pickled water that escaped from crevices in the leaf plates. The walls around were stained with random showers of betel spit and urine. Expectant cinema goers squatted in the company of empty potato chips bags, squished banana peels and strewn peanut shells. The blistering sun seemed to accentuate the overbearing odours of open gutters, perspiration and street food.

Nonetheless, Lovely's eyes were blind to the revolting filth around her, ears deaf to the restless noise, and nose blocked to the nauseous stench. It was as if her brain was a powerful colander—filtering out the unwelcome stimuli of sight, sound and smell, while allowing only for pleasant reveries to register and install.

Those reveries were of escaping somehow to the west, where everything the eye met was idyllic, the ears heard was symphony, and the nose smelt was roses. She stood long gazing at the billboard looming over the crowds and clutched tighter at her ticket. This, indeed, was her ticket to visit London and Switzerland for three long hours. And it cost only 18 rupees and 50 paise! She was already several light years away from her primitive town of Ramnagar, imagining herself riding piggyback on Shahrukh Khan in the backdrop of pristine Alps, instead of Kajol. How lucky these actors are, she ruminated, gawking over the billboard of *Dilwale Dulhaniya Le Jayenge*. Would a handsome groom take her away to the west too? Her journey back to Ramnagar took merely a split second, with a light tap on her shoulder.

"Sheetal!" cried Lovely disbelievingly. "When did you come back?"

"I'm here for a week," shouted Sheetal, pointing at the cinema doors that had just opened, and disappeared into the wild crowds.

"Okay, Okay!" Lovely shot back at the top of her voice. "Come home before you go!"

The sun was beginning to set when the matinee show got over, and staggering crowds spilled on the streets. The honking intensified, sending confused cows choking busy intersections. The filth of the city was temporarily cloaked under dark shadows of humans and stray animals staking claim over the planet they co-inhabited. In a few hours, the humans would retire to concrete homes or mud hovels, according to their station in life, whereas the animals— cows, dogs, rats and pigs, among others—would wander the dark streets to scavenge them of peels and plates, paper and plastic. Thus, a new dawn would break, and this cycle would be perpetuated.

Lovely's station in life had been scaled down from an unplastered, red-brick, rectangular godown-like house to a house barely visible through the thick cover of weeds and stray grasses. When strong blowing winds parted the overgrowth, slivers of red flashed through the shiny green vines of ivy climbing the walls and trailing around the tin roof. It was hard to tell that the house existed, much less, if it was inhabited. And yet, only three years ago, the dominating brush had been a trim front yard where Lovely's mother could often be seen pounding spices in a big, stone mortar and pestle.

Paradoxically, it was the backyard that was the centre of activity all day long at the Seth household. Scattered visitors during the scorching summer afternoons turned into a constant trickle at sundown. Groups of people—chiefly men—clustered together, awaiting their turn. Sitting on their haunches, some lit up *bidis* to pass the time, others ground tobacco with their thumb on their palm, dusting it lightly with the other palm before placing the earthy powder under their lower lip. Nobody seemed to be in a rush for their turn as they gossiped about neighbours, soaring food prices and political parties. Children were entertained by Lucky, Lovely's younger brother, who would gather water in a bucket from the hand pump and splash it on his playmates. The only person oblivious to the hubbub in his backyard was Lovely's father, Mr. Seth.

Face framed in a small window with neither glass nor rods, his customers received unhindered interaction with their repairman. Old watches, clocks and radios were turned over to the welcoming hands of Mr. Seth, who diligently dismantled them, examining their interior with the most discerning eye before pronouncing a diagnosis. He would explain the symptoms to the owner by rotating the hands of the clock, or by winding the watch and putting it to the customer's ear, or by simply thrusting the open side of the radio to their nose for them to sniff the burnt smell of wires. Mr. Seth was as famous a repairman in Ramnagar as the physician Dr. Akash. None was ever known to have faltered in their prognosis. But this was *then*. Three years ago. Now, the pumping rod of the hand pump was scarcely visible in the thick brush surrounding it. The window was inaccessible due to the natural fence of thorn bushes barricading it. The opening where Mr. Seth's plump, double-chinned face drooped pensively over timepieces and radios was closed off tentatively with a carom board, pressed in place by a big boulder.

Lovely entered the house to find her father hunched over his wheelchair, head in his lap that resembled a skinned coconut. The loud snoring emerging from under his bent head seemed to reprimand the illusory interaction created by the television, which, refusing to court defeat, aired program after program despite Mr.

Seth's menacing snorts. Lovely pressed the power button off and granted unconditional victory to her father. A victory he was incapable of achieving himself, after being paralysed in a gruesome road accident three years ago.

Lovely stared long at the piteous figure in front of her, folded between two big, cold, grey wheels of metal—trapped inside life itself, yet ashamed to face life—with head hung low, as if in shame for not fulfilling his obligations towards his wife and children. She passed to the kitchen where her mother stood, head bent and hands folded in prayer to the framed photo of the goddess of prosperity, Lakshmi. As the elaborately ornate goddess sat comfortably on the pink lotus of the photo—raining gold coins from two of her four palms—Mrs. Seth offered her humble food to the image in small bowls of steel. The oil lamp cast a glow on the lotus, giving its petals a semblance of dangerous red tongues of fire. Lovely bowed her head in deference, although she was reluctant to believe that these age-old Hindu rituals had any power to turn fortunes around.

She finally went to her modest bedroom, only to find another hung head: this time that of her brother Lucky, who, despite his name, and the fact that he was reading his weekly horoscope in the local Hindi newspaper, had failed to charm his lucky stars.

The hung heads congregated at dinner. Seated around an old, scratched plywood table, all heads stared at the basic dinner of lentil soup and rotis. Only the expression on faces concealed under the hung heads had changed. Mr. Seth's had nuanced from shame to helplessness as Mrs. Seth fed him with bowed head—not in deference, but browbeaten by destiny. Lucky hung his head to stare long enough at the food, in case it might change into something sumptuous by magic.

Only Lovely's head was hung in perceived culpability. She had passed high school with distinction the same year her father was crippled. Not only were her dreams of higher education ruthlessly hijacked, all eyes in the family turned to her unwittingly to make ends meet. Her English education, coupled with a fancy for Bollywood songs, earned her a small income by way of tuitions to neighbourhood kids in English music (for, she composed her own songs in English on Bollywood tunes). But, of late, her students had dwindled: girls her age already married off, and boys having moved to metropolis of Delhi, Mumbai and Bangalore to pursue a college degree.

Lucky had been pulled out of his English-medium private school for lack of resources and admitted to a local government junior school. From a promising, bright A-grader, he plummeted to being a reckless truant: plying marbles, flying kites and throwing stones at street dogs.

"How was the movie, *didi*?" he asked, head still down and hand playing with the spoon immersed in his lentil soup.

Lovely ignored the wry undertone in her brother's question which sounded more like an allegation.

"It was good," she quipped. "Excellent value for 18 rupees and 50 paise." With her lowered head Lovely noticed a brief freeze of her mother's hand at her remark, but it recovered gradually and she continued feeding her husband.

"So many—er—beautiful songs—" stammered Lovely, scrambling to justify entertainment expense in a family struggling to fulfill basic necessities of life.

"—T—that I can compose a dozen English songs on those eternal melodies for my students."

"You mean for your class of Mahak and Razia?"

Mrs. Seth stared frigidly at her son's brash brown eyes.

"Okay, okay," he sang in jest, raising his spoon as a flag of peace, his braced teeth flashing a disingenuous metallic smile.

"Let's hear *didi*'s signature song!" he announced loudly, tinkering his spoon on the side of his steel bowl containing the lentil soup.

The clinking noise seemed to create a sudden rush of excitement in Mr. Seth's mind, for he signalled his wife with his limp hand to stop feeding him, and bobbing his head latched to his left shoulder, prodded his daughter to commence singing an impromptu song. "Gaaa—O—O!" were the only inarticulate sounds that escaped his arduously convoluted mouth.

Lovely felt trapped—like a mouse in a mousetrap—her brother having laid the bait inside it, while her father clamped its door shut on her. Perplexed, she looked at her mother. What she saw was a stone statue. Frozen in time. Like a photograph that's not supposed to change its pose until infinity. Hand where it was when she was told to stop using it to feed. Eyes vacant as they were when Mr. Seth was declared quadriplegic for life, three years ago. Lovely hung her head. This time, in contemplation. She desperately wanted to compose a song and sing it. Right away. Even though she dreamed her songs after a long night's sleep, when wings of imagination flew her to a cherished land of thick wooded forests with streaming blue rivers; and just when twilight was breaking in her real world, she would wake up and dig her hand passionately under her pillow to retrieve the notebook where she recorded her songs. She would scribble line after line, humming a sleepy hum, like that of a bee intoxicated on nectar.

Lovely cleared her throat, unsure of the lyrics of her song. However, she started singing softly the two words that formed naturally in her heart, and breathing up her mouth, exited the delicately shivering pink cleft of her lips.

Forgive me . . . forgive me . . .

Her face burnt with the intensity of three pairs of eyes observing it from different angles. She soon realized that despite her sucked cheeks and the perfect O formed by her lips, her vocal chords failed to produce any sound. She swallowed so hard that two flawlessly rounded globules of water fell from her eyes and shimmered under the light bulb; sitting side by side—just like the eyes that shed them—yet, trembling with uncertainty like her voice, as she sang her improvised song:

Forgive me, father; I'm but a mundane daughter,
With no means of restoring your bygone life of laughter.
But if I had the nimble hands of a magician,
I'd have brought to supple blossom, every pore of your skin . . .
I'd have reversed the fall of your life to spring . . .
Yet, I'm a mundane daughter, who can't do a thing.

Forgive me, mother; I'm but a selfish woman,
Who, instead of partaking in your grief, dreams of my man.
Across the oceans, nestled in a leafy countryside . . .
He awaits my arrival by the lamp on his bedside.
Alas! If I had the charm of a fairy godmother,
I'd have eradicated your worries altogether.

Forgive me, brother; I'm but a helpless sister,
Whose cherished dream is to see your life glitter.
Yet, I fancy being a bird to fly o'er the moon . . .
And rest my wings in my beloved's leafy cocoon.
Oh! Only if I had the magic lamp of Aladdin,
I'd have summoned the genie to make your life serene.

Forgive me, Lovely; you're neither mundane nor selfish,
You lack the means for the miracles you want to accomplish.
To cure papa's handicap, mummy's worries and Lucky's cynicism…
So life becomes vibrant again like the colours through a prism.
Then you can fly unhindered to your leafy bliss,
And destiny shall give everyone its eternal kiss!

Lovely buried her face in her hands and dashed out of the room. The globules on the table lost their identity; hugging the new ones shed around them, they clustered together for support—and stopped quivering.

A few days later, on a predictably trite evening, a vigorous knocking on the front door evoked a tizzy in the Seth household.

Mr. Seth awoke with a start on his sagging floral sofa.

"Tell him I'm not at home if it's Sukhram asking for past due payments on groceries," hollered Mrs. Seth in a voice loud enough for the visitor to hear, and, possibly act upon.

But the knocking continued.

"Go get the door, *didi*!" shouted Lucky peevishly. "It might be your students."

"They don't come on Fridays," retorted Lovely rather irately. "Might be one of your playmates," she sighed, laying aside the classified jobs section of the newspaper from her lap.

"Sheetal! How nice!" Lovely beamed joyously as she held the door open, blocking entry to the house in her absent-minded delight.

"Will you invite me in, or do we have to do all the catching-up in the doorway?"

"Of course," flushed Lovely as she ushered her small town friend, transformed unrecognizably into a modern metropolitan diva.

"*Namaste*, aunty," said Sheetal to Mrs. Seth, with a gentle bow of the head instead of folding her hands.

Mrs. Seth dubbed Sheetal's impudence as city life adaptation that requires an abbreviation of traditional gestures. "No time for anything Indian, I guess?" she remarked sympathetically, inspecting Sheetal's jet-black drainpipe jeans and a tight-fitted sleeveless top with curiosity rather than disdain.

"How about Indian food?"

"Oh, aunty, who has time to roll rotis when there are so many fast food joints in the city?"

"Ok, then, today is your home food day with roti and *daal*."

Mrs. Seth turned away and busied herself with forceful kneading of flour dough as the two girls disappeared into the bedroom.

"I'm going out to play!" jumped Lucky, clearly embarrassed at the sight of a modern city girl in his modest room.

Lovely observed her friend intently as the latter sat on the bed, glancing at the newspaper where it lay open. Her eyes were lowered, and Lovely couldn't help admiring the well-defined features she had only seen in Bollywood actresses in films. The metallic violet shadow on the eyelids blended seamlessly with a deep blue eyeliner, under which thick brushy eyelashes curled upwards. The lips sparkled with a natural lustre like clear river water under moonlight. Then, Lovely's attention drifted to Sheetal's manicured hands resting on the coarse newspaper that paled in front of her milk-white blunt-edged nails.

"So, are you planning to be a banker or an engineer?"

Sheetal's candid question broke Lovely's trance.

"Nothing in there for a high school graduate," lamented Lovely, eyeing the newspaper with apathy.

"Listen," began Sheetal, folding the newspaper and looking straight into Lovely's doleful eyes.

"Why don't you come with me to Delhi?"

Lovely didn't answer, just looked down at her worn rubber slippers.

"I mean, you know, I'm a 12th pass too. But what you don't know is how much money I'm making in Delhi."

Lovely looked up at the genuine expression in the made-up eyes.

"And think of the freedom," continued Sheetal, dabbing the lip gloss at the extremities of her lips with the soft pads of her thumb and forefinger.

"You can meet educated, rich, open-minded men that *you* choose from to get married, not wait for Ramnagar's generosity to send an orthodox, semi-literate villager your way!"

"And maybe, go abroad," fantasized Lovely without articulating her fancies.

"But mummy-papa will not hear of it," she fumbled, casting a sly sidelong glance at her mother's curvaceous back bending over the scratched plywood table in the living room. She saw her mother space out the stainless steel bowl of *daal* and the tray containing rotis, to create an illusion of a full table. A thin film of haze blurred her eyes momentarily, and she saw a clear vision behind the mist: her mother running to the door at the knock, signing a bearer's paper, retrieving an envelope. And then the scene changed. Three beaming heads held high at dinner: Lucky proudly showing his report card from the English-medium private school as Mrs. Seth fed a hearty three-course dinner to her husband seated on a power wheelchair.

"When are you leaving?" spurted Lovely in an unfamiliar gritty voice.

Before Sheetal could answer, Mrs. Seth came and stood in the doorway, pealing off the sticky remains of wheat flour dough from between her fingers. "Food is ready," she said in a meek voice.

"Let's go!" exclaimed Sheetal perkily, winking mischievously at her friend.

Just then, there was a loud bang on the door. Mrs. Seth winced. "It's Lucky; I'll get it," she mused, hoping her son wouldn't make a public show of his resentment towards the repetitive meals. Her fears were immediately mitigated as Lucky quietly washed his hands and occupied his seat, without maintaining eye contact with anyone.

When everyone had served, Sheetal saw her opportunity to pitch the case for Lovely.

"Aunty," she began, in her trademark casual voice, dipping a morsel of roti into the soupy yellow lentils. "If Lovely was to go to Delhi, she would definitely make Indian food every day."

Lucky looked up, excited, and gasped, "Wow! *Didi*'s going to Delhi?"

Mrs. Seth's face fell, and it was as if the pallour of *daal* had spilled all over it. "We have enough food to feed her here," she contended, brushing off the idea as preposterous by a violent shake of her head.

"Please, ma," supplicated Lovely, staring at her mother's side face that was turned to feed her father.

"Ask your father," replied Mrs. Seth curtly when their eyes met.

"*Naaa beta*," howled Mr. Seth fearfully, cowering behind his wife's shoulder.

Sheetal made a last-ditch effort to overcome the objections. "Aunty, I had gone to Delhi all alone. I looked for a house, got a job, and now make enough money to support myself and my family here in Ramnagar."

Mr. and Mrs. Seth remained grim, but Lucky's excitement bubbled over.

"So, *didi* can live with you and work in your company?"

"Yes," assured Sheetal, pressing Mrs. Seth's cold hand whose blue veins criss-crossed like meandering rivers.

"Lovely will live with me, and I will help her secure a good job."

"Do as you please," blurted Mrs. Seth helplessly and left the table.

"When are you leaving, *didi?*" shouted Lucky as the two girls followed Mrs. Seth in the kitchen.

The next two days passed as if the earth had suddenly stopped orbiting, leaving the Seth household in a perpetual day-like frenzy. The weekend was all they had to prepare for Lovely's unprecedented departure to the capital city, New Delhi. Suitcases lay open on the floors, and the whole house looked like a chaotic laundry with clothes and bed linen strewn everywhere. Lucky got a splendid opportunity to make some pocket change from his frequent trips to the market—Mrs. Seth being too preoccupied to add bills or balance accounts.

Mr. Seth, for his part, didn't fully comprehend the reasons behind this unexpected frenetic activity in the house. His acute amnesia prevented him from remembering accurately where or why Lovely was going—if he remembered her departure at all. So much so, when Lovely touched his feet on Monday morning, he regarded her numerous bags with a mix of pride and concern.

"Be k—care—ful on the—the road to school," he cautioned, stammering. "Your s—s—studies have become b—burden—sssome."

Lovely rushed to the storeroom, overcome by emotion. Suddenly, she started feeling suffocated by time; choked by its presence all around her: hanging on cobwebbed walls, stacked on the sticky floor, and scattered carelessly on the dusty wooden table facing the window barred by the carom board. She didn't know which one to believe. The bulky, aluminium-finish metal alarm clock resting on one foot on the table, leaning against the wall, had its hands frozen at eight-thirty. A small rectangular slit on its face indicated the date as Jan-03-03. If she were to believe this time, her father's memory would be impeccable. Three years ago, at eight-thirty, she would be packing her bags for school. Then, she glanced at the wall. Hung below the blotched yellow ceiling smelling of damp mould, was an intriguing circular wall clock with four small clocks impregnated within it. Lovely wiped with her bare hands the tangled trap weaved by a spider on the face of the clock. It was as if this clock was its prey, the gauzy silken threads potent enough to arrest not only the *mother* of Indian time, but also the four *babies* in its belly.

Now, the impossible had become possible: East and West stood united in that abstract continuum called "Time". Lovely shook her head. Of course, it was impossible for it to be sharp 12 O' clock in India, New York, London, Paris and Tokyo at the same time!

Time stood still for Lovely, just as it had in the clocks she stood staring. Yet, even though there was no ticking sound of life from the scores of time pieces around her, she could feel its ceaseless passing with the wild thumping of her heartbeats. She clutched her wrist nervously, and the pulsating of her vein reinforced the fluid nature of time. It had *never* stopped and never would.

"Time to go, *didi*," came a shrill call as Lovely jerked around unsteadily.

Timeless memories were left behind as she bid a tearful farewell to her family to begin an uncharted journey.

* * *

As long as they were still travelling to Delhi, Lovely was starkly conscious of the passing of time—second by second—as the train chugged slowly on the fringes of overcrowded stations, expansive farmlands and remote villages. Every second took her further away from her predictably stagnant life of Ramnagar.

However, once in Delhi, it was as if the light-footed time, that until now seemed to be tip-toeing stealthily around her, had acquired mighty wings, and lifting her up in its transcendent embrace, soared over life with the speed of light.

Lovely didn't see the time passing as she scrambled to adapt to the fast pace of life in Delhi. She felt as if she was in another country. Gone was the exhaustion of working the hand pump to fill water— now the faucet obeyed your instructions. Needless to say, she was fairly intimidated by urban living. Sheetal often took her to huge shopping malls in an autorickshaw after work. Lovely would lean nervously on the escalator railing, or huddle behind people in the queue at checkout. The only time she watched a movie at a theatre in the mall, she couldn't suppress her astonishment. There was no pushing or jostling. People disposed of their garbage in designated plastic dustbins, soliciting their use by big bold stencilled letters of USE ME stuck on both sides of their bulging bodies. The cool, fresh air conditioning ensured there was no stench of perspiration as people ate pizzas and popcorns from trendy cardboard boxes, instead of *paani puri* from leaking leaf plates.

A month passed since her arrival in Delhi, yet Lovely failed to secure a job for herself. Despite Sheetal's insistence, she refused to trade her traditional attire of *salwar kameez* for creased trousers or dress skirts. The few employers who showed interest in hiring her, did so with the explicit intention of using her as an escort after hours.

"He could've been my grandfather's age!" she bursted one evening amid persistent sniffles, as she sat on the bed narrating her humiliating job interview experience to Sheetal.

Sheetal was just finishing her make-up before the van came to take her to the call centre in Gurgaon. From the mirror, she could read defeat writ large in Lovely's distraught eyes. She felt helpless that she couldn't refer her friend for call centre or office jobs, given that Lovely was completely computer illiterate. But that's not what she told her.

"Toughen up, Miss. Ramnagar; this is Delhi," she winked naughtily at a red-faced reflection in the mirror that was wiping its eyes with the sides of a *dupatta*. "What d'you think, the society respects me for working at night?"
Sheetal slobbered another coat of shimmering wet burgundy gloss on her lips in retaliation.
"But I know that I'm not sleeping the night away with some old hag's fantasies; just parroting, *thank you for calling*, nearly eighty times a night! And now, missy, *how can I help you?*"
Lovely's lips parted for a frail smile, but just then, there was a loud honking from outside and Sheetal grabbed her leather satchel and dashed out. "See ya t'morrow!" was all Lovely heard as the door of the sleek black Tata Sumo slammed shut before zipping out into the smoggy twilight of Delhi.

Days rolled into weeks, and Sheetal too became increasingly concerned about Lovely's future in Delhi, especially when her applications at malls and stores started getting turned down. Sheetal was convinced that Lovely's image of a village girl was standing in the way to her financial independence. The moment managers saw an unpolished face, framed by shapeless long hair, wearing a flowing Indian *kurta*, they typecast her as "out-dated, hindi-medium, *behenji*-type" who would not gel with the hip mall culture of Delhi. But there was nothing Sheetal could do to transform her friend into a fashionable city girl. She knew the day was not far when they would be packing her bags for her return to Ramnagar. Only now, she dreaded the next time she'd be in the town herself.

Lovely seemed to have accepted her fate with resignation. She smiled rarely, called home less frequently (which left Sheetal puzzling over whether her friend was ashamed of herself, or was only being frugal, given that she would be with her family shortly, anyway).

Sheetal's most disturbing observation of Lovely, however, was that she had stopped watching Bollywood films altogether. It was as if she didn't believe in her dreams anymore. Sheetal, for her part, hesitated to broach the subject of Lovely's departure, as she didn't want to give her friend the impression that she was a financial burden. So, the same routine played out day after day: Lovely would labour at household chores with the diligence of a beaver, and even though Sheetal was too tired to notice sparkling floors, clean laundry, and cooked food when she returned at dawn after her night shift at the call centre, she silently prayed for her friend every day.

Ironically enough, the prayers seemed to have been answered the same day Lovely had gone to inquire about train tickets to Ramnagar. When Sheetal saw her friend's face in the doorway, she sprung up from her chair at breakfast table and hugged Lovely. Then, unhooking the gold chain from her slender neck, she challenged her friend: "Sell this to me, ma'am!"

Bewildered, Lovely broke free from the embrace and started arranging the dishes on the table. "How can I sell you something that is already yours?" she questioned in a subdued voice, head lowered.

"Just as a practice, silly," Sheetal shot back impatiently.

"Sleeper class was too expensive," said Lovely with a serious tone. "I'll buy the regular ticket tomorrow."

"You wouldn't have to," beamed Sheetal. "Unless you hate selling jewellery from an air-conditioned showroom in posh South Delhi!"

"What d'you mean?" demanded Lovely in a loud, quivering voice.

"Vohrasons?" teased Sheetal, wrapping her chain playfully around her index finger by swinging it round and round in circles.

"They may never take me," prognosticated Lovely, sadly reminded of her recent succession of failed interviews.

"I tell ya missy, you're hired!"

Lovely shrugged sceptically at her friend's unexplained confidence.

"I know the boss," Sheetal joked boisterously. Then, with a more sombre tone added, "You're hired because the guy who left the phone message emphasised that *sari* was the dress code there!"

Lovely chuckled. "Really? Did he say when the interview was going to be?" Without waiting for Sheetal's response, she dashed to the phone.

The following day, Sheetal couldn't get any sleep in the daytime, so she called in sick for her night shift. She had concentrated all her make-up skills on Lovely's face that day, and the end result was a sophisticated young woman in a traditional sari with a polished face. She was surprised Lovely didn't protest when she blow-dried her hair to give it volume and buoyancy. "I'd have gone with you, baby," she said, holding back warm tears that welled in her eyes. Then, changing her mood instantly to her signature buffoonery, she quipped, "I just can't handle this sari-shari business, and my attire might be quite a scandal for them!" Lovely smiled amid her tears, and hugging Sheetal with a racing heart, set out of the house.

Her first reaction was that of intimidation when she stood outside the imposing glass doors of the upscale jewellery shop in South Extension. The tinted glass soothed her eyes from the blinding glare of the sun above. She ran her fingers nervously through her hair and pressed her lips together. The guard stationed outside did not open the door for her, as he had keenly observed her getting off a noisy autorickshaw, and waiting for the driver to return her small change. Lovely was habituated to this differential treatment based on social status in India. She glanced at her dark silhouette in the glass, hitched up her sari and pulled the door open. A whiff of cool air sucked the perspiration from her face, armpits and scalp. She trembled involuntarily at the glittering opulence of the showroom. Case upon case of royal blue velvet lay open behind sliding transparent glass windows shielding multifarious sparkling incarnations of the precious yellow metal. Elegant young women clad in lemon-yellow saris were helping elite customers choose the right pieces of jewellery for their needs. Lovely blinked hard to adjust her eyes to this new sun-like glare, without its attendant heat. She inched cautiously, trying her best to look comfortable in her luxurious surroundings. Just then, a dark man with a shiny bald scalp and a well-rounded tummy approached her with a broad smile on his betel-stained lips.

"Gold in this section, ma'am; diamonds at the back," he gestured with his stone-ringed hand.

"Actually," began Lovely reluctantly. "I came for an interview."

The bald man reflected silently, his thick eyebrows furrowing upwards.

"Job interview?" questioned Lovely with appreciable concern in her voice.

"Oho! I see," figured the bald man immediately. "Come with me, we'll go to meet Sinha sahib in the back office."

Lovely followed the round man, who seemed to throw his shoulders back while walking, as if he were pregnant. They passed through the guarded section of diamond jewellery, where, much to her astonishment, the guards saluted Lovely. Embarrassed, she was relieved to be ushered into a bright, well-equipped office that was presently empty.

"He should be back from lunch soon, *beta*."

Lovely was glad the bald man had left when she wiped a tear that escaped without warning from her eye. "Did he just call me *beta*?" she second guessed herself, as this endearing name for a *child* had just reminded her of her father.

Her interview with Mr. Sinha was brief, professional, and to-the-point. Everything was predetermined: the store hours were from 12 p.m. to 8 p.m. Monday through Saturday, the uniform of yellow sari was provided by the store management, and the base salary was 8,000 rupees per month.

Mr. Sinha was quite impressed by Lovely's English, and gave only a cursory glance to her high school certificate that she had brought along in a crisp white envelope.

Back at home, Sheetal had already organized a victory lunch for her friend. She had spent the morning arguing with a sandalwood cut-out of the elephant god Ganesha sitting atop her television.

"So, you do agree that Lovely is a determined young woman, only trying to help her family tide over their financial crises?"

As was to be expected, the statuette didn't answer.

"You at least agree that if she got this job, Lovely would be a very honest worker?"

After staring hard at the light brown elephant, Sheetal thought she noticed its trunk nod in consent.

"Thank God!" she sighed. "At least this is not a one-sided discussion."

"So," she continued with forced patience, "give me one good reason why Lovely should have to go back to Ramnagar empty-handed." Just at that moment the doorbell rang and Sheetal jumped to answer it.

"Yummy, smells darn good," sniffed Lovely, standing in the doorway and craning her neck to the distinctive odours of fresh-baked pizza.

"It's the sweet smell of success I get from your confidence, missy," remarked Sheetal, who saw a smile on her friend's face after agonizing long weeks.

Lovely dropped her bag and hugged Sheetal. "Yes! Yes! Yes!" She exclaimed, the intonation of her soft voice climbing higher with each affirmation.

"O-k-a-y!" sang Sheetal, swirling her friend to make her sit on the dining chair. "You should be starving," she judged, serving a tempting triangle of cheesy bliss onto Lovely's plate. Lovely's eyes dampened.

"I baked it!" triumphed Sheetal, biting into the side crust of her own piece. "No, just kidding; Pizza Hut did!" She poured beer into two glasses and raised a toast to Ganesha before clinking Lovely's glass. "This proves God exists, and one only has to corner Him in an argument to see results!" she joked, downing her beer in one neat gulp.

* * *

Time went on, and Lovely's new job as if transformed her personality. She not only interacted with affluent people in the showroom, but also saved a portion of her pay every month to buy herself a delicate gold chain she had been eyeing for a few months. Although the staff discount gave her a break on the price, Lovely justified the indulgence by convincing herself that a rich, well-settled groom was to be had only if she looked prosperous herself. Now, she embraced with gusto the urban life of Delhi, shopping confidently at malls and eating fast food with friends more often than previously.

Months rolled by, but Lovely's Mr. Right didn't cross her path. She sold jewellery mostly to married couples, or would-be brides accompanied by their mothers, or even white people from the west, but the professional dealings seemed to end abruptly after the clients had made their payment.

"I want to sell my gold chain," she confessed to Sheetal over a Sunday brunch at home one morning.

"Of course not, missy!" cajoled Sheetal, twisting her face distastefully as if she had just crunched an egg shell in her spinach omelette.

"I mean," she continued, relaxing her expression back to normal gradually, as she explained with a raised fork.

"You gotta try harder. Like the white guy who came to by a—?"

"Bracelet," filled in Lovely flatly.

"Yes, bracelet; thank you. So, instead of saying here's your bracelet and that's how much you pay at the counter, ask probing questions like 'Who is it for?' or even, 'Won't that look pretty on your wife's wrist?' That way you know if they're available or not."

"He told me, without my asking, that it was for his daughter," responded Lovely rather defensively.

"Just an example, dear," clarified Sheetal, taking her empty plate to the sink. Then, looking over her shoulder she added, "the more proactive you are, the better your chances."

From that day on, Lovely took her friend's advice seriously. Every white-skinned male customer who looked relatively young and potentially single, received special attention from the gullible groom-hunter camouflaged behind the mask of a savvy sales woman.

So, when a tall, thin foreigner with a British accent came and sat on the slender cushioned bench in front of her in the store one day, Lovely prepared for the kill.

However, when she steadied her gaze to look into his eyes and start a conversation, she couldn't get past his shiny mop of thin golden hair. She blinked hard as she would when staring at the sun, and looked away. She cleared her throat to speak, but the words forming in her mind were suddenly swept away by a massive undercurrent of emotion. Random words from the signature song she had sung at dinner table for her family came rushing forth to jumble her thoughts. "Was *he* the one who lived in a leafy cocoon and waited for her by the lamp on his bedside?" Lovely was tongue-tied. Her face burned with the luminous rays of the new sun that shone so close to it. Sweat droplets spattered on her face despite the cool air conditioning.

"Rich. You can call me Rich."

Lovely's ears filtered the unhurried casual words as she extended her delicate shivering hand to shake the outstretched bony white.

"However, I'm not all that rich," he joked, playing with words mischievously.

Lovely's strained face muscles loosened into a genuine smile, and her stiff posture resumed its supple quality.

"Ring, please," Richard answered her questioning eyes. She opened and closed a few boxes from under the glass countertop, unsure of which one to produce for her client.

"Sorry, my bad," he apologized, understanding her quandary. "Ladies, I should say."

Lovely's heart stopped beating. She was instantly transported to her father's abandoned clock room. Absolute vacuum engulfed her as time stood still again. "He was *not* the one for her." This stinging realization jolted her back to reality and she regained her composure. "Sure," she whispered, reaching for the cases with a decorative slant lettering of 'L' rounded from all corners. She opened the boxes and demanded weakly, "What size?"

"Oh, I don't know," came the frank reply as Rich scratched his mop of gold. "Maybe yours," he blurted out harmlessly.

The next couple minutes that Lovely spent modelling gold rings with stars, hearts, butterflies or letters crafted from gems or diamond stones, she did so from the safety of her subconscious niche. She had, as if, curled herself back into her mother's protective womb where nobody and nothing could hurt her. She remained floating there until Rich selected the ring she liked most, paid at the counter and left.

Sheetal tried her best to cheer her up at home, but eventually gave up, considering time would be Lovely's best healer. Which it was. After a few weeks, she almost forgot about Rich and regained her lost hope of finding the right match for herself. In the months that followed, Lovely's discerning eye quickly separated prospective candidates from mere clients, just like a sieve separates wheat flour from husk. The first thing she would mentally speculate on was the approximate age of the man, by intently observing how far back the hairline had receded from his forehead. In the same glance, she would size up additional giveaway signs like crow's feet, laugh lines or wrinkles. If this preliminary examination scored well, she would gaze all the way down to the prospect's hands. If the ring finger appeared free from any engagement or matrimonial shackles, she would steer the conversation into productive probing territory. Otherwise, it would tread wearily into the mundane wasteland of business decorum.

One winter evening, just before 8 p.m., Lovely was eager to return home, but the lady she was helping choose earrings seemed quite indecisive. Lovely kept aside the pairs the lady had shortlisted, but after trying on every single one twice in both ears, she wanted to see more designs. Lovely was beginning to get frustrated, and believed she would be delayed at work when the guard flung open the store door to a foreigner. Lovely gaped disbelievingly at the emaciated figure of Rich, who was scratching his scalp awkwardly to get service right before closing time. Although a few salesgirls were available to help him, he stood behind Lovely's client, awaiting his turn. Lovely's face lost its colour. Her heart ached to talk to Rich, but the limited time and the presence of another customer vitiated her prospects. As if on cue, the lady sighed in exasperation and got up to leave.

"Thank you, but I'll come with my husband," she apologized with a sidelong glance at Lovely. "Thank *you*," responded Lovely in a daze.

Rich explained matter-of-factly that he had come to exchange the ring for himself, as his fiancé had moved on in life after his prolonged absence from Britain.

"Guess I don't have to ask you to try it on this time," he joked, although Lovely could clearly hear the distinct sad undertone in his forced laughter.

"You've grown quite thin," she remarked, after all the rings Rich tried were too big for him.

"I can have it sized for you," she suggested, as he paused over a plain gold band without answering.

Just then, a few lights of the showroom were turned off, enhancing the air of privacy between them.

"It's okay," he sighed finally, getting up to go. "Maybe next time."

Lovely's eyes followed the luminous gold light of his hair as Rich's body merged with the darkness of the background. She stood transfixed until he turned and retraced his steps. Digging out a visiting card from the wallet in his back pocket, he extended it to her silently and left. Flustered, Lovely thrust the card in her purse and ran out of the store through the back door.

The Perfect Match

The bus was overcrowded, as all buses in India are, regardless of the time of day or night. Lovely was holding on to a sour-smelling metal support when she got reminded of the card in her purse. Balancing her weight deftly to another hand, she struggled to pull out the small card from her purse amid insane swaying and screeching of the bus.

Richard Henley
Instructor, English as a second language (ESL)
British Council, Connaught Place, New Delhi
Telephone: 91 11 4168543570
Fax: 91 11 6477120149

*   *   *

A year passed. Lovely was still working at the jewellery store. Sheetal had been promoted to a customer service coach position within the same call centre, which meant she no longer had to work night shifts. But that privilege didn't automatically translate into a peaceful night's sleep for her. Sheetal would be jarred awake systematically from her sleep every night by Lovely's relentless screaming. Evidently, time had not been her best healer this time around. She had been unable to accept the grim reality that Rich had left India after her parents rejected their decision to get married. Night after night, with uncanny frequency, Lovely would scream uncontrollably, "Don't leave me!" Then, she would plead hoarsely, "Take me o'er the moon, please!" Sheetal was a strong woman with steel nerves, but even she feared for Lovely's sanity when she heard her laugh cynically in her sleep and mumble, "I'll fly to your leafy cocoon—across the oceans—o'er the moon!"

Consequently, she hatched a plan to free Lovely from her tormenting memories, and rekindle in her friend's aching heart a renewed passion to find a match settled abroad. She lost no time to create an internet chat ID for her friend on her laptop. Now, the only challenge was to transform Lovely into a computer savvy 21st century woman. This training took weeks, and Sheetal explained to Lovely the advantages and perils of befriending absolute strangers over the internet.

"It's like finding a needle in a haystack," she would draw an analogy to emphasize the abundance of scammers and hackers in chat rooms. "The diamonds are scattered among countless stones," she cautioned her naive friend, who was trying to absorb the myriad intricacies of the World Wide Web.

"So, the mantra is to *extract* more information than you *give up*."

Lovely pondered hard over her friend's bottom line advice. "Does that mean we never meet?" she ventured uncertainly.

"I'll tell you when that stage comes," Sheetal reassured a rather perplexed Lovely. She sure kept her promise, as Lovely's online activity was closely supervised by her mentor.

"Setting yourself up for another heartbreak?" Sheetal would reproach Lovely when she started getting too friendly with white men. "If you're so adamant to get married with your parents' blessings, you'd better hunt for a *desi* guy settled abroad."

Like most things, Lovely took Sheetal's advice and started chatting online with Indian origin men settled in the US, Canada and Australia. She knew these countries housed large Indian populations, and she hoped to adjust better in these destinations as opposed to Europe.

The only problem was that Lovely's elusive diamond was buried deep within the labyrinth of virtual friends with aliases.

After a few months passed without any success at befriending a genuine guy with noble intentions of marriage and family, Lovely began to seriously doubt the efficacy of new technology to bring two people together from different corners of the planet, and unite them in the sacred bond of matrimony. She would often wonder, while looking at sparkling diamonds in her jewellery store, how labour-intensive it would have been to excavate these precious stones from the core of the earth. "I shouldn't give up," she determined once again, and re-launched the search for *her diamond* with doubled vigour. Within two weeks she was chatting daily with a Punjabi guy settled in Canada. His name was Gursharan, but she called him Guru, while he called her Love.

Soon their online chat transitioned to long telephonic conversations, after Sheetal forbade Lovely from using the web camera so early into their relationship. But her fears were allayed when Guru proposed marriage to Lovely less than two months after their initial acquaintance.

"Express train, that Guru of yours!" Sheetal jested after Lovely broke the news to her the same morning the proposal was made.

"He can't wait," blushed Lovely, wondering what her next steps should be. As always, Sheetal came to her rescue with sound and practical advice.

"Just ask him to come down to India," she said breezily with a light shrug of her shoulders. Then, remembering to add something important, she stated, "and you, missy, ask for leave from your jewellery store."

"Why are you smiling like that?" Lovely asked bluntly. "We're serious about marriage."

"No, I know missy," Sheetal replied sheepishly. "I was just wondering if your employer will gift you bridal jewellery!"

Both of them broke into chuckles, and Lovely relaxed in the carefree comfort of her friend's attitude.

As natural instinct would have it, she started paying special attention to bridal jewellery in her store. She would picture herself in elaborate gold chokers, diamond chandelier earrings and precious stone bracelets—pieces she knew she could never afford for herself.

"Maybe your Canadian prince can buy them for you," Sheetal would joke naughtily at home. "That is if your store manager doesn't gift them to you already!" Lovely knew in her heart that Guru didn't care about her financial status. She was convinced she had found true love at last. Her family back in Ramnagar was delighted with her choice this time, and started preparations for an early marriage. Soon, the eagerly awaited day arrived, and both friends boarded the crowded train to head back to their native town. Guru and his family were to arrive on the eve of the marriage, as they could only spare a week in India owing to a busy schedule. They hoped to take Lovely with them to Canada, and had already spoken to their contacts in embassies to expedite her visa formalities.

Although Sheetal enjoyed herself thoroughly in the rather frugal wedding ceremony hosted by Lovely's parents, the reality of her own new life only struck her when Lovely was departing from her family once more, this time with people she had met for the first time. "I hope they take good care of her," she prayed silently as a vacuum settled in her stomach. Almost immediately, she reverted to her bubbly self, cracking jokes to elevate the mood of visibly emotional Mr. and Mrs. Seth.

"Teach ma how to chat online," Lovely instructed Lucky, as she finally sat in the car with Guru and his family.

That thought assuaged Sheetal's dilemma too. "I'll chat with her regularly," she spoke aloud, as if trying to calm her rankled nerves that dreaded the prospect of returning to Delhi alone to an empty house.

Lovely's introduction to Canada was through the bewitchingly beautiful British Columbia. She gazed awestruck at the clear blue ocean she had flown over to reach the wooded green bliss of her dreams. Her new house in White Rock had all the amenities she could have imagined, and when she saw the small crystal lamp on the side table of her bedroom, tears of joy rolled down her cheeks.

At first, Lovely didn't despise the endless household chores that were assigned to her by her relentless mother-in-law. She also justified her father-in-law's indifference towards her as natural age progression. As for Guru, he was scarcely at home, and Lovely wondered if his admission of being a retail store manager was actually true.

The only person she guarded against was Guru's younger brother, Avtar. Not only had he dropped out of school and spent all his time playing video games or loafing with friends, he also passed indecent comments and made lewd passes at Lovely. She couldn't be alone in the kitchen without having her bottom pinched or back scratched. Her in-laws turned a blind eye to her shrieks when events like these happened, and made her feel guilty of overreaction. Desperate, Lovely turned to Sheetal for help via online chat. She waited anxiously for night to fall so her in-laws would retire to their bedroom. Guru mostly returned home around 4 in the morning and left immediately after breakfast. So she would steal into Avtar's room when he was away at night, and log on to his computer with shaking hands. Briefly typed messages from Sheetal coming from a world away restored Lovely's courage and instilled new confidence in her.

"What do you mean you never ask Guru where he spends his nights?"

Lovely's cursor blinked a few minutes as she groped for an answer to Sheetal's question late one night. "Are you there, missy?" came a worried second question as Lovely fumbled on the keys of her keyboard.

"I never dared to ask," she typed laboriously, but quickly erased the line with a swift stroke of backspace.

"We never have a conversation," she wrote finally.

"Why????" came another pat question with multiple interrogation points that made Lovely anxious to find a convincing reply. But before she could do so, she was bombarded by a string of questions from Sheetal.

"Did he marry a wife or a housemaid? Tell me when you're going to ask him? Are you sure he's not having an affair?" Lovely buckled under pressure and typed a reply she regretted as soon as she had sent it.

Sheetal's reaction rang with exhilaration. "That's like *my* friend! Tell me tonight, then, how he reacts."

It was too late to retract. Sheetal had already logged off. Lovely stared at her screen, reading the transcript of their conversation several times over. She couldn't believe what she had just promised, and wondered if she could somehow erase her last line. But she couldn't. It sat there obstinately in royal blue ink: "I'll talk to him this morning."

It was 2 a.m. when Lovely finally lay on her bed, reflecting. Her dilemma was twofold: if she accosted Guru immediately upon his return, she risked igniting the cinders of his ire. Instead, if she let him sleep normally and confronted him at breakfast, the whole family would join in ridiculing her, and the result would be as devastating as a massive forest fire. After much deliberation, she opted for immediate confrontation. The result was that she couldn't go online to chat with Sheetal that night. When her mother called from Ramnagar, she just laughed a throaty laugh in an attempt to appease her mother's fears about her unusually nasal voice. "It's

Canada, ma. It's beginning to get cold here." Lovely pushed the big swabs of cotton deep into her nostrils and pressed the cellotape securing them on the bridge of her nose. "I'll be fine," she whispered into the phone she cradled with the other hand. Convinced that she had not disclosed Guru's vicious beating that morning, Lovely's mother-in-law stopped eavesdropping and retired to her room.

With time, the frequency and severity of beatings intensified. Lovely was forbidden from calling or receiving calls from her family in Ramnagar. She secretly talked to them through Avtar's webcam, but never revealed the torment she was enduring daily. She would dim the lights of the room so that her bruises would be concealed, and forced herself to sound blissfully cheerful. Sheetal, however, knew the real story; only she didn't know how to help her friend.

Lovely was slowly suffocating within the walls of the house. She started sneaking out after dinner when Guru and Avtar were not at home. She was too preoccupied with her physical and mental abuse to appreciate the clean winding roads of White Rock bordered with immaculately manicured lawns. She would walk silently through the gathering darkness that effortlessly cloaked her scars and gashes. The black-blue bruises too blended seamlessly with the pall of night. Somehow, walking on the wooden pier at White Rock beach seemed to liberate Lovely, albeit momentarily. Every advancing step brought her closer to the endless waters of the ocean, extending past the horizon, into a land free from torment and toil. The ocean was inviting—promising to drown with her a life fraught with lurking dangers and ignominious deceit. Yet, she invariably turned away from the end of the pier, and retraced her steps back to the outwardly picturesque leafy trails leading up to her hideous cocoon, where every tree threatened to choke the life out of her being with its entwining roots; where the blossoms were poisonous berries, and the lamp by her bedside only a stark testament to her ongoing agony.

Thus, Lovely continued walking alone on this perilous trail—suffocated, poisoned, and in unspeakable pain—only so her family in India could rest easy with the thought of a daughter well settled in a country of her dreams. But very soon the trail became increasingly treacherous, and as Lovely persevered on, she eventually fell facedown into a black pit whose sticky mire pulled her down in its profound obliteration.

It all happened one evening when the family was getting ready to go to Fairmont Hotel in Vancouver for Guru's birthday celebrations. Lovely was wondering what to do when her mother-in-law solved the puzzle. "No need to cook dinner tonight," she instructed. "There are leftovers in the fridge from the afternoon." Lovely knew she couldn't leave the house when she heard the key lock the door from outside.

She didn't know how long she had been sleeping in her dark room without eating anything, when forceful rough hands hauled her out brutally. She screamed loudly and scrambled to reach frantically for the lamp by her bedside. It was swept to the floor in the wild tussle and crashed to pieces. She screamed again, and tried to break free from the heavy hand gagging her mouth, while she was being shamelessly undressed by her persecutor. Gasping for breath, she continued struggling as the last of her clothes was ripped, and body scratched as if a sharp knife was slitting it randomly. Excruciating pain numbed her senses as her legs were parted wide with brute force, and she was raped savagely again and again. After what seemed a gruelling long time, the massive weight lifted from above her, and she heard the door open. With a gigantic effort, Lovely opened her watering eyes and blinked weakly to catch a glimpse of her assailant. In the vertical slit of light from outside, she recognised the familiar figure.

"Avtar!" she muttered subconsciously.

The slit of light grew as the hardened face peered in. "Don't you dare take that name to anybody, you fucking bitch!"

Lovely tried to cover herself with the blanket as the light from outside illuminated her shame.

"What fun were you having with that gay husband of yours, anyway?"

The menacing voice and the shocking revelation hung in Lovely's dark room long after the perpetrator was gone.

The next time she awoke, she was completely disoriented. Her room was pitch dark, and as she moved a little to feel the lamp by her bedside, traumatizing memories of her nightmare came flashing through her mind in violent gushes. She lay sprawled on the bed, legs parted as they were when she was ruthlessly attacked, one hand stretching to the side table where the lamp used to be. Acute pain shot up her vagina as she gingerly tried to move her legs together. The deep sharp gashes on her body throbbed with a piercing dull pain, and Lovely felt stiff from the blood that had clotted around them.

She was too weak to sit up, having had nothing to eat or drink for hours. She had lain unconscious for a full night and day. Lovely knew she had to contact her family somehow, so they could arrange for her return to India as soon as possible, given that she had no money of her own. She pressed both hands tightly over her mouth to prevent accidental shrieks that most certainly would accompany her herculean effort to get up on her feet. Slowly and painfully, she rolled down the bed and fell on the carpeted floor with a muted thud. She lay there a few minutes as the fall had enlivened her numbing pain and sent pointed needles like chilling pricks throughout her body. Her feet wobbled unsteadily as she tried several times to put her body weight on them with the support of the bed frame. As she blundered through the dark room in a dazed stupor, her foot landed on the smashed pieces of the crystal lamp. Lovely felt thick warm blood oozing copiously from the new wound. Undeterred, she faltered towards the door with one massive leap to avoid the scattered glass pieces. She waited and listened before turning the knob to open the door. Even the familiar sounds of night insects made her blood curdle. Holding her breath in the dim light of the living room, she pressed her lips together to withstand the insane pain that shook her after she valiantly pulled out the cruel wedge of glass from under her swollen foot. She clutched the door knob tightly as the tremors caused by the stunning pain made her feel faint. Collecting herself gradually, she released the door knob and hopped silently towards the computer room, leaving behind telltale footprints of blood. Although she opened the door fearlessly, Lovely was incredibly relieved at finding the room empty. The simple task of logging on to the computer appeared like a mammoth effort to her, as she plunged lifelessly into the chair facing it.

Within seconds of connecting to the webcam, the smiling faces of Lovely's family members changed into death-like gloom. Despite the dim light, they clearly saw deep, violent, blood clotted gashes cruising her frail body behind brazenly ripped clothes. The bruises and scars of past and present injuries peered in full view of the camera. Their daughter was unrecognizable. Mrs. Seth buried her face in her hands and howled inconsolably. Lucky was aghast. "Call the police right now!" he yelled helplessly, his face covering the entire screen of the camera. Lovely quickly lowered the volume of the speaker for fear of rousing her in-laws. When Lucky backed off a little from the screen, throwing up his hands in despair, Lovely shrieked loudly in horror. Her father was holding the left side of his chest with an iron grip, as his sweat-soaked face contorted with pain. Violent seizures overpowered him, shaking him out of his wheelchair so that he collapsed on the floor, hitting his head first.

"What happened to papa?" Lovely hollered, forgetting all her pain and the nagging anxiety of waking her in-laws. Mrs. Seth and Lucky had surrounded her father, and were trying to lay him on the adjoining sofa. Lovely froze. She heard noises in the next room and saw light through the bottom slit of her door.

Nervously, she glanced at the wall clock. It was a quarter to four! Guru would be home anytime, and would beat her before throwing her out of the house. "What would she do without money?" she panicked. "Where would she go?" In a nano second, she turned the light on and hobbled to disconnect the computer. Unfortunately, it was too late. Her mother-in-law had slammed into the room, ire dominating her sleep-puffed face and sunken eyes. She promptly pushed Lovely forcefully against the wall and got a good view of the computer screen. Furious, she rushed out, locking the door after her. Momentarily, the door opened again, and Lovely shielded her head with her arms as her father-in-law rained kicks on her with his heeled boots. Lovely screamed in pain as her distraught family in India swung between attending to Mr. Seth and witnessing her mindless flogging through the webcam. Before long, Guru arrived on the scene and pulled the computer plug off the wall. Lovely heard him yell frenetically, "Shut this bitch up, or she'll bring us big trouble!" Immediately after, she lost consciousness as a blunt object struck the back of her head.

*　　*　　*

Lovely shuddered when she awoke. She felt she had been sleeping for days. All was foggy when she opened her eyes. She tried to sit up, but felt a big weight pulling her, as if deep down the floor of an ocean. Seeing her retch, a woman advanced a bag in which Lovely vomited. The mist around her eyes cleared a little, and she perceived an angelic figure dressed in white clothes, with a caring smile on her face.

"Where am I?" Lovely demanded almost inaudibly.

"You're lucky to be alive," the nurse answered, touching Lovely's shoulder in a way that made her lie back down on the bed.

"It was a long surgery," continued the nurse with a painful grimace. "The hair on your head will grow back; they had to shave it off to dissolve the multiple blood clots and other damage."

The relief of unfamiliar surroundings relaxed Lovely and she fell back into a deep slumber. The room was dark, except for the faint dispersed light of a night lamp by her bedside when she awoke again. She let out a terrified low whine when she saw the silhouette of a man in the faint red glow. "It's okay," reassured the voice calmly. "You're safe here."

Lovely recognised the voice as being familiar, but the heavy medication in her system impaired her memory. She signalled the man with her index finger to come closer. He obeyed, and Lovely lost her composure instantaneously. "Rich!" she exclaimed, with all the vigour her battered body allowed. "How did *you* come here?"

Rich held her hands together and pressed them tightly. "I've been teaching creative writing at Humber College, Toronto for a few months."

Then, he added somberly, "I couldn't believe my eyes when I saw your pictures on national news two days back."

His face was flushed red with emotion and Lovely felt the burning heat of his hands. "God alone knows what would've happened to you if your neighbour hadn't called 911."

A sarcastic hoarse laugh escaped Rich's throat involuntarily. "To think that the neighbour's dog was disturbed by your shrieks and woke his owner—"

Rich shook his lowered head, appalled at what some humans had come to represent. Then, wiping both eyes with his fists, he dug into his trouser pocket.

In the red glow of the night lamp, Lovely recognised the ring that Rich's warm hand had just slipped into her left ring finger. It was the same heart-shaped golden leaf studded with a diamond, she had helped him choose for his ex-fiancé. Warm tears soaked their firmly clasped hands as Rich whispered softly in her ear, "Will you marry me?"

The Pied Piper of Jaipur

"**M**a! Grandma!! Wake up, snake!!!" Dolly's high-pitched cries brutally pierced the stony early morning silence enveloping the Bansal household. She ran amuck, hopping on one black unlaced shoe, a navy-blue tie hanging unknotted around her neck, as she jerked the shoe off and jumped on her grandmother's bed.

Grandma sat cross-legged on a jute rug on the floor, facing a panoply of Hindu gods fogged by smoke wisping from a claw of incense sticks.

"Get up from the floor before you die of snake bite!" shrieked Dolly testily, terror crawling into her vivacious black eyes squinting under frowning bushy eyebrows.

Grandma turned her arched back slowly, revealing a broad priest-like face, mild brown eyes and puckered lips moving in prayer as she whispered the mantras in intone. A benign smile flickered across her toothless mouth, ironing out temporarily the creases surrounding it, but sagged back into a cluster of waxy skin as she spoke.

"Today is *Naag Panchami*, my child, and our house has been blessed by none other than God Himself." She touched lord Shiva's feet in the framed photo garlanded with marigold and looked reverentially at the snake coiled around the god's neck.

"Didn't they teach you in school that the entire universe rests on the hood of *Vasuki?*"

"Call ma to have the snake killed!" commanded Dolly biliously, huddling to the far end of the bed and unheeding her grandmother's idiosyncrasies.

Grandma maintained a placid countenance as she endeavored to mollify the pythonic fear seizing her granddaughter.

"Don't fear the venerated being, my child. Lord Shiva drank all the venom of snakes, and therefore, his throat is blue. Snakes henceforth became innocuous and protectors of gods and humans alike." She let out an exhausted sigh from the strain of talking and counting her abacus beads in mental meditation simultaneously.

Dolly had always wondered why lord Shiva's neck was blue, but finding the answer under such excruciating circumstances dissipated its significance. Instead, her attention riveted on the dangerous reptile lurking in the house.

"If snakes are so saintly, why then do oodles of them swim in spirits of closed glass jars in our science laboratory? Surely our teachers know more than you to treat them that way?" Dolly's tone was pugnacious and left grandma groping for words to ward off the verbal attack. She closed her eyes queasily, as if to blind herself to the image of holy beings butchered without compunction.

"Tell me where the snake is," she asked in a deep bass voice, giving Dolly an icy glance and resolving to seek penance for obdurate humanity all by herself.

"I have locked it in the study where it was hiding behind my shoe," said the thirteen-year-old with an air of accomplishment.

Grandma strode towards the study, her trademark white sari of a widow trailing behind her, exposing her mountainous bosom adorned with a string of dark *Rudraksha* berries. Upon reaching the door of the study latched from outside, she prostrated on the floor, her forehead touching the scraping of the door paint that flaked on her semi-bald pate.

"Get away from the door!" screeched Meenal raucously, hitching up her sari and standing barefoot on her toes, as if to allow space for the snake to slither through her feet instead of getting muffled in the folds of her sari.

Dolly was squeezing her mother's hand tightly, her rheumy eyes twinkling with ironic glee, as grandma gathered the mounds of her body and slumped on the bed with her feet up, after being upbraided by her daughter.

Meenal rushed to call Shankar, the servant, using both hands to free herself from Dolly's clasp. The vermilion in her centre parting was smudged after the night's sleep, and the small bells on her silver anklets jingled sonorously as she flitted in and out of rooms.

Dolly crept on the bed—avoiding grandma's steely glint—and from there, leapt on to the table, oscillating a little before balancing herself. She surveyed the room in a sprightly manner from her fortified bastion crenellated by books and spare boxes.

Her cocksureness that she wouldn't have to attend school today was concretized when she glanced jauntily at the oval wall clock. In another ten minutes the school bus would hoot outside the house, but how could she be expected to retrieve her school shoe from a room vandalized by a deadly snake?

She visualized her swarthy classmates bending endlessly over complex geometry problems she loathed most, their notebooks pitted with holes from pointed compass needles in an effort to draw accurate angles and spheres.

Presently, Shankar entered Dolly's bedroom, followed close on his heels by Meenal, who pointed the closed door to him authoritatively with her forefinger.

He cowered—careening—and almost missed falling over the festooned bronze *Nataraja* hanging from a dowel close to the door of the study. "I can't kill a snake, *memsahib*!" he implored, his face ashen and eyes bulging with horror.

Grandma concurred wholeheartedly, and her eyes gleamed with joy as she spoke. "Believe me, if you inflict harm on this envoy of god, it will spawn infinite offspring that will infest our house and be omnipresent," she warned with foreboding.

"Moreover, Shankar, your name itself comes from one of the many names of lord Shiva. You will walk on razor-edged swords, and if you were to lose your balance, you would fall into simmering hot vessels of oil, should you sully your karma by hurting the snake. In no rebirth would you attain *Moksha*!"

A shiver travelled the fifteen-year-old's spine as he glanced at the metal cut-out of the "destroyer" Shiva in the trinity of Brahma the creator, and Vishnu the preserver. He closed his eyes in prayer to entreat the Mighty God to condone his sins, and eulogized Him for redeeming his benighted soul from committing a hideous crime.

All this while, Dolly was stroking her jetty tresses tied in a braid that resembled a gnarled saw rope. She gave the room a cursory glance, pinching her eyes to picture snakes dangling from the ceiling, coiled around fans and wrapped around lampshades, as preordained by grandma. She thought her grandma to be a queer fish to uphold such dogmatic views and expect an intelligent girl like her to believe in the existence of ogres and monsters from fairy tales. She remonstrated against her granny's apocryphal dogmas with the force of a maverick. "If your snakes are so powerful, why do they hide in straw baskets and dance to flutes?"

At this profane remark by Dolly, grandma waddled out of the room, bearing a mortified look on her face and muttering, "Believe me, if you kill *naag devta*, you are all doomed!"

Meanwhile, Meenal straddled between the two polarized arguments concerning the snake and wished her husband was home. Mr. Bansal was travelling to Frankfurt to showcase his semi-precious stones to potential importers at the International Trade Fair, and was scheduled to return in a week. As she teetered between the two camps—represented by the two conflicting generations of her mother and daughter regarding the snake's destiny—she asked Shankar if he knew anybody who could help.

"Bunty was talking about some snake charmer who lives in the slum, and who successfully charmed a snake out of their house sometime back," said Shankar, feeling both important and relieved.

As he set out for the slum in quest of the snake charmer on dusty blanched roads, Shankar exulted at the divine significance of his name. In all his fifteen years, he had never wondered if his name meant anything more than the banal names of his seven siblings who were named after the days of the week.

He had known all along that he was especially blessed by gods, or why else would he be the only one selected to work at the Bansals'? His siblings listened to his exploits in rapt awe, when he visited home and boasted about watching TV and playing cricket in between mopping floors and scrubbing dishes.

Now, he shared the same name as the god who could annihilate the entire universe by simply opening his third eye on the forehead, and breaking into a cosmic dance!

Shankar swaggered, magnifying the hitherto trifling details of the bronze *Nataraja*.

He ran his fingers through his tangled crop to see if his hair was long enough like Shiva's flying locks that formed two wings in the violent frenzy of his dance.

He skipped playfully, synchronizing his flying hands with raised legs, wondering if he was capable of balancing the cycles of creation and destruction in this universe by the swaying of his torso, like the supreme Shiva.

Shankar entered the shanty hovels of the slum contumeliously, gloating in his newfound celestial affiliations. He looked disdainfully at semi-nude kids playing barefoot on sewers clogged with trash and plastic. Thick smoke billowed from earthen stoves as women burnt coal to bake rotis for the afternoon meal. It was in one such shack, covered tentatively by a tin shed, that Shankar found Nagesh, the snake charmer.

Although Nagesh was expecting company, he lay nonchalantly on newspapers spread on the mud floor of his ramshackle hut. A man of forty-five, he looked over sixty, his scythe-like moustache white as milk; silver hair sprouted from his ears like water from a fountain, and his emaciated body appeared to cling on to mortality by a tenuous strand of cobweb.

Nagesh had recently been released from jail: incarcerated for practising the banned profession of snake charming. With neither money nor education, the hapless widower had adopted the unwonted profession of releasing his harmless snake at the crack of dawn in an affluent house every once-a-few-weeks, to keep his body and soul together.

He reminisced with rancour how his once blossoming family got chewed by the callous jaws of poverty. He used to earn enough to provide his family the luxury of onions with rotis twice every day, when he roamed the city enchanting onlookers with the hypnotized dance of his snake to his flute.

He returned from prison to learn that his twins had perished—one after the other—from untreated diarrhea; and his wife had succumbed to malnutrition during her second pregnancy, thus snuffing out any hope of posterity.

Gripped by a morbid fear of starving to death in his four mud walls, he started hoodwinking wealthy bungalow dwellers by first planting, then offering to rid their house of the dreaded reptile for a fee.

He adjusted his tattered saffron turban as he followed Shankar through the scorched stubble of grass leading to the posh colony inhabited by his opulent clients. He lurched, trying to keep pace with the well-fed Shankar, as a dusty beam of sunlight fell obliquely on the gourd flute he carried: his last hope of survival.

A cacophony of clamorous noises emanated from the Bansal bungalow as the two approached it.

Grandma's cumbersome body blocked the doorway, as if to stand between the snake and its liberty.

Dolly was bubbling with anticipation and fear like Mount Vesuvius—ready to explode anytime—as she jumped on the chairs in the verandah.

Meenal was heard bellowing that the snake had slithered out of the study and entered the scullery.

Grandma folded her hands repeatedly, praying for the God Incarnate to knock over the milk pot she had left unattended in the scullery after making her morning tea, so that she could consecrate the milk transformed into ambrosia by the savoring of the anointed snake.

A feeling of salvation swept across everybody upon seeing Nagesh, except Grandma, who could not comprehend how the guardian of gods could be accused of wreaking havoc. She had even opened the door leading to the terrace, hoping the snake would escape and find refuge on one of the imposing mango trees in their backyard. She secretly nurtured the ambition of offering it milk everyday, should it make good its escape into one of the burrows around the house. She was plagued with scepticism though, concerning the snake's ability to climb stairs, but she instantly chided herself on underestimating its divine powers. "It could fly out of the house if it wanted," she thought, suppressing a smile.

Nagesh squatted on the floor at the entrance of the house, producing melancholic notes from his flute by inflating his cheeks as if two tennis balls were trapped inside them. He had laid in front of him a grimy home-spun cotton pouch in which he intended to transport his possession back with him.

The poignant music frayed Dolly's nerves as she thought it to be a travesty of all she had learned about snakes in her science lessons. "Snakes are deaf to rock-and-roll on your music!" she affronted, giving Nagesh a censorious glare.

After an agonizing wait, just when everybody was about to tag him impostor and curse him out of the house, a groggy black mass quailed at the entrance, its eyes burning like embers.

Dolly screamed loudly and pushed a chair at it, making the snake skulk behind the door.

Nagesh sat unruffled, knowing well that his snake was as docile as a dove, after he had removed its venom glands and partly stitched up its mouth. He swayed his body violently, playing his flute behind the door to gather his object and return home with the fee to buy something to eat.

But this habitual repertoire did not entice the sluggish snake out of its hiding; it made several staccato movements, but squirmed back, twirling its body behind the door. Nagesh realized the uphill task of extricating his superficially imposing shiny black cobra, stuporous from months of starvation.

He finally lunged behind the door and goaded the snake with his flute. Sensing danger, the cobra wriggled out of the house and plopped on to the forested garden.

Nagesh was rankled by this effrontery of his snake, and chased it under tall palm trees and behind decorative flower pots, amid screeching yells from the females of the house.

The snake writhed laboriously, crawling as arduously as an acrobat tightrope walking in a gale. It camouflaged itself behind creepers replete with fragrant white jasmine flowers.

Nagesh was irked with his foible to let the animal tyrannize him. With a massive force of his flute, he flailed the bushes, sending broken petals and leaves flying in the air. He was about to gather his snake when he fell back, startled.

A shaggy, long-faced grey mongoose had crept in front of the snake, challenging it into a duel. The muzzy snake spat left and right with its forked tongue, but soon burned out. Seeing its adversary frail and non-combative, the mongoose seized its head and wrenched it.

Nagesh lay on the grass debilitated, as he watched impotently the coarse bushy tail of the predator disappear into the thicket with its meal.

The family members were appalled by this inordinate turn of events and rushed into the house, slamming the door noisily.

The Pied Piper of Jaipur

Nagesh picked his way, flute in hand, and the empty pouch in the torn pocket of his flared tunic. After reaching the crossroad, he instinctively turned on a road leading away from his hut. He walked vigorously, despite feeling delirious from hunger and the sweltering sun. So unparalleled was his mental agitation that he walked hours in the gruelling sun, until he reached the foot of the high Amber Fort perched on a hilltop.

He paused for a split second, then, smiling wryly, attacked the steep stairs of the fort like lightning in his determination to avenge the animals that had outdone him.

He envied his snake that had embraced death and terminated its earthly misery.

He despised the mongoose who quelled its hunger effortlessly.

He ran up the stairs—two at a time—in his frenzy to reach the top, sneering at effervescent tourists riding on exquisitely decorated elephants climbing languorously. Once on top, he scaled the rampart, panting noisily. Fat beads of sweat trickled from all parts of his body, soaking him from head to toe as his head throbbed violently. With one despairing look, he flung his flute down the gaping deep valley. As he peered dangerously at his free-falling flute, it struck a pointed rock and split into two, before disappearing out of view.

The Compromise

Cookie and Monica walked across the street from Starbucks on Davie, towards English Bay, sipping extra large lattes. Despite the sunny fall afternoon, it was rare for the mother-daughter duo to go out together. They would meet for family dinners during Christmas, or Easter, or Thanksgiving, or even when Cookie and Tina hosted extravagant parties for their Indian friends in Vancouver during Diwali, Holi and other Hindu festivals, that gave them an opportunity to escape temporarily from their adopted western cuisine and indulge in native delicacies of basmati rice *biryani*, spicy curries, and calorie-soaked desserts of *halva* and *gulab jamuns*.

The sidewalk was teeming with pedestrians crowding around a hotdog stall as cyclists slowed down to make way for them. From that vantage point the seawall looked like an ocean itself, forever changing colour as waves of people moved across its vista, some on bicycles, others on rollerblades, and most others on foot. Even the waters of the Pacific wore a festive look as white sail boats drifted sleepily along the blue background, yellow kayaks rowed past leisurely, and crimson freight ships stood anchored, waiting patiently to enter Vancouver Port.

The Compromise

"I'm hungry," announced Monica, joining the burgeoning queue behind the yellow-and-red umbrella with the lettering *"The Dogfather"* in black—the only part of the hotdog cart visible from behind heads with straw, cloth and baseball hats.

Even though the appetizing odour of fried onions, mustard and pickles wafting through the air was tempting for Cookie, she had spent way too many years in India to appreciate western snacks, which she always found uncooked, or bland, or not filling enough.

"How do they eat sandwiches for lunch?" she would wonder with like-minded Indian friends, who couldn't conceive a meal without rotis, or rice, or both.

"You go ahead," she said to Monica, knotting the scarf around her neck as a steady breeze blew from the water, kicking up dry fallen leaves on its way and accentuating the odours emanating from the steel roll grilling sausages.

As they waited in line, Cookie glanced perfunctorily at her emerald Jaguar sparkling handsomely under an evergreen tree on Davie Street, which, instead of camouflaging its splendour, served as a befitting shade for her proud possession.

Shortly after, they were walking down the slope leading to the seawall, looking for a place to sit.

"There, on that log," Cookie said, pointing to the cylindrical wood that had just been vacated by a young couple who seemed to have finished their picnic, as the woman closed plastic boxes and stowed them away in a broad-wheeled high stroller they were now pushing, its front curtained off by a pink floral towel.

Monica let her coffee mug sink in the sand for grip as she settled beside her mother on the log, facing scattered sun bathers lying on their stomachs, on sheets and towels of varying hues and sizes. "This is good stuff," she remarked, biting into the oblong bun oozing a confused melange of sauces and condiments at its seams.

"You must cook at home more often," advised Cookie, taking extreme caution not to sound like a typical possessive and controlling Asian mother, for she knew there was more important advice she wanted to dispense to her daughter today, besides the obvious health hazards of eating too much fast food.

"We can go to a restaurant, you know," she suggested, after a long sceptical gaze at Monica's ketchup-smeared hands. "There are plenty on Denman street, one just behind us—*The Boathouse*, I think it's called."

"They're expensive!" exclaimed Monica, licking her fingers and then wiping them off with Kleenex.

Cookie did not comment. Instead, she relapsed into memories of her past, when purchasing even the basic ingredients to cook a decent meal for her family of three had seemed formidable. Yet, after marrying Mark, a successful family physician, her fate of penury had turned around a complete 360 degrees. Together they went to the fanciest restaurants in downtown Vancouver—whisked away in glass elevators of the Revolving Restaurant—lost in the glow of each other's eyes, oblivious to the glowing city beneath them over five hundred feet below. There, she marvelled at the array of variety displayed artistically on their table: the soups cleared away courteously for appetizers of smoked salmon and fresh oysters, only to be followed expeditiously by seared duck breast, marinated teriyaki and crab legs. Needless to say, it was always Mark who ordered; her knowledge of western food being limited to hamburgers and hotdogs. She never complained that the food was bland or raw by Indian standards, or if it was beef or pork—meat she didn't eat prior to converting herself to Christianity.

Now, after fifteen years of their marriage, she ordered and recommended the exact same dishes that were Mark's favorites, even though he rarely accompanied her to Indian buffets, where she longed to go at least once a week to satiate her cravings for deep-fried *pakoras* and butter chicken with naan.

It's because Cookie hadn't forgotten her humble beginnings and a protracted struggle, that she considered as trivial the unguarded mockery of some Indian friends condemning that she abandoned her religion, that her girls were too western, and that she married a man almost two decades older than herself, only for money.

That's precisely why she couldn't fathom how her younger daughter Monica could even contemplate separating from a successful man providing her a secure and respected life. Josh was a scientist with Health Canada, a federal job envied by most who knew him, for, when his friends juggled two jobs or adapted to graveyard rotations, he would slip out of his 9 to 5 Monday through Friday routine to sleep in, or watch the NHL match during his 5-week vacation. "What more stability could a woman look for in a man?" Cookie would wonder.

"Let's walk, ma," said Monica, stretching her arms in front of her languidly as the hotdog cover and napkins crumpled into balls in her hands. They started walking towards Stanley Park, disposing of their empty coffee mugs and trash in one of the numerous park bins.

Even though a lot of years had elapsed, Cookie was still astounded by the stark cleanliness of her new home country. She wished Monica could've remembered where she was born and lived for five years: the filth-ridden narrow alleys of *Dharavi* slum they called home, the single room a little more than the size of a washroom stall they were crammed into, the squatting over open sewers every morning, adding to the unbearable stench of human excrement floating everywhere, the stinking landfill they called playground.

But both Monica and Tina were quite young when their nightmare ended. At 5 and 7 years, they used to be jarred awake when the planks above shook violently in the middle of the night, and the moaning from the tin wall separation made them think someone was sick—much to Cookie's relief. However, at every such occasion, she missed her husband; reliving memories of the last time they made love before he was shot dead by the mafia gang members he worked for, when he fell into the hands of Mumbai Police. Cookie was only 33 then, a single mother providing a hand-to-mouth living to her two kids with the little she earned as an *extra* on Bollywood sets.

Nevertheless, she had big dreams and aspired to become a glamorous megastar, in whose shadows she danced with dozens others, merged in big crowds, hardly distinguishable, in take after endless retake of scenes.

Her aspirations defied her age and were totally out of touch with reality. Not only was her stomach flaccid after two unsupervised childbirths, the fact was that even if afforded a role, she couldn't render her lines in Hindi, for her literacy was limited to local Marathi and the ability to sign her name in English.

It was, however, on one such set of a Hindi film, ironically called "*Kismet*," that her destiny transformed radically, like Cinderella's had after wearing the golden slipper. But unlike Cinderella's prince charming, Cookie's had not descended royally from an ornate chariot to seek her, but approached her casually, a photo camera garlanded around his neck.

Ryan was a freelance photographer with leading Canadian journals, and was visiting India for extensive coverage on Bollywood and Asia's largest slum—*Dharavi*.

After an early pack-up was announced by the director, owing to below satisfactory dance moves by the leading lady who had a minor sprain in her ankle that day, the *extras* were preparing to leave when Cookie—then known as Khushi—felt a tap on her shoulder.

The Compromise

"Somebody told me you live in *Dharavi?*" he had asked in a reserved, unimposing manner.

She instinctively felt lucky, as if the question had been, "Madhuri has a sprained ankle; can you replace her in this dance sequence for the film?" and it had come from her film director, instead of this strange man who now faced her, mesmerizing her with his decency and grace, more than his pale long face, grey sideburns, dishevelled hair and a pair of tired green eyes.

"Yes, why do you ask?" she had shot back curtly, for, despite the hard life she endured, she had refrained from getting lured into occasional offers of being an escort to earn extra money, like most her colleagues did.

Once the harsh lights were out, the greasepaint wiped, and the illusion of belonging to the world of riches broken the moment she changed out of glittering bright costumes into her nondescript cotton sari, she would jostle her way into the local train with people hanging from every door, and return home to cook for her girls.

In the course of the next week she bonded with Ryan incredibly, despite the gaping chasm of social status that separated them. The language barrier forced them to communicate with gestures, amid peals of laughter when one or the other exaggerated their body language in this seemingly endless game of charades. He had even nicknamed her "Cookie," a name she embraced eagerly, for it allowed her to escape her past life which had hardly had any consistent happiness, unlike her name "Khushi" suggested.

The week passed quickly, like a fleeting night when two people in love spend it together. And yet, none had the courage to acknowledge the irrepressible desire to not say goodbye.

While she ensured he got the best shots of the slum, rattling off permissions in Marathi to enter mouldy hovels or overcrowded workshops of pottery and cloth dyeing, he had spoilt Monica and Tina with battery-operated walkie-talkie dolls, enticing red Kit Kats and blocks of Lego.

The night before his departure, she had wept silently on her floor bed comprising a mat covered by an old sari.

When he came to meet her the following morning, she avoided all eye contact: her face shone red from the excess crying, her fish-eyes were glazed, and her nose frosted. Even her voice was hoarse, mismatching starkly her feminine curves draped elegantly behind a shocking pink sari with a golden border. It was the one she had worn for her wedding with Birju, eight years ago. Yet today, it cast on her the same charm of an alluring bride: the *pallu* covering her head of jet black hair parted in the centre and pulled tightly behind her ears—fragrant oil holding every strand of it in place—so that the half-moon bindi on her forehead stood out, undistracted.

When she learnt that he was going to stay in Mumbai for as long as it took to get her papers ready for immigration to Canada as his legal wife with the kids, she had neither smiled nor hugged him. She just stood still, pearly tears dripping down her sore eyes to settle on her silk sari in beads before getting absorbed by the weave to wet it.

"Ma, look, how beautiful!" exclaimed Monica as they approached an aboriginal who had displayed hand-chiselled carvings of polar bears, seals and stone Inukshuks on the curb of the seawall leading to *Second Beach*.

What arrested Cookie's attention, however, was not the Inuit sculptures, but the abject poverty to which this craftsman appeared to be subjected. His ragged jeans had holes on the knees, and his buttonless denim jacket didn't look like it could weather the chilly fall or the bitter winter.

The Compromise

"You must not separate from Josh," she announced, more like a court order than motherly advice.

"But ma," began Monica, evidently irked by her mother's interference in her personal matters. "We've grown apart."

"Then learn to grow close."

"You don't understand," retorted Monica, clearly vexed. "We're like housemates living under the same roof." She exhaled forcefully, looking away from her mother and towards a flock of Canadian geese see-sawing on undulating waves, dipping their beaks in the water every now and then.

Despite the monotonous drone of bicycles passing them, they were both listening intently to each other. When her mother didn't react to the analogy she had drawn of her relationship with Josh, Monica seized the opportunity to elaborate, now looking further away, at the horizon of houses across the water which was once mountains—serrated pine trees jutting over the tallest skyscrapers.

"He's such a couch potato," she began, in a dismissive tone, turning suddenly to look into her mother's shrunk eyes on a drawn face.

"You always knew he wasn't an outdoor person—a camp counsellor—like yourself," argued Cookie passionately, her eyes expanding. Even though she was secretly admiring the dedicated joggers panting their way up and down the winding seawall, she had experienced poverty and deprivation at such close quarters, that she was unwilling to let her daughter renounce a well-settled partner only because he was a recluse.

"It's not *just* that," interjected Monica, looking a little subdued. She was a much sought after camp counsellor, animating campfires with impromptu rap parodies, organizing fiercely contested talent shows and adventure hikes.

"I mean, when he's not cheering the Vancouver Canucks or Whitecaps on TV, he's either sleeping or playing with Meow."

There was a long silence, interrupted only by the barking of a few dogs pulling at their leashes to play with other dogs, thus forcing their owners to fall into easy conversations, first about the dog's gender or breed, gradually giving way to general topics—weather being the most common of them all.

They stood waiting as a black-and-tan dachshund leapt playfully on a snow-white poodle whose ears looked like two furry ponytails framing an elongated mouth.

As the owners of the dogs moved closer together, Cookie and Monica resumed their walk, stepping on crushed leaves that had clustered together to form hollow, almost weightless matted balls.

They halted again to take a closer look at some amateur paintings displayed by budding artists on the elevated grass covered cliff, just before *Second Beach*. Sundry scenes of cruise ships, sunsets, and the Vancouver skyline were standing on wood-framed canvases, etched into the soil by thin wooden tails hammered to their backs.

Even as Monica nudged Cookie to continue walking, Cookie was unable to take her eyes off the life-size painting of a charming red-tiled cottage with a huge sundeck and a cobblestone driveway. "Where will you live if you leave him?" she asked finally, joining her daughter, her voice grim and apprehensive.

Monica didn't answer, but continued staring at the greenish-black algae that was reeking strongly during the low tide, covering smooth round stones around which water lapped in swirls, making them look like shiny semi-bald heads.

"Look, Monica," began Cookie sternly. "You don't even have a permanent job. This part-time camp counselling can be fun, but it doesn't buy you the luxury of a secure home like the one Josh is providing you."

The Compromise

Monica was still quiet, though visibly disturbed, as her frolicsome gait was more measured now, and her plump impish face bore a pinched introspective expression. She slipped her hands into the pockets of her khaki capri pants, buttoning her beige cardigan close to the neck as the sea breeze showered more wilted dry leaves from trees on their heads and over the trails.

She looked up at the forest in different stages of fall: maple trees blazing with orange foliage, birch trees still lime-green, whereas many others were a spectacular tricolour: ochre yellow, maroon, and grass green—all at once.

And then she looked down at the twisted dry leaves, crushed under shoes and wheels of bicycles and rollerblades: the obvious consequence of quitting their home trees. Soon enough, those trees would be green again with spanking new leaves; the absence of the old ones replaced and forgotten.

Suddenly, she became stiff, and her 5-foot-3-inch tall frame straightened out, pushing slender shoulders away from her pronounced collar bones, as her glossed mouth drew open to allow more air for her accelerated breathing.

Josh would replace her with somebody else, she frowned, raking the semi-circular fringe of straight black hair away from her face with one hand. Her eyes narrowed at the dreary prospect of sharing the same fate as the shed autumn leaves: crushed and trampled upon the street.

They had now reached the Children's Park, and as Cookie stood gazing longingly at toddlers crawling up yellow tunnel-like slides, to be caught at the other end by mothers or grandparents, Monica glanced at the abandoned swimming pool, closed after Labour Day. A definitive neglect had set in since, as the water looked a muddy brown; the cemented floor strewn with shells and mollusks had invited a flock of crows pecking at them for food, and the colourful plastic tortoise with a diving slide running through its dome shell lay abandoned with a perpetual imbecile smile.

They walked to *The Concession* cafeteria behind the pool, and as Monica joined the line-up, she looked at Cookie and confirmed, "Cappuccino?"

"Yeah," replied Cookie, nodding, as she sat on the stone bench running around a pink stone chip table on all sides that looked like an inverted lotus.

A little while later Monica returned, holding two small porcelain cups—one in each hand. She had barely settled down opposite her mother, when Cookie spoke out rather affirmatively.

"I think you should both get married and have kids. That changes everything, you know."

Monica didn't react, as she had just burnt her upper lip in her haste to drink the coffee, by taking a big sip that allowed the steaming hot liquid below the deceptively cool froth on top to sting her.

"I mean, look at Tina: married and settled with two lovely kids. She never complains that Greg is out all weekends fishing or hunting in Vancouver Island." Cookie continued staring at Monica, even though her daughter had turned her head to look at dogs swimming after sticks flung into the water by their owners, and children filling small plastic buckets with sand.

"I mean, think about it," continued Cookie, joining her daughter's gaze focussed on a small group of young boys making mud houses and then flattening them by stamping on their creations.

"Life's all about *compromise*. We'd all have had to return to India— back to our life of destitution—if I wouldn't have stuck it out and persevered after Ryan's death, just two years after we landed in Canada. Have you forgotten our struggle before Mark came into our lives? The garage in which we lived on welfare cheques doled out by the government?" Cookie's face was flushed, and she drank her coffee at one go like one would drink neat whisky. Pressing her temples, she stood up, grabbed her genuine leather satchel and waited for Monica with her back turned towards her.

The walk back to the Jaguar on Davie Street passed without any communication between the two, and each one looked straight ahead, or in opposite directions to pass the time.

It was only when Monica undid her seatbelt, after the car stopped outside a tall apartment building of grey cement and spacious balconies on a tree-lined street in Yaletown, that Cookie said in a low bass voice—one hand on the gear—"watching some television with him won't hurt you, and cats can be adorable if you make an effort."

Monica stepped out without a word, the lyrics of Phil Collins' *Another Day in Paradise* still ringing loud in her ears. She couldn't help thinking that her mother had purposely played that song on the car stereo, yet she knew it was one of Cookie's favorites, reminding her perhaps of the horrors of homelessness she had faced, with two dependent children to feed alone. She had only turned her fate around with the strength of her ability to compromise on everything she held dear, focussing on the sole aim of keeping poverty and destitution at bay.

Hard as she tried—humming the latest song of Norah Jones, and raising her pitch to imitate Celine Dion's *My Heart Will Go On*— Monica was unable to repress the lyrics of the car, and when she took the elevator, they climbed with her, following her to her 10th floor apartment. As she shut the door forcefully behind her, they had already entered, lurking in the hallway lined with potted plants, and beckoning her to the bedroom, echoing aloud—every word repeating itself *three* times of the same *three* lines:

Sir, can you help me?
It's cold and I've nowhere to sleep;
Is there somewhere you can tell me?

*   *   *

A week had passed without any news of Monica, so Cookie thought she'd check on her daughter.

"You're washing the *what?*" screamed Cookie with a mix of delight and amazement, carrying the handset to her couch from the study table in the living room.

"It's Meow, ma," came a resigned voice from the other side. "He looks so shrunk after a bath."

"I was really worried," said Cookie, concealing her joy. "Hadn't heard from you in a while."

"Actually, I was trying out some recipes from the cookbook Josh gifted me on my birthday, a few years back."

There was complete silence as Cookie tried to absorb this drastic transformation of her daughter.

"In fact, Toronto Maple Leafs beat Vancouver Canucks 2/0 last week, so I was trying to lighten the mood with some good food— nothing fancy—just homemade Poutine. And now, don't start lecturing me on the hazards of fried foods," Monica added with a chuckle.

*   *   *

The flurry of activity in Cookie's house was unmistakable. The detached split-level luxury bungalow in elite West Vancouver, whose numerous rooms had remained unoccupied since Marks's only son moved to Harvard for graduation, now buzzed with activity.

It was the annual Diwali get-together time of the year, and over 50 guests had been invited for dinner. Monica and Tina had come early in the afternoon to help Cookie with flower decorations, wrapping prizes for card-game winners, and doing each other's make-up. A famous catering service had been hired for food, with separate vegetarian and non-vegetarian choices to accommodate people who didn't harbour compunctions about eating meat on Diwali, and relished tandoori chicken and mutton tikkas.

The white men of the household had been particularly excited about the meat dishes, lifting giant lids of silver cutlery resting on low flames to keep the food warm at all times.

Sundry aromas filled the air, hanging under high ceilings and hiding behind plush velvet curtains that resembled perfect hourglasses after being knotted in their middle with plaited tassels.

The bar had already been pressed into service; members of the family downing cokes and juices after the animated chatter left them thirsty. Men had gone to pursue their separate interests after a collective drink of bourbon, whereas women clustered together at all times—helping each other wear a sari, selecting jewellery and overseeing preparations.

Josh had retired to the media room to watch soccer on the home theatre; Greg had gone up to the exercise room to lift weights after tucking the kids in for their afternoon nap, and Mark had descended to the billiards room to savour some solitude before the hustle and bustle of the evening began.

At first, Monica was clumsy with her sari, as she wore it only occasionally for special functions or weddings, even though she felt and behaved in a more feminine way in the traditional attire. On the contrary, Cookie and Tina had wrapped heavy, bead-embroidered saris, having the expertise and skill to manoeuvre their way around in them even in large gatherings.

A certain nervousness gripped Cookie when the clock struck 6, leaving just an hour before the guests would start pouring in. "Monica, go and light the candles along the parapet of the patio, and turn all the bulbs on; it's getting dusky already," she said, baring her teeth in the mahogany-framed mirror of her Victorian-style dressing table. She wiped the stains of lipstick from her front teeth with the edge of a Kleenex, and spraying her hair with a few pumps of mist in a bottle, headed towards the kitchen.

Monica left the room promptly, fidgeting with the delicate topaz pendant hanging between her cleavage in a thin gold chain—an elegant piece of jewellery she had chosen to wear—much in contrast to the heavy sapphire choker Tina wore to match her turquoise sari. Cookie had gone with diamonds: solitaire earrings and a *cross* pendant in white gold chain—something Monica thought could offend the Indian guests and give them spices for juicy gossip in private.

Cookie was strolling in the broad driveway, having entrusted the final layout of crystal flower vases to Tina on pretext of getting some air outside. In reality, she was waiting to greet personally whoever arrived first, in keeping with her reputation of being an exceptional host.

The driveway was still dark, and she was about to flip the switch to light the two elephant-shaped lampshades on either side of the sharp-speared wrought iron gate, when she stopped herself and slunk behind the tall box-hedge separating the drive from the patio.

In the flickering light of dozens of candles, she saw Monica seated majestically on the cedar garden swing. She understood immediately what had kept her daughter from turning the lights on. Kneeling on the ground in front of her, she recognized Josh's head forming a black silhouette against the natural curtain of tall palms and ferns of their garden.

When her daughter's outstretched hand retreated, and both Monica and Josh were only visible as one dark figure coalesced by a tight embrace, Cookie looked up at the sky. A thick cloud cover had obliterated the presence of the infinite stars huddled under its cloak, so that when she saw a twinkling light getting brighter, she thought it was a shooting star. As the airplane flew overhead, she followed its trajectory until it was swallowed up by the clouds. She let out a mixed sigh of relief and content as her life journey finally reached its desired destination; and, as if to celebrate this realization, she flipped the elephants to light.

The Camel Trader

Makhan Singh surveyed the scene. Despite one material difference, everything was essentially the same: the same frenzied pace of camel traders he was so familiar with—feeding, shearing and decorating the camels to command the highest bid for their valued possessions—only this time around, after 20 years of being the best camel trader, *he* was forced to join the ranks of *spectators* visiting the annual Pushkar fair in Rajasthan.

For four days Makhan Singh had waited for his camel supplier Ranjit Rathore, who had unfailingly made him the most sought after trader for two decades. Now, Makhan Singh sat cross-legged on the cooling fine sand of the desert as the sun set on thousands of cattle and human beings, signalling the shift of priority from business to family.

The dust hadn't fully settled when thick smoke from outside countless makeshift tents obscured the nearby mountains. Women dressed in psychedelic orange, pink, yellow and red *ghagra-cholis* busily prepared mounds of wheat rotis on handmade stoves of firewood under mud bricks. Animals stopped bellowing and munched on bushes and hay as men dressed in long shirts, *dhotis* and bright turbans huddled around small fires, keeping warm until the modest dinner of rotis and chutney was served.

Makhan Singh had made up his mind. Tomorrow being the last day of the fair, he would head out to Ranjit Rathore's abode, seeking answers for his unexplained and bizarrely unexpected absence from the fair.

Nothing could deter Makhan Singh. Not even the fact that Ranjit Rathore lived in the remote interior of Thar Desert, the details of which were sketchy for Makhan Singh.

The bazaars in Pushkar were dressing up to lure customers on the final day of the fair as Makhan Singh navigated its meandering narrow alleyways on his faithful camel Veeru. Merchants had congested the already constricted streets by displaying their treasures of colourful glass bangles, *bindis* of varying shapes and sizes, dazzling bright costumes of assorted textures and a wide array of houseware like earthen pots, glassware and utensils. Veeru's arching long neck was especially drawn to street stalls frying blazing orange *jalebis* and golden-brown samosas in huge black *karahis*. Patrons seemed unaffected by the effortless commingling of thick plumes of smoke from these street kitchens with wafts of dust rising from the sweepers' traditional brooms.

Makhan Singh reined Veeru to a tentative halt and tossed a small coin in the direction of a street stall brewing steaming hot chai in a large open saucepan. A clay cup half-filled with the spiced sugary concoction was advanced towards him without much delay.

Makhan Singh pulled the rein with one hand, sipping his hot chai with the other, and Veeru reluctantly moved away from the tantalizing odours, his dilated hairy nostrils contracting gradually.

Makhan's sun-beaten face sombered as he passed his sweaty hand over his white sickle moustache and stubble beard. He pulled down his carefully twisted turban of red tie-dye muslin and let the warm breeze caress his shiny bronze balding pate. The aerated head performed a quick mental math: the bag each of wheat flour and raw onions he was carrying should last him the almost week-long trip to Ranjit's home, provided there were opportunities to restock in the villages on the way. To confirm his survival kit was well in place, he pressed his calves against the bulging packs of rations and utensils saddled on either side of Veeru's humped back. Now Makhan replaced the turban on his head and relaxed in the rhythmic chiming of bells tied around Veeru's curved neck.

Gradually, the hustle and bustle of honking vehicles, wayward cows, noisy children on creaky wooden merry-go-rounds, and shrill calls from mobile vendors of ice candy and spiced chick peas were replaced by quieter outskirts of town. Veeru quenched his thirst at a farm pond and Makhan refilled his leather-skin water bag. The crisp evening breeze chilled Makhan's senses, as he was gripped by another haunting fear: soon he would have to camp for the night in frigid desert temperatures. He decided to take refuge in the next village that came in view beyond miles of scrubland, after Veeru arduously climbed a steep hillock riddled with spiky thorn bushes. The sun went down, leaving rose pink streaks in the sky that were gradually consumed by the enveloping darkness. Makhan would have been directionless, had the joyfully bobbing flames of lanterns in the approaching village not guided the way. After almost two hours of relentless trekking, the first signs of the village appeared in sight: a small well with a rusted iron bucket hanging from the rope of the pulley attached to the side of its wall. Not far, under a shady neem tree, rested a fiery orange statue of the monkey god *Hanuman*, the tree trunk festooned with matching marigold garlands. Businesses were obviously closed, although a lively garbled chatter emanated from the few liquor shops serving their clients. Makhan heaved a sigh of relief for making it on time, as the lanterns illuminating the huts and a few concrete houses were being blown out—their residents preparing to retire for the night.

He was walking randomly with Veeru, wondering where to spend the night, when a villager with a stack of hay on his head stopped to ask, "Are you a traveller?"

"Yes!" replied Makhan in a sceptical yet elated tone.

"Sleep in my hut if you have nowhere else to go," proposed the nonchalant voice with a simplicity Makhan could not suspect.

"*Shukriya*," bowed Makhan, overjoyed at the relatively smooth start to his journey.

The silence of the night was broken only by Veeru's ringing bells as they followed the villager through dark fields of what looked to Makhan like corn ears in the haloed light of the crescent moon. Makhan felt the fields end when his feet started sinking in the familiar desert sand, until finally the ground became firmer, and a dim flickering light from inside a small hut revealed a modest courtyard in giant black shadows.

"*Aa gaye?*" came a questioning, high-pitch female voice, and Makhan heard the soft jingle of her anklets before he saw the veiled face holding a fading lantern.

"Prepare a *charpoy* for the guest," commanded the villager mildly as the veiled woman disappeared indoors, taking back with her the jingling sound and the flickering light.

"Narayan. Villagers call me Naru." The hut owner squatted against one of the dung reinforced walls painted with geometric motifs, and lit a *bidi*.

"Makhan—Makhan Singh, and my camel, Veeru."

Makhan took the *bidi* advanced to him, and pressing it between his lips, craned his neck forward until his *bidi* puffed to life after touching the smouldering tip of Naru's.

Both men blew small illusory moons into the black night, until they dissipated out of shape and hung in the cold air like thick tobacco-smelling fog.

"Where are you headed?" coughed Naru.

There was a heavy silence as Makhan pondered over his destination.

"I'm going to Ranjit Rathores'," he began, his smoke bubbles dancing like distorted witch faces as his memory of the address became hazy.

"In the next village?" Naru's voice was casual.

"No, in the Thar." Makhan strained his cheeks to blow uniform circles in an attempt to fake control over his jangled nerves.

Naru didn't answer. He bowed his head in thought, and the smoke rings met an early demise by hitting the ground. But they bounced back for revenge.

"You could die!" Naru coughed belligerently, uttering profanities and butted out his *bidi*.

"They won't find your body for months." He spewed a wad of phlegm into the courtyard.

"Nothing but sand for days . . ." he warned ominously.

"It's an emergency." Makhan blew the last of his shivering rings as he thought mournfully of the advance payments he had to return in full to prospective clients of Ranjit's camels. Resolved to pursue his treacherous journey, he tied Veeru to a flagstaff in the courtyard and followed Naru inside the pitch dark hut.

The following morning, Makhan started early to cover more ground during the day. Naru's words didn't take full impact, as he made it to the next village a little after dusk. He ate a hearty supper of lentil soup, rotis, vegetable curry and rice. Veeru feasted on the trees and drank water from an open tank that the village restaurant used to wash dishes. Not being fortunate enough to get an offer like Naru's in this village, Makhan paid a small fee to the restaurant owner in exchange for enough space to spread his blanket on the sooty kitchen floor shared by half-dozen workers. Despite the putrid smell of undisposed garbage and constant rattling of utensils by rats and lizards, Makhan Singh slipped into a deep slumber, exhausted from his day long trek.

Early next morning, after purchasing breakfast of deep-fried bread with spicy potato filling and a mug of extra sweet chai, Makhan set off for the Thar. To his knowledge, there was no other village for at least a week, but he hoped to find Ranjit's house in the next few days. With his craving for answers from Ranjit Rathore taking precedence over nagging thoughts of foreboding, Makhan's mood was rather upbeat, even though the full day of trekking removed him further away from any sign of habitation. So far, Veeru found scant food of declining thorn bushes and intermittent *Khejri* trees, but Makhan knew that soon he would have to open up his stack of fodder. However, his optimism turned bleak when the illuminous hot ball of fire sank below the horizon, transforming the harmless looking wasteland of sand into a vast desert fraught with inexplicable dangers lurking in every speck. That night, Makhan couldn't sleep a wink, his ears sensitive to eerie sounds of the chilly howling wind and the call of an occasional black buck. He didn't dare to dismount from Veeru for fear of poisonous snakes and annoying beetles. As was to be expected, every muscle in Makhan's body twinged with pain. His back was stiff from lack of rest. His throat felt sore from the dramatic drop in night temperature. Even before dawn broke, Makhan resolved to make some hot tea for himself, the violet blue sky radiant enough to guide his aching body to some trees in the distance whose branches he could axe for firewood. His matchsticks had become soggy from the night dew, and he had to waste precious few sticks to finally get the life-sustaining fire going. After greedily gulping the hot tea, Makhan felt a little energized to bake a few rotis on his flat cast-iron pan.

He flattened a raw onion with his fist and gulfed down the rotis with the pungent wedges of the layered red bulb. Shortly after this hearty breakfast, the two set off again under the steadily increasing warmth of the rising sun.

The fierce intensity of the afternoon sun made Makhan's exhausted mind and broken body delirious. His head swam in the seemingly infinite ocean of sand, carved meticulously into static ripples by the hot blowing wind. He lost all sense of distance and direction. Whichever way he looked, he found himself alone on a planet whose water had been annihilated by the blistering rays of the sun. The only colour his dusty dry eyes could discern was the deathly pale yellow of sharp, flawlessly curved or angular dunes. But just when Makhan was convinced that his recollections of endless oceans brimming with soothing turquoise waters were a mere illusion, the same oceans beckoned him from every side. Crystal clear blue waters swelled and danced before his eyes amidst gently swaying lush green trees. Before Makhan could reach for his leather-skin water bag, he fell to the ground and passed out.

He must have been unconscious for a long time, for when he awoke, he was sprawled on the cold sand under the ebony canopy of brilliantly twinkling stars. The temporary blackout of his senses had chased the fear out of his embattled self. He lay motionless next to the calmly relaxing Veeru, whose head was blissfully lowered between his long folded legs. "Where did I bring you, Veeru?" he lamented balefully as he painstakingly stretched one arm to pull a blanket from Veeru's saddle.

Then, coiling inside the blanket like a snail, Makhan drifted back into a feverish sleep. When he awoke the next morning, he couldn't understand why he felt so lifelessly feeble. One glance at Veeru gave him the answer. Veeru was monotonously chewing his cud, sticky fine threads of saliva weaving between his wide toothed jaw. Makhan realized immediately that in order to make it alive out of this hostile desert, he too needed to replenish his body fuel. He promptly unknotted the sturdy jute bag containing Veeru's fodder and laid it in front of his ruminating companion. Veeru hastily sank his hairy muzzle into the bag, and Makhan could hear the constant clicking of his teeth at work. With a weak smile, he set about preparing his own meal. He had to unwillingly eliminate chai from his predictable menu of rotis and raw onion, in order to ration the precious little water he was left with. Boiling it for tea would mean letting priceless few sips evaporate ruthlessly into the atmosphere.

He had scarcely settled down to devour his modest meal when he noticed a beeline of beetles tunnelling through the soft sand and creeping on his blanket to share in his food. Jumping up with a start, Makhan whisked his treasure of rotis high into the air. Placing them deftly on Veeru's safe saddle, he shook the blanket violently. The beetles flew in different directions, and resumed their fine embroidery on the sand as their needle legs moved randomly through the desert. Makhan finished his food standing, and wet his mouth with a few drops of water. He regarded Veeru with doleful eyes. "Alas, if you were a female, I could've milked you to quench my thirst!"

A few hours into their trek, the commonplace azure sky took on a threatening rusty-brown hue. The simmering hot air felt cooler, and Makhan's instincts kicked in before a whopping mushroom of gigantic proportions buried everything in sight under its ferociously blowing sandy embrace. Makhan had ducked under Veeru, face covered tightly by his blanket. At most times, the strong grainy wind felt overpowering enough to sweep anything on its way, and Makhan clutched ardently to his unperturbed camel Veeru's firmly planted legs. He knew Veeru would face the storm better than him, given his natural adaptation of thick eyelashes, and his ability to close his ears and nostrils to the menacing sand swirling at incredibly high speeds. Had Makhan not been so long and deep into his journey, now was the time he felt an irrepressible urge to return without confronting Ranjit Rathore. He prayed reverentially to all Hindu gods he had known since childhood, beseeching them to pardon his life *just this one time.*

The gods relented, but not without putting up an intimidatingly spectacular show of natural might. Thunderous fiery streaks of lightning criss-crossed the darkened sky as if an unseen force was stabbing its massive chest. Finally, torrents of rain fell from the wounded sky, transforming the parched landscape into a vast chocolate-brown ocean of blood. Huddled under the unswerving umbrella of Veeru's stoic body, Makhan stared awestruck at nature's unbridled prowess from sky to earth. He gathered fists full of god's precious lifeblood and drank the fresh rain water until all the dying cells of his body sprang to life. He instantly knew his life had been spared. Veeru too drank incessantly from the muddy puddles all around him. When the intensity of the rain subsided, Makhan gathered some water for the remainder of his journey. He knew full well that his wheat flour was too wet to roll into rotis, so he would have to rely solely on raw onions and chai for survival. Chai! He still couldn't believe his luck. He would've definitely died of dehydration had God not opened up His profuse heart to rain the blessed liquid on his shrivelled body. Even though it was impossible to camp for the night on the soaking wet desert, Makhan was so rejuvenated that he didn't feel a shred of fatigue or fear while traversing the solitary desert in the eerie night silence.

After two more days of erratic travelling—persevering in the bitter cold nights if the days got too sweltering, and plodding wearily in the day if his burnt out body forced him to sleep in the night— Makhan Singh spotted the elusive stone pillar that was the only landmark to Ranjit Rathore's house. Etched on the rough grey boulder with pointed stones were ominous warnings: "If you're still alive, you'll die before finding a house," and, "Welcome to the point of No Return!" Paradoxically, there were also symbols of hope painted in saffron that looked like earnest prayers to god offered by desperate travellers like himself. On its own, the impressive stone didn't offer much respite, sitting as it did in the middle of the desert. Even though all directions from it led to the now familiar barren wilderness, Makhan veered his camel to the right, as per his hazy recollection of Ranjit's address.

They had travelled almost three hours without any trace of home or humanity near by. The portentous warnings of the pillar echoed loud in Makhan Singh's ears. His heart sank at the prospect of undertaking the gruelling return journey. Was he really at a point of "No Return"? So engrossed was Makhan in his own dark thoughts that he failed to notice Veeru's deathly slow pace. What would he do if Veeru fell sick or died? He would be doomed to die too, and they wouldn't find his body for months, as Naru had predicted. Makhan pulled the reins hard but Veeru threw his neck back in retaliation and bellowed loudly. Furious, Makhan whipped the reins on Veeru's neck, to no avail. Instead of advancing, Veeru roared angrily and kicked up his forelegs into the air. Then, howling hoarsely, he backtracked a few steps.

Makhan's patience ran out. He jumped down from Veeru's back, and without a word of admonition, started pulling his reins while walking. Veeru obeyed, following his master silently for a few yards, but soon burst into an uproarious bellowing and broke free from Makhan's control. Not paying any heed to his camel's unusual temperament, Makhan sailed along wearily on the murky sand. He was descending tardily down a steep dune when his eyes met a sight that froze his feet. Littered in front of him were, what looked like severed carcasses of camels. Fleshless rounded bones of rib cages detached from hollow skulls sent a chilling shiver down Makhan's spine. Empathising with Veeru's dilemma, Makhan fled the horrific spot as fast as his fear-paralyzed legs could carry him over arduous dunes. He found Veeru staring at him with bulbous terrified eyes. Turning him around, Makhan decided to make a U-turn to locate Ranjit's home.

Dusk was falling heavily upon the scene, mitigated only by a thin silver sliver of the moon that barely distinguished the black outlines of curvaceous dunes from what lay ahead. After going downhill for a few hundred metres, Makhan jubilated at the sight of a mud-coloured concrete house that blended seamlessly with its prosaic surroundings. It stood out like an oasis in this deep dry desert, and its mere sight brought indescribable peace to Makhan's abused body and voided mind. He contemplated long conversations with Ranjit Rathore under the luxuries of a sturdy roof and the amenities of a functioning household. Makhan's pace quickened as he approached the serene inviting house, whose front gate of shaving discoloured wood lay open, as if the residents of the house were expecting him intuitively.

"You owe me a good explanation and decent home food," he smiled smugly after finally reaching his destination, despite gargantuan challenges.

"You'd better leave a good impression," he instructed Veeru amiably, tying him to the flagstaff beside the front gate. "Ranjit has a professional eye for well-bred camels."

Wondering why the lantern was still unlit, Makhan Singh pounded hard on the main door shouting out loud, "Ranjit! It's me, Makhan." There was no reply, but Makhan continued knocking persistently. "It's okay; don't hide, my friend. I'm not angry with you anymore." Still, no answer. Now, Makhan grew anxious. An unsettling feeling dawned on him that there was probably nobody home. He quickly drew out his matchbox from the pocket of his long tunic and lit the lantern hanging from the ledge. Its unsteady flicker settled to a certain flame when he turned the sticky knob around a few times. The door was only ajar, and opened with a laborious creak as Makhan peered inside reluctantly through the wavering shadows cast by the glimmer of the lantern.

The living room was empty, yet Makhan found solace in the sight of two easy chairs upholstered with the pre-eminent brown colour of the desert. Facing the chairs was a darkwood chest hammered with nails on all sides, and covered with a dusty grey bedspread. It was supposed to serve as seating, for right in front of it was a rather fragile-looking yellow cane roundtable with two levels.

Makhan carried on his search of the house, although, for some strange reason, he felt the need to tiptoe across it, holding his breath subconsciously. The next room was a rather simple bedroom, with a mahogany wood queen-size bed that looked slept-in from the crumples on its linen. Makhan Singh welcomed it as a good sign. "Maybe they've gone somewhere," he contemplated.

Then, sighing loudly he thought, "No need to even lock your house in this solitary wilderness." He smirked, "How often do the likes of Makhan Singh embark on a perilous journey through the Thar to visit Ranjit?" He suddenly felt an odd sense of ease permeate his body, and an urge to find the kitchen overtook his curiosity to explore any other room of the house. Breathing easily—even confidently—Makhan hummed a folk tune as he groped his way out with the help of the swinging lantern. The hallway was dark, and when he came upon a tightly latched worn-out wooden door, he assumed it was the kitchen.

"Locking up your rations when all the house doors are open?" Makhan chuckled at his own witty remark as he unlatched the termite infested door. When the lantern illuminated the inside of this room, his lilting hum changed into a muted cry of disbelief. The kitchen looked as if nobody had used it for ages! The small window the size of a ventilator had been pushed open forcefully by gusty winds, raining dry leaves and twigs on the grimy floor carpeted with sand. Moving the lantern to the corners of the wall, Makhan noticed giant cobwebs dangling from utensils stacked haphazardly in open cupboards. His appetite as if evaporated with this unwholesome sight. Stepping back hurriedly with the lantern, Makhan latched the door firmly and rushed headlong into the last room of the house.

The upkeep of this guest room, even in the abandoned state of the house, drew an admiring whistle from Makhan's lips. The maroon rug under his feet read, "Welcome," and the linen on the single beds opposite each other was so immaculate as if nobody had ever slept in them. There was even a rectangular coffee table between the beds, with a tinted glass top. On it sat a small, blue ceramic clutch-like ash tray that resembled a young animal's paw. The ruby-red plaited curtains of starched cotton looked fixed on the windows to one side of the room. "I'll sleep here, tonight," decided Makhan, yawning widely. He was standing on the welcome rug with his back turned to the guest room, when the lantern shone on a sturdy iron backdoor secured with a rusted interlocking chain that looped around a black hook projecting from the ceiling. Suddenly, Makhan was overcome by an intriguing curiosity to discover what lay beyond that forbidding door. Raising the lantern cautiously to the hook, he freed the chain, but the solid gate did not budge. Unwilling to give up so easily, Makhan scoured the gate visually by shining his lantern slowly over its fortified frame. Close inspection yielded that the hinges securing it to the wall had somehow become stuck to it due to the vagaries of weather. The difficulty with which the door gave way was indicative of its long disuse. Makhan could hardly believe what the obstinate door was concealing. Nestled around a clear blue pond was a sprawling vegetable garden! "Who says the arid desert soil yields no produce?" Makhan demanded satirically as the lantern cast dappled light over lush green vines of tomatoes and lemons as big as oranges.

"That solves my dinner problem rather beautifully," he exclaimed, tugging at long cylindrical leaves of spring onions whose bulging huge bulbs were the size of tennis balls. He couldn't believe the tomatoes were for real, either. Drooping under their own weight, they sat on the soil like juicy red apples from far. "Just one is good enough," Makhan bemused, biting into its soft tart flesh. Feeling quite full after his healthy meal, he strolled back to the house and closed the metal backdoor firmly behind him. Not wishing to retire immediately for the night, he made his way to the verandah.

Veeru was chewing his cud gleefully when Makhan offered him some leftover fodder. Feeling relaxed at the prospect of a good night's sleep, he dragged the wicker armchair from the far end of the verandah and went to hang the lantern back on the ledge. The lantern swayed sideways like a pendulum, and its moving light danced on a small black-and-white framed picture of Ranjit's family on the ledge. The spotlight moved systematically from Ranjit's young face in the old photo to that of his wife's, who looked like a bashful new bride. Makhan held the lantern still, and a full glow brought into focus a chubby toddler cradling between the blissful couple. He released the lantern, and was about to lie back on the armchair when he noticed a folded piece of paper tucked under the photo frame. Lifting the frame gently, he pulled the paper and went back to rest on his armchair. He gave a start when the chair rocked by his weight, but soon began to enjoy its soft cradle, even though the occasional squeak of its wicker alarmed him every now and again. Rocking back and forth in the crisp evening breeze, Makhan unfolded the paper under the whimsical light of the lantern, and read:

"Dear traveller,

The comfortable house you find yourself in, was, 30 years ago, an unsightly mud hut whose straw roof would get blown away by monstrous dust storms of the Thar. My wife Fatima used to huddle close to me when buckets of water poured mercilessly into our roofless hut. Yet, we were happy, despite living on the edge: ostracized for marrying outside the dictates of caste and religion, and banished from civilised world. But when our son Kanwar was born, he didn't understand Hinduism or Islam. He only felt the raw, basic sensations of deprivation—of food, shelter, clothing, and later, education. As years rolled by, our anxiety for his future mounted exponentially. That's when we gave him away to a rich trader who could provide for our son's growing needs."

Makhan Singh sighed sympathetically and gazed at the faint picture of Kanwar before reading on:

"My wife and I had no means of a livelihood. We'd have been killed by the villagers had we dared to return. We'd have been killed by the Thar had we not made a damning decision: *to kill for our own survival.* Not many traders passed by our hut as the route was very treacherous. But some brave ones dared, as it saved them a precious few days of travel time to and from Afghanistan. Fatima and I murdered the lone traders who broke their journey at our place. We used their cash to build this cement house, and I started selling their finest camels at the Pushkar fair every year."

Makhan's body was overpowered by involuntary seizures of fear and revulsion, as a result of which the letter escaped from his hands. The only sound audible was the uncanny squeaking of his rocking armchair that grew more intense as his body convulsed violently. A rat slithered through his feet furtively, and Makhan fell to the ground in terror. The noise made Veeru raise his head from between his folded legs, and this sight gave Makhan the strength to reach for the fallen letter. Grabbing it with trembling hands, he continued from where he had left off:

"Early this year, a rich traveller stopped by our abode, riding the finest breed of camel you ever saw. Just one look at that camel told me that he would be the show-stopper at Pushkar. Fatima remarked how royal the trader looked in his classic jewellery of gold and precious stones. He had stacks of the purest silk that was ever made, and he hoped to sell it at a great profit to purchase dry fruits from Afghanistan, that he would then sell back in India. Our clothes were quite worn, and we were indeed tempted by the riches of jewels and silk, but this man became our friend in just one day. When night fell, Fatima and I lay in bed a long time before mustering the courage to suffocate him in the guest room. When he stopped struggling, Fatima brought the lantern. We couldn't bear the look of joyful composure on his lustrous face, so we hurriedly dug up a pit in our backyard and buried him with unspoken regret. The next morning, upon rummaging through his belongings, we found the same framed picture from under where you retrieved this letter."

Makhan felt so dizzy that only the strong urge to know what happened after, kept him from passing out. So, he continued reading, still sprawled on the ground.

"Fatima collapsed at seeing this picture, and I almost lost my mind. When she regained consciousness, she begged me tearfully to exhume the body to identify whether it carried a tattoo of the letter K she had got inscribed on his left arm as a child. Insane with grief, I dug up the grave. Fatima stared long at the lifeless body of our son who looked so content and youthful even in death, that it seemed he would start talking as soon as his sleep broke. Wiping his body clear of dirt and dust with her bare hands, she collapsed on it with a tight maternal embrace, never to get up again. I buried them together in the same position, and threw tomato seeds on the soil."

Makhan couldn't stop himself. Holding one leg of the armchair, he retched loudly and vomited repeatedly. His eyes glazed over the reddish-green mess that his system had emptied.

A brisk breeze was about to carry the letter with it when Makhan's weakened fist fell over it. These last few words danced in front of his rheumy eyes:

"Please tell my story to all you know, so man learns never to ostracize another, or kill another, or kill his own. As for me, I must use my forefathers' sword to join my family with the ill-gotten camels that await my arrival in the desert."

Next book

Vinita Kinra's next book **Live and Let us Live** will blow you away by the unstoppable force of its storyline and characterization.
www.vinitakinra.com

Made in the USA
Charleston, SC
15 September 2013